THE GUILD CODEX: SPELLBOUND / THREE

TWO WITCHES AND A WHISKEY

ANNETTE MARIE

dark owl
fantasy

Dark Owl Fantasy Inc.
PO Box 88106, Rabbit Hill Post Office
Edmonton, AB, Canada T6R 0M5
www.darkowlfantasy.com

Cover Copyright © 2019 by Annette Ahner
Cover and Book Interior by Midnight Whimsy Designs
www.midnightwhimsydesigns.com

Editing by Elizabeth Darkley
arrowheadediting.wordpress.com

ISBN 978-1-988153-27-8

BOOKS BY ANNETTE MARIE

THE GUILD CODEX

The Guild Codex: Spellbound

Three Mages and a Margarita
Dark Arts and a Daiquiri
Two Witches and a Whiskey
Demon Magic and a Martini

STEEL & STONE UNIVERSE

Steel & Stone Series

Chase the Dark
Bind the Soul
Yield the Night
Reap the Shadows
Unleash the Storm
Steel & Stone

Spell Weaver Trilogy

The Night Realm
The Shadow Weave
The Blood Curse

OTHER WORKS

Red Winter Trilogy

Red Winter
Dark Tempest
Immortal Fire

THE GUILD CODEX

CLASSES OF MAGIC

Spiritalis
Psychica
Arcana
Demonica
Elementaria

MYTHIC

A person with magical ability

MPD / MAGIPOL

The organization that regulates mythics and their activities

ROGUE

A mythic living in violation of MPD laws

TWO WITCHES
AND A WHISKEY

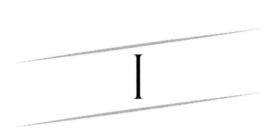

DARIUS WAS a man of unshakable and unquestionable authority. As the leader of the Crow and Hammer, he set a steadfast example of integrity and composure. Of *dignity*.

"Personal Protective Equipment," he announced to the room. "Every job is different, and that means wearing appropriate PPE." To emphasize his point, he lifted a leather trench coat with studded cuffs.

I looked from the goth-lord coat to Darius's somber gray eyes, set in a handsome face with chiseled features and a short salt-and-pepper beard. Biting the inside of my cheek, I fought back a snigger.

"We've had several incidents this month that the proper selection of PPE could have prevented." He stretched out a shiny sleeve. "Your personal style takes a backseat to safety. Leather may not be the most comfortable choice in summer, but it's necessary."

No one was looking at me, but I nodded gravely just in case. The fifty other people in the pub watched Darius with equal solemnity, their unbroken attention a sure reflection of the gravity of—

"Keanu Reeves just called," someone said in a mock whisper. "He wants his *Matrix* outfit back."

Laughter rang through the room, and I noted the time. We'd managed to go six minutes without a wisecrack. New record.

Darius's mouth twitched but he didn't break. "Vampire bites are no laughing matter, which you can attest to, Cameron."

As Cameron coughed awkwardly and more snickers erupted, my humor faltered. Right. Vampires. Maybe it wasn't so funny after all.

The man perched on a stool with his back to the bar, elbows braced against the wooden top, angled his head to bring me into view. His blue eyes sparkled mischievously, the color heightened by his tousled copper-red locks.

"Go ahead," Aaron murmured as Darius continued his lecture on PPE. "Ask."

I glanced around to make sure no one was listening in. "What happens if a vampire bites you?"

"You turn into a vampire, of course."

My eyes widened with horror.

His smirk bloomed. "Just kidding. Vampire bites aren't a death sentence or anything. A whole nest could chew on you and you'd be fine. Well, aside from getting chewed up. That part would suck."

Why wasn't I surprised that the unfairly powerful pyromage saw no need for concern? He could roast his attackers into crispy piles of undead ash.

The guy lounging on the stool beside Aaron cast a look my way. "Aaron is downplaying the danger. A vampire bite increases your chances of converting by forty percent."

Trust Kai to have the facts. Not that he had anything to worry about either. I didn't know if he could stop a vampire's rotting heart with his electramage powers, but he could snap one in half with his martial arts skills.

The third man, sitting on Aaron's other side, turned on his stool. "Don't worry, Tori. If a vampire ever bites you, our healers will know exactly how to fix it."

His meltingly smooth voice rolled over me, soothing as always. Seriously, Ezra could convince me the earth was flat if he talked long enough.

I propped my arm on the bar top. "Aaron, Kai, please take notes."

The pair looked at me. "Notes on what?"

"How to reassure the magic-less human." I beamed at Ezra. "If it weren't for you, I'd have nonstop nightmares."

His eyes, one iris brown and one pale white—the result of an injury that had left a scar running from his temple to his cheekbone—lit with amusement.

"Nonstop nightmares, eh?" Aaron's grin grew wicked. "Tori, ever heard of an allucinator?"

"Uh … no?"

"They're dream manipulators. They can—"

"Aaron Sinclair." Darius's voice cut through our whispered conversation. "Thank you for volunteering."

Aaron snapped around in alarm. "Volunteering for what?"

Darius pointed at the woman standing beside him. "Zora is about to demonstrate how to break a vampire's jaw to prevent a bite. You'll be the vampire."

Aaron's eyes flicked to the petite sorceress and went even wider.

Before he could protest, Darius snapped his fingers. "Now, Aaron."

With a grumble, Aaron heaved himself off his stool and slouched to the front. Kai, Ezra, and I shared a gleeful look, then settled in to watch the show.

The rest of the hour-long meeting passed quickly, and Aaron didn't sustain any serious injuries in the demonstration. Darius wrapped it up at eight o'clock—and then my work began as fifty restless, thirsty people swarmed my bar.

As I zoomed in and out of the kitchen, my spirits soared. This was what I loved: fast pace, slinging drinks, cracking jokes with customers, and giving winning smiles as my tip jar filled up. It hadn't always been like this, but since I'd started working here three and a half months ago, well, let's just say *everything* had changed.

The Crow and Hammer wasn't just a bar and I wasn't just a bartender. This place was a *guild*, and everyone in it was a mythic—a magic-user belonging to one of five magic classes. Actually, four classes, since our membership didn't cover the full spectrum of abilities, which suited me just fine. Who wanted to deal with literal demons?

Me, I was special because of how *un*special I was. In a guild of talented mythics, I was a human. Yep, a regular human without a single drop of magical blood.

I lost track of my three favorite mages over the next hour, but as things settled down, I spotted Aaron, Kai, and Ezra with a group of sorcerers. They'd pushed several tables together and were sitting in a big circle, shot glasses and whiskey bottles in the center.

My eyes narrowed. When had they swiped those bottles? They were showing some serious disrespect for liquor law, but with a guild motto of "any rule can be broken"—and a guild officer sitting right at the table—yelling at them wasn't likely to achieve results. Didn't mean I wouldn't yell at them, though. Just not this minute.

"Tori!" A blond girl my age dropped her purse on the bar top and slid onto a free stool. "How are you?"

"Sabrina!" I gave her a one-armed hug over the bar. "How was your trip? You just got back, right?"

"Yesterday." She whipped out her phone. "Sir Fluffle won first place!"

Before I could ask, she proudly displayed a photo of a floppy-eared bunny posing with a blue ribbon. She rapidly scrolled through another dozen images from the rabbit breed show.

"Isn't he wonderful?" she gushed.

"Amazing!" I agreed, not entirely sure how to compliment a bunny.

"I predicted the show would go well," she added. "Rose warned about inclement weather and untrustworthy judges, but *clearly* she had no idea what she was talking about."

I nodded, determined to stay neutral. The competition between the guild's two diviners was a thing of legend, and I'd experienced their conflicting predictions firsthand. Funnily enough, both fortunes had turned out to be accurate in their own way.

"Anyway," Sabrina sighed. "How was your week? I heard you—"

As she reached for her purse to put her phone away, it tipped over. A deck of black and gold tarot cards spilled across the bar, and a couple fluttered off the edge, landing on the floor beside me.

"Got it." I crouched and grabbed the two cards. As I held them out to her, I glimpsed the top one—and my good mood snuffed out in a rush of cold prickles. Dropping the cards on the bar top, I glared at the detailed rendering of a grim reaper and muttered, "You again."

Sabrina picked up the Death card. "This is very strange behavior for my deck. Why does this card keep showing itself to you?"

Dogs could have behavioral issues. Rabbits could have behavioral issues. I'd even say vehicles could have behavioral issues. But *not* cards. Cards were just cards, end of story.

Sabrina reached for the second one, face down on the counter, and flipped it over. On it, a young man with a rucksack had his face turned skyward, unaware that he was about to step off a cliff. Beneath the drawing were two words: *The Fool.*

My scowl deepened. "Your deck has nothing nice to say about me. It's prejudiced."

"The Fool isn't an insult." Sabrina pondered the card. "It's all about opportunities and potential. About starting a new journey. It means to keep an open mind and embrace your sense of adventure."

I twisted my mouth doubtfully. "The card's a bit late on that one. Pretty sure I'm already well into the 'new journey' thing."

"Hmm, I'd have to agree. Unless …" She canted her head, then slowly rotated the card 180 degrees. "Did it present the right way up or reversed? The reversed Fool warns that your journey is headed toward failure."

My shoulders stiffened. "Failure?"

"Mm." She scooped the deck into a neat pile. "Either you've stalled because something is holding you back, or you've bitten off more than you can chew and your new venture is threatening to come crashing down."

"Those are very different things."

"I could give a clearer prediction if you let me do a full reading." Brightening, she started shuffling the cards. "How about it?"

"Uh …"

"Hey Tori!" Aaron called from across the pub, his voice rising above the loud rumble of conversations. "Can we get another bottle of whiskey?"

Oh, *now* he was asking my permission? Suppressing an eye roll, I waved in acknowledgment, then composed my face into an expression of disappointment. "Sorry, Sabrina, I need to get back at it."

Her shoulders drooped. "Sure. Maybe another time."

Squashing my guilt, I hastened into the kitchen and high-fived Ramsey, the cook, on my way by. In dry storage, I grabbed a bottle of whiskey. The guys were going to clean me out, sheesh.

When I pushed through the saloon doors, Sabrina was animatedly describing her victory at the rabbit breed show to Sin and Riley, who'd joined her at the bar. As Sabrina pulled out her phone for another round of photos, Sin shot me a pained look.

Chuckling, I poured her a coke and slid it into her hand as I stepped out from behind the bar, whiskey cradled in the crook of my elbow. Out of nowhere, a man and a woman appeared on either side of me.

I bit back a groan. "Hi Zhi. Hi Ming."

Zhi stared at me, his intensity at nuclear level. With short-cropped black hair, cheekbones sharp enough to cut glass, and a terse mouth that never smiled, he wasn't winning any friendly neighbor awards. His sister, Ming, had similar features, slightly softened by her long raven hair and bright red, over-the-ear headphones.

"I'll be right back to serve you," I continued hastily. "Just give me a minute to—"

"We aren't here for drinks," Zhi interrupted in his usual monotone. An intense monotone. Don't ask me how that worked. "We're here for the information you refuse to share."

"Yeah, well, as I said before, I can't—"

"Every day you hold your silence is a chance for the Ghost to abduct another victim."

I inched backward, but Ming was blocking my retreat. "I've got nothing to share. If you have a problem with that, take it up with Darius."

Was I hiding behind the guild master? Damn right I was. This human girl knew better than to tick off a sorcerer, especially a prodigy who'd completed his apprenticeship years ahead of schedule.

"Where do your loyalties lie, Tori?" he asked coldly. "Have you and Darius discussed *that*?"

I shoved past him and marched away, ignoring his glare singeing my back. He and his sister could nurse their grudge against the notorious Ghost without my help. Even if I'd wanted to share, I couldn't spill a single detail about the rogue mythic without ending my life. He'd made me swear a black-magic oath to keep his secrets, then swear I wouldn't reveal said oath.

Irritation flashed through me at the thought. Every few days, I'd get annoyed enough to send him an insulting text message, but he never responded. Jerk.

Shouts burst from Aaron's table in a mix of triumph and dejection. Half the table lifted their shot glasses and tossed them back, Aaron included. He slammed his glass down and growled.

"That one wasn't fair," he complained. "Lyndon, your turn."

Surveying the gathering, I counted most of our top combat mythics—from mages like Aaron, Kai, and Laetitia, to sorcerers like Andrew, Lyndon, Gwen, and Zora. Even Girard, the first officer, had joined in. This was the elite faction of the guild— the ones who claimed the toughest jobs and took on the deadliest opponents.

Ezra was part of the circle too, but he'd slid his chair back and didn't have a glass. He never drank much, stopping long before he got tipsy.

Whiskey bottle in hand, I leaned against his chair. "What's going on?"

"Drinking game," Ezra replied with a grin. "Going around the circle, each person shares something they've done or experienced on a job. Anyone who hasn't had a similar experience has to drink."

"Since Darius covered it so thoroughly," Lyndon declared, "I want to know. Who's been bitten by a vamp? If you haven't, cheers!"

Groaning, Aaron downed his refilled glass. Wasn't he happy to be vamp-bite-free? Or maybe he was so many shots in that he'd prefer pointy fangs over more liquor. Laetitia, Gwen, Andrew, and two others drank as well, but Kai didn't.

Zora pushed her sleeve up and displayed an ugly half-circle scar on her forearm. "The bastard nearly ripped a chunk out of me. It happened back at my old guild and their healer wasn't top-notch."

As various mythics whistled appreciatively, Lyndon pulled his shirt collar aside. A similar scar marked the spot where his neck and shoulder joined. "She drained a solid pint before my team caught up. I don't normally relish a kill, but that one didn't bother me."

They passed the whiskey around, refilling their shot glasses.

Andrew, a skilled defensive sorcerer and frequent team leader, leaned back in his chair. "I want to see who *hasn't* tripped and fallen on their face in the middle of a fight. And when you drink, we'll all know you for the liar you are."

As everyone laughed, Kai alone lifted his shot and downed it. Smacking it on the table, he raised his chin in challenge. "Who's calling me a liar?"

I snickered when no one said a word. If there was ever a mythic who hadn't wiped out in a battle, it was super-ninja Kai.

Girard stroked his beard. "My turn, isn't it?"

Aaron and Kai exchanged despairing glances.

Smirking, Ezra half-whispered to me, "Girard will try to make *everyone* drink."

The officer shot him a grin, then lifted his glass in a mocking toast. "Not to get too macabre, but Lyndon brought up kills, so. If you haven't seen at least six bodies in one place, drink."

"What?" Gwen pointed accusingly. "What kind of horrific shit have you been sticking your greasy beard in, Girard? Who stumbles across *six* piss-reeking corpses?"

Ah, Gwen. Every time she opened her foul mouth, I had to fight the urge to laugh. With her sleek blond ponytail and penchant for designer business attire, she looked like a high-end executive—an impression she ruined whenever she spoke.

Girard wagged a finger. "Drink, Gwen."

Scowling, she tossed back her shot. Everyone else lifted theirs—except Aaron and Kai. Their smiles had vanished, their expressions grim as they stared at their shots like they wished they could drink too.

An uncomfortable silence settled over the table, then Zora grabbed my arm and pulled me in front of Ezra's chair. "Tori, you do one!"

"Uh, me?"

His drunken grin back in full force, Aaron took my replacement whiskey bottle and stuffed a full shot into my hand in its place. "Give us a good one, Tori!"

I blinked around the table, packed with the guild's best warriors. What could little ol' human me say? What had I done that none of them had? Well, there were a few contenders. Flown with a dragon? Made a darkfae scream like a sissy girl? Punched a rogue druid in the nose? Problem was, I couldn't talk about any of that.

My gaze dropped to Aaron. "Who here has thrown a drink on three mages at once?"

Laughing groans circled the table. Even Girard had to take a shot.

"Wait!" Laetitia lowered her whiskey. "I spilled a coffee across Darius, Tabitha, and myself once. Does that count?"

The table debated, then decided it counted. Zora gave me a commiserating slap on the hip, making me stumble backward into Ezra, still seated in his chair. He steadied me with a hand on my waist.

"Good try!" Zora exclaimed. "You almost had it, but no one's managed to make everyone drink yet."

"Tori *could* have," Kai interjected. "All she had to do was say 'kissed Aaron.' Then we all would have lost."

The guys howled with laughter and Aaron snorted.

Zora turned to Alistair, an older man I knew only as the most powerful mage in the guild. He was rarely here, too busy hunting the scariest bad guys both in the city and outside it.

"Last round, Alistair," she said. "I can't handle any more whiskey, so this is your final chance to claim ultimate victory. Go big or go home."

Alistair tugged thoughtfully on his snow-white beard. Deeply tanned and weathered, with full-sleeve tattoos on his sinewy arms, he oozed badass-ness. I leaned forward, eager to hear his challenge.

"Hmm. All right, this is mine: Who among us has fought the ultimate opponent?" His dark stare roved around the table. "Who's fought a demon mage?"

No one moved. A wordless ripple passed among the mythics as they assessed their comrades' reactions. Cold, tangible fear crawled through the eerie silence. Then, in near perfect unison, they lifted their shots and drank. Only Alistair didn't move.

Andrew set his glass down with a clink. "Not sure that one was realistic, Alistair. If any of us had met a demon mage, we wouldn't be here to talk about it."

The formidable mage lifted his eyebrows. "You asked for my best. I suppose, out of fairness, I could've asked who's faced a demon and needed a change of pants afterward."

The tension broke as everyone chuckled and began sharing their most frightening encounters. As the game devolved into conversation, I slid a step closer to Aaron.

"What is a—" I began.

A hush fell at the other end of the pub and swept through the room, silencing all conversation. Heads turned as everyone homed in on the front door.

Two people stood just inside the entrance. Both the man and the woman wore identical dark business suits, his hair buzzed short and hers tied in a simple ponytail. The guy carried a leather document case under one arm. I squinted, trying to place them. They weren't guild members arriving late to the party.

Crap, what if they were inspectors from the liquor board come to bust me for letting customers pour their own alcohol?

The man took a half step forward, plucked the white ID card off his lapel, and held it up. His severe voice was quiet, but it pierced the entire bar.

"Agent Harris of the MPD. Where is your guild master?"

2

AT THE WORD "MPD," people jerked straight and some leaped out of their chairs. I didn't move, gawking and paralyzed. Oh, how I would've preferred liquor-law inspectors. This was worse. *Exponentially* worse.

The MPD. MagiPol. The all-powerful organization that ruled over mythics and guilds. I'd never seen an agent in person, and for good reason. Me being human meant I wasn't allowed to work at a guild. My employment hinged entirely on the MPD's ignorance of my existence.

As fortyish mythics flailed at the agents' appearance, hands clamped around my waist. Ezra yanked me down and pushed me under the table, then ducked under it with me. He held a finger to his lips.

I sucked in a silent inhalation, my head bent sideways under the tabletop. Hiding. Yeah. That was a smart idea. Good thing

Ezra's reflexes were better than mine. I frowned at him. Why was *he* hiding too?

"The guild master?" Agent Harris prompted again.

"Good evening, Brennan," Girard said calmly over the uneasy murmurs filling the pub. "Darius might be upstairs, but I suspect he's gone home for the night."

Footsteps thumped against the floor, heading toward Girard—and toward me and Ezra. Agent Harris's shiny dress shoes appeared in my line of sight, stopping a few feet away.

"And you are?" Agent Harris asked in a low voice.

"Girard Canonach, first officer of the guild." Amusement mixed with a sharp note of displeasure in his voice. "I'm surprised you don't remember me, considering our numerous communications over the years."

"I deal with many officers," Agent Harris replied dismissively. "If Darius is here, I will speak with him immediately."

"Laetitia, can you check upstairs, please?"

She pushed her chair back and hurried toward the staircase in the corner. The rest of the mythics at the table stayed put, their chairs and bodies forming a curtain around my and Ezra's hiding spot.

"How've you been, Brennan?" Girard asked conversationally, the sharp note lingering in his tone. "You're working late tonight."

"I have a demanding job."

"You have lucky timing. We're not usually this busy at ten o'clock on a Saturday."

My questioning gaze snapped to Ezra, and he gave a tiny nod of confirmation. The MPD agents had shown up precisely *because* it was meeting night.

Quiet, nervous conversations were picking up around the room and chairs creaked as people got to their feet.

"Girard," Agent Harris said. "Tell your people that no one leaves until we're finished."

"Everyone, please take a seat while we see what the esteemed MPD agents need from us. Thank you." Lowering his voice again, Girard said to Harris, "If you're going to hold us here, I'd like to know why."

Papers rustled. "We're here regarding Case 18-3027, the investigation into Albert and Martha River, and the Crow and Hammer's involvement in their apprehension."

Ice flooded my veins. Those names were all too familiar. I'd played a major role in the couple's capture, but that had been four weeks ago and I'd assumed it was all a done deal. The MPD was only getting to it *now*?

"We're investigating in conjunction with Case 03-1622, the disappearance of Nadine Emrys from the Bellingham Sorcerers Guild in England fifteen years ago." Agent Harris shuffled his papers. "You, Girard, are required to appear for questioning regarding the Rivers' apprehension. I have your summons here, though as per procedure, I need to present it to your guild master first."

"I see," Girard replied flatly. "Do you have summonses for anyone else?"

"Aaron Sinclair and Kai Yamada, for their roles in the interrogation." Another shuffle of papers. "Ezra Rowe also faces a summons, as well as pending charges for using undue mythical force on humans."

I looked at Ezra in horror, my lips silently forming the words, "*Pending charges?*"

He leaned close and put his mouth to my ear. "Not criminal charges," he breathed almost soundlessly. "They'll fine me unless we can convince them that the Rivers should be tried as mythics."

His whispered words calmed my anxiety, but my heart didn't slow. If anything, the stupid thing raced even faster. As if I didn't have enough to worry about, his lips brushing against my ear had sent ridiculous tingles running down my neck and spine.

"Why is that woman taking so long to fetch Darius?" Agent Harris demanded.

"Laetitia will be back any moment, I'm sure," Girard answered coolly. "Is there anything else I can assist you with?"

Ezra turned sharply, scouring the empty space beneath the table.

Agent Harris cleared his throat. "There's one more matter I'm investigating."

Ezra focused on a spot beside me. Catching my eye, he again put his finger to his lips. Uh, yeah, duh. I knew to stay quiet. I didn't need a reminder to—

A man appeared beside me.

I started so hard I fell over, and Ezra caught my elbow before I could bump a table leg. I gaped in disbelief. Darius crouched beside us, head bent under the table, his expressive eyebrows arched. What the actual hell? The dude had materialized out of thin air! What kind of mythic *was* he?

"We have a summons," Agent Harris continued, oblivious to the growing group concealed under the table, "and pending charges for use of an illegal artifact on a human. The woman in question goes by the name Patricia Erikson, but we believe that's an alias."

Oh, shit. That was *me*.

"Do you have any members with red hair?" Agent Harris asked Girard.

A moment of quiet.

"Ginger, checking in," Aaron announced. "You've already got me on a summons, though."

"A *female* member with red hair," Agent Harris corrected irritably. "We'll be questioning you and Kai Yamada in detail about your associate Patricia Erikson."

Oh shit, oh shit, *oh shit*.

Agent Harris's feet shuffled with impatience. "We'll also be discussing how this woman is connected to the rogue known as the Ghost. The Rivers insist the woman intimated that she works for him."

I pressed both hands to my face. Why, oh why, hadn't I kept my big mouth shut? While interrogating the Rivers, I hadn't even considered they would describe my every word and action to the MPD.

Reaching past me, Darius touched Ezra's shoulder, then pointed at Aaron's legs. Ezra tapped Aaron on the knee.

"You can save your inquiries for the official questioning," Girard cut in firmly. "It seems Darius has left for the night. Why don't you return at a more reasonable hour?"

As Girard spoke, Aaron slid his car keys out of his pocket and passed them to Ezra. Holding them tightly so they wouldn't jingle, he tucked them in his pocket.

"Actually," Agent Harris replied, "we'll be inspecting the premises before we leave. I have the paperwork here."

Beside Aaron, Kai held up three fingers under the table, then folded one down. He was counting? Three, two, one—

He shoved his chair back and stood.

"This is *bullshit*," he declared loudly, slurring the words. "Why the hell are you bursting in here and ruining our night?"

I choked on a gasp. Kai was not the "belligerent outburst" type—nor was he drunk enough to slur like that.

"Calm down—" Girard began.

Kai slammed his hands on the table, rattling the shot glasses. "Bullshit! Who does this prick think he is? He's not even following procedure! This is intimidation, that's what it—"

"Shut up!" Aaron shouted, leaping to his feet. He staggered drunkenly. "You're just making it worse!"

Darius took my elbow, distracting me so I missed Kai's snarled response. As the two mages yelled at each other, the guild master pushed me toward an opening between chairs. Panic rushed through me, but I didn't resist his guiding touch. Surely Darius knew a shouting match wouldn't prevent the MPD agents from spotting us.

I skooched out, Darius right behind me. Two feet away, Kai and Aaron were ranting back and forth while Girard ineffectually tried to separate them. Harris and the female agent watched with stiff annoyance.

Not a single person so much as glanced our way.

Ezra popped out of hiding last. Hands on my shoulders, Darius steered me between tables. No one noticed us walk past. We circled the bar, then Darius gestured for me to duck under the saloon doors that led into the kitchen. I crawled under them and jumped up on the other side.

Darius slid under next, followed by Ezra, and together we hastened through the empty kitchen. Darius pushed the back door open and balmy night air rushed in.

Ezra puffed out a breath. "Well, that was fun."

I looked between him and Darius. "Uh, how did no one notice us?"

Darius winked. "Trade secret, darling."

My mouth went slack. Darling?

"He's a luminamage," Ezra told me. "Concealment is his forte."

Darius frowned as though Ezra had spoiled his game, then glanced at the door. "It's time I make an appearance for dear Agent Harris. You two get moving." He placed a hand on my shoulder and squeezed gently. "For now, Tori, you'll need to take a holiday from work. We'll be in touch once the heat is off."

"But—"

"Take her home, Ezra. You should stay out of sight as well."

"Yes, sir."

As Darius backtracked into the kitchen, Ezra linked our hands and pulled me across the small lot toward Aaron's old red sports car. He dug out the keys and bounced them on his palm, then asked, "You drive, don't you? I try to limit my driving to emergencies."

"This doesn't count?" I reluctantly took the keys from him. "Let's hope I'm not too rusty."

We climbed into the car. I adjusted the mirrors, half expecting the MPD agents to burst through the doors, then reversed the car out of its spot and pulled into the sporadic traffic. It felt weird. I hadn't driven in a year and my shit-mobile had handled like a geriatric barge compared to this old but eager speedster.

At least I wasn't stranding Aaron at the guild. Considering the amount of whiskey he'd consumed, he would've been walking home anyway.

As the three-story building disappeared from the rearview mirror, I tried to contain the shivering dread in my gut. Funny thing was, the threat of MPD charges wasn't what had my hands quivering.

"It's over, isn't it?" I whispered.

Ezra twisted in his seat so he could see me with his good eye. "What's over?"

"Everything." I swallowed painfully. "The MPD found out about me. Darius will have to fire me, and I'll never be allowed back …"

I'd known from day one that my employment at the guild was temporary. The MPD didn't allow humans and guilds to mix except under specific circumstances—criteria the Crow and Hammer couldn't meet. My job had been supposed to last a few weeks at most, but it had somehow stretched into months, and I'd gotten really good at not thinking about the future.

"No," Ezra said sharply. "Darius won't give up that easily. He'll fight to keep you, Tori."

"But what can he do? He can't break the rules indefinitely."

"I don't know, but Darius will figure it out. Have some faith." He lightly brushed my shoulder. "Even if you lose your job, you won't lose us."

My fingers tightened on the wheel, my aching heart threatening to split. How I wanted to believe him, but I'd experienced this scenario too many times. No matter how friendly I was with coworkers or customers, once I lost my job and our only connection was severed, the friendships fizzled out in a matter of weeks.

Ezra studied my profile, then leaned back. "All the MPD knows is that a red-haired woman called Patricia Erickson participated in a single interrogation. We'll come up with an explanation that'll send them searching elsewhere for 'Patricia.'"

"Like what?"

"Kai has a few ideas." At my surprised look, he added, "We were expecting this. It's why I got out of sight too. Darius doesn't like us being taken into custody. It makes negotiating more difficult."

I pulled up to the curb in front of my place—then realized this might not be the correct destination. "Oh! Should I take you home first?"

"No, this is fine. I can drive now—it's all quiet streets from here."

Leaving the keys in the ignition, I climbed out.

"We might have to delete your contact info again," he warned as he met me in front of the hood. "MagiPol has been known to surprise-inspect our phones."

"Right. Sure."

"We'll let you know as soon as it's safe. Hopefully, it won't be long."

"Okay."

"Tori," he sighed.

Stepping closer, he pulled me into a hug. I buried my face in his shirt. Damn, the man smelled heavenly. Whatever soap or cologne he used was worth every penny.

"This is only temporary, I promise." His voice rumbled through his chest and into mine. Too soon for my liking, he released me. "I need to get going. Will you be okay?"

"You bet," I said brightly.

He searched my face, and I rather doubted my optimistic tone had fooled him. Just in case it had, I held on to the smile as he slid into the car. The engine growled to life, and with a final wave through the window, he pulled away. I watched the taillights disappear around the corner.

No matter what he said, what he promised, my heart believed that had been our last hug. Tonight had been the last silent joke I would share with Kai, exchanged with nothing more than a glance. Tonight had been my last kiss from Aaron, stolen across the bar top when no one had been looking.

Sabrina's tarot card flashed in my mind's eye. The Fool, blindly stepping off a cliff. The warning, so clear but too late.

Standing alone on the sidewalk, I stared at the spot where the car had vanished and wished this magical dream could have lasted longer.

3

A WAVE OF AIR CONDITIONING rushed over me as I walked into the coffee shop. Getting in line, I watched the baristas with interest. Hmm, barista. Not a job I'd tried before, but I could learn. After three days of radio silence from the guys and the guild, I was contemplating desperate measures. Rent wouldn't pay itself.

With an iced latte and a cranberry muffin in hand, I chose a window seat. Absently watching the passersby on the sidewalk outside, I nibbled on my muffin and waited.

The door jingled and a man walked in, his dark blue uniform and the gun holstered on his belt catching the eye of every patron. I waved and he gave a quick nod, then stepped into line. A minute later, he dropped into the seat beside me and unwrapped a thick slice of banana bread.

I nudged him with an elbow. "At least say hello before you stuff your face."

"Hewwo foree," he managed through a bulging mouthful. He swallowed hastily. It looked like a challenge. "Sorry. I haven't had lunch yet."

"How's the shift going?"

When his shoulders sagged forward, concern sparked through me. Justin wasn't a mere cop. He was my older brother, and anything that made him unhappy made me unhappy.

"I didn't get the promotion," he muttered. "They chose someone else."

"Bastards," I growled, slamming my latte down. "How could they pass you over? You graduated top of the academy, you work like a dog, you take every shift they give you no matter how shitty—"

"Thanks, Tori," he interrupted with a wan smile, knowing my rant would only gain momentum if he let me go on too long. "I'll have to aim for the next one."

I shredded my muffin wrapper. "Why would they snub you like this? Do you know?"

A grimace, almost hidden behind his short beard, contorted his mouth. "I think I was asking too many questions."

"Questions? About *what*?"

"About … certain rules. Stuff I didn't know about until after I joined the force." He glanced around, suddenly tense. "I can't actually talk about it. I signed an NDA."

A chill washed over me. Special rules. Something he wasn't allowed to discuss. *Oh.*

The mythic community kept well out of the public eye, but law enforcement was a big exception. The MPD had made … special arrangements for mythics. Their ID cards were marked with an MID number, and police weren't allowed to arrest anyone who carried one. Instead, they had to take down the person's information and submit it to the MPD.

I'd wondered how much the average cop knew about mythics, but for some idiotic reason, I hadn't clued in that my brother, as a police officer, would be in on the secret. How much did he know?

Justin forced a smile. "Enough about me. How's work going? Do you have a shift this evening?"

I wanted to back the conversation up and quiz him on his knowledge of magic, but that would raise all sorts of alarm bells. Better to leave it for now.

Then again, that meant talking about *my* work.

"I'm on leave," I said lightly. "They're doing renos at the bar, so I get a mini vacation."

"Time off? Nice. I hope you're getting holiday pay."

"Yep," I lied guiltily.

"What about … that guy?" Justin wrinkled his nose like he was asking about my digestive health. "Aaron?"

"What about him?"

"Aren't you two dating?"

My expression froze. I quickly smiled. "Sort of. Casually, I guess. Nothing serious."

The furrow in Justin's brow reappeared. "You've mentioned dates with him over the past few weeks."

I nodded.

He waited for a moment, then prompted, "So?"

"So, what?"

Huffing, he leaned back in his chair. "I know I don't have ovaries and am therefore incapable of proper girl talk, but can't you at least gush about his manliness or rave about your latest date or describe your future wedding or something?"

"Is that what you think girls talk about?"

"It's a highly educated guess. Don't you have *anything* to say about this guy?"

"You don't want to hear me gush—you want dirt so you can convince me to dump him. That's what you always do."

"That's what I *usually* do, since you usually date pricks who deserve to get dumped. This guy seems decent, but"—he arched his eyebrows pointedly—"if he's stringing you along, that isn't cool and you should think about whether—"

I held up a hand. "Stop right there. Aaron isn't stringing me along. We're casual because we want to be casual, simple as that." He opened his mouth and I hurried to ask, "How's Sophie?"

Justin's mouth hung open, then slowly closed. He looked down at his coffee. "We broke up."

I almost dropped my latte. "*What?*"

"She ..." He cleared his throat. "She moved out two weeks ago."

"Why didn't you say anything?" Sympathy welled inside me. He and Sophie had been coming up on their one-year anniversary and as far as I'd known, they'd been deliriously happy. "What happened?"

"She moved in shortly after you moved out. It was great for a bit, then ..." He slumped. "I don't know. Suddenly, nothing I did was right. She wanted everything a certain way and I tried to follow along, but ..."

I patted his shoulder, inwardly seething. Justin was easy to live with. To make him miserable, Sophie must have gone full control-freak harpy. If I saw her again, I would give her a facial in the nearest mud puddle.

After consoling him for a few minutes, I changed the subject to sports and let him rattle on animatedly about rookie camp and draft picks until we finished our drinks and his break was over. I saw him to his squad car, gave him a goodbye hug, then headed home.

Even on a Tuesday afternoon, Robson Street traffic was insane, and I dodged pedestrians until I could duck down a side road. Skirting the edge of Chinatown, I entered my neighborhood, the streets lined with small apartment buildings and a few bungalows, mature trees casting welcome shade over the sidewalk.

The house I rented squatted on its slip of grass, looking tired but comfortable. I cut through the backyard and unlocked the outer door, then the inner door that led to the basement. As I swung it open, a blast of raucous laughter echoed up the staircase.

How many times had I told my roommate not to turn up the TV? My upstairs neighbors traveled most of the year, but I didn't want anyone wondering why my television was on twenty-four hours a day.

I trotted down the stairs, ditched my purse, and strode into the living room. "Twiggy! What have I told you about the volume?"

Huge leaf-green eyes pried themselves off the screen and turned my way. The two-foot-tall faery thrust his lips out in a pout, then pointed the remote at the flat-screen TV. His large green head, adorned with crooked branches in place of hair, bobbed as he pressed the volume button exactly twice. The noise level scarcely changed.

A flat-screen TV wasn't in my meager budget, but Aaron had shown up one day with it tucked in his back seat.

According to him, it was an extra one from his basement, but I'd still resisted the donation until I realized it was as much for him as for me. He wanted the option to watch TV when he was over here, which was a weekly occurrence—him *and* Kai *and* Ezra.

Kai could cook when motivated, but that wasn't often. Aaron's skills were limited to following instructions on a box, while Ezra avoided kitchens at all costs. So, the guys showed up at my house most Sundays and Mondays—my days off—to mooch dinner.

I teased them mercilessly about being helpless bachelors, but secretly, I loved it. First, I enjoyed cooking and always made too much food, and second, what woman *wouldn't* want three hot, funny, mostly charming mages in her apartment as often as possible? If I didn't work five evenings a week, I'd cook for them more.

My gaze traveled to the worn sofa, facing the television with its back to the rest of the room. Another gift. The guys had, apparently, been planning to get a new sofa, so they'd given me theirs and replaced it with a reclining leather monstrosity.

Ducking into my bedroom, I pulled on a loose tank top and yoga shorts. Another round of fake laughter echoed from the TV, and I shook my head. I had no idea whether Twiggy was enjoying the sitcom—he never reacted to the gags, just stared intently as though committing every scene to memory. I could only guess what the little monster was internalizing. I'd already banned horror movies and rom-coms. I'd thought the latter was safe, but then I came home one day to find a message. Spelled out *on my bed*. In *rose petals*.

The word? *BACON.*

After recovering from my shock, I'd informed Twiggy that, one, flower petals were a terrible form of communication, and two, if he wanted to make breakfast requests, he needed to tell me in person.

Should a woodland faery be eating bacon? Who knew. Just one more way I'd corrupted him. The other faeries would never take him back now that he was addicted to meat.

An hour later, I was perched on a stool at my breakfast bar, unenthusiastically scrolling through job listings. Though I hadn't *quite* abandoned all hope that my job at the Crow and Hammer would survive the MPD investigation, no shifts meant no pay. It was time to put on my big-girl pants and look for employment.

Chin propped on my palm, I scrolled past three bartender listings. Blah. No, no, and definitely no. I wouldn't last an hour at an upscale steakhouse. "Hey assclown" wasn't an acceptable way to address customers in places like that.

Giving up on the job hunt, I wandered around my apartment, searching for something to do. Restless energy buzzed through me, but I couldn't settle on an activity. As the clock ticked closer to four, my tension increased. Three times, I pulled my phone out and checked it to be sure I hadn't missed a call.

I came to a stop in the middle of my kitchen and stared at the microwave as the glowing green clock turned from 3:59 to 4:00. It was official: the first shift I'd missed since starting at the Crow and Hammer.

Okay, not quite true. I'd missed two weeks of work while a notorious rogue held me captive, but I wasn't counting that.

I didn't move, watching the time. 4:01. 4:02. When it flipped to 4:05, I opened a cupboard and pulled out a shot glass.

I grabbed a bottle from the cupboard above the fridge, poured a shot, lifted it, and tossed it back. The whiskey burned all the way down to my stomach.

I poured a second shot and downed that too, then smacked the glass on the counter. Enough moping. There was only one solution to this level of self-pitying restlessness.

Twiggy ignored me as I strode past him to my bedroom. He ignored me as I popped out again in an even rattier tank top and shorts. He didn't react when I dragged a bucket and rags out of the closet or when I pulled on yellow rubber gloves.

The moment I cracked open the bottle of cleaning solution, his head jerked around.

"Not again," he hissed angrily. "Why do you wipe poisons on everything?"

"It's called cleaning, and if you don't like it, you can leave."

He minced closer, his petite nose scrunching. "You *cleaned* last week. The floor reeked all night."

"I clean every week."

"Humans are stupid." As I poured cleaner into the bucket, he backpedaled, his oversized feet smacking the floor. "Stupid human! Put it away!"

"I've warned you about insulting me."

Snarling in another language, he disappeared.

I squinted at the spot where he'd vanished—sometimes he just pretended to leave—then I shut off his TV show and put on my favorite playlist. After turning the music up until the beat thudded in my chest, I got to work.

First I scrubbed every surface in my kitchen, stopping twice for another shot, then headed for the bathroom. Late afternoon morphed into evening, and I only checked the clock three times an hour.

Dumping and refilling my bucket, I hauled it into the main room, hips swaying in time to the beat. After four shots of whiskey, I was feeling pretty good. Or was it five? I might have lost count. Jacking up the music another few notches, I sat cross-legged on the floor and wiped down the baseboards.

"*Na na na na,*" I sang enthusiastically. Reaching for the baseboards behind the TV stand, I paused, my head cocked to listen. "Twiggy?" When no one answered my call, I shrugged. "*Na na na na—*"

I stopped singing again, straining to hear over the music. Stripping off my gloves, I pulled out my phone but it showed no missed notifications. Was I losing it? Exasperated with myself, I marched to the kitchen. The whiskey bottle waited patiently, and I hummed as I poured a shot. Just one more.

Lifting the glass in a salute to no one, I belted out the song's chorus, then brought the glass to my lips, tipped my head back—and heard it clearly: knocking.

I lowered my glass without drinking. The loud rapping sounded again. Bewildered and hopeful, I trotted across the room—and didn't realize I was carrying my shot until it sloshed on my bare feet. Oops. At least I was already in cleaning mode.

Zooming up the stairs, I opened the basement door and stepped into the vestibule, but my hand hesitated on the exterior door. Fuzzily, I considered whether this was a good idea. Maybe they guys were here. And they hadn't called first because, uh … because the MPD had confiscated their phones! Yeah, that was it.

Grinning, I swung the door open.

Two people stood on the step, but they weren't Aaron, Kai, or Ezra. They weren't even men. So disappointing. I scrunched my nose as I looked them over from head to toe.

"You," I announced. "I don't know you. Who are you?"

The women stared at me. Their pretty blond hair hung in pretty waves around their pretty faces, and annoyance bubbled through me. Their flowery blouses and ankle-length skirts were so nice, and I was dressed in a stained tank top and yoga shorts with a hole in the crotch. Why did pants always rip in the crotch first? Stupid.

"I'm Olivia," the taller of the pair said, offering her hand. "This is my sister, Odette."

I squinted at her hand, her nails buffed and filed into perfect half-moons. "Those're your names, not who you are."

"My apologies," Olivia-or-Odette said. I'd already forgotten who was who. "I should have started with that. We're from the Stanley Coven and … well, we were hoping to speak with you, if possible?"

"Stanley Coven," I repeated slowly. "Coven. Ah, so you're *witches*." Of course. Covens had witches. That's how that worked. See? I knew my mythic shit.

She gave a hesitant nod, still holding her hand in the space between us, waiting for me to shake it. I peered at the shot glass I held, half empty after my race across the apartment. Shrugging, I tossed the whiskey back, then gestured grandly.

"Come on in, witchy girls, and let's hear what you've got to say."

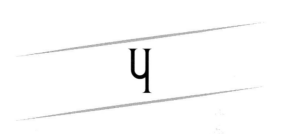

4

"WANT A DRINK?" I asked over my shoulder, leading the way down the stairs.

"Thank you for the offer, but I'm afraid we don't drink," O-one said.

"That's no fun. Just sit down then, I guess." I ditched my shot glass in the sink as they perched gingerly on my sofa. Pretty blouses, long skirts, timid mannerisms, and disinterested in alcohol. Suspicion dawned on me. "Hold on. You aren't here to convert me to Wicca, are you?"

O-two frowned delicately. "We aren't Wiccan. Most witches aren't."

Oops. "I knew that. It was a joke."

"Of course." She forced a laugh. "How clever!"

I might be a bit tipsy, but I wasn't drunk enough to believe that for half a second. Dragging a stool away from the breakfast bar, I positioned it in front of the TV and sat facing them. Then I stood, turned the music down, and sat again.

"So," I prompted, "what brings a pair of witches to my house?"

An uncomfortable prickle ran down my spine. Huh. Now that I thought about it, that was an important question—one I should have asked *before* letting them inside.

Eyes narrowing, I looked them up and down. Meh, I could probably take 'em in a fight. I'd faced worse odds.

O-one folded her hands together. "Odette and I came in the hope that you and your guild could assist us."

Ah, so *that* one was Odette. I committed it to memory. What was the other one's name again?

"I'm aware we aren't following the usual procedures—"

Ofelia? Or was it Odessa?

"—and I apologize for our rudeness in coming to your home unannounced—"

Opal? Oakley?

"—but we felt we had no choice after—"

"Olivia!" I exclaimed triumphantly.

Her brow pinched. "Yes?"

Coughing awkwardly, I composed my expression. "Let's back up. First question: How did you find me? Like, seriously?"

Along with being unknown to MagiPol, I was also unknown to the magical community outside the Crow and Hammer. I wasn't registered in the MPD database, wasn't an official employee of the guild, and for all intents and purposes, I didn't exist in the world of mythics.

So, what the hell were two witches doing here?

Odette offered a weak smile. "As Olivia said, we apologize for intruding. We inquired among the local fae, and several smallfae told us of the witch who lives with a forest sprite, and through them, we found your house."

Twiggy, that leaf-brained gossiper. What had he been telling his sprite friends about me?

She leaned forward. "We're delighted to meet a spirit sister. We thought we knew all the—"

"I'm not a witch." The words were out of my mouth before I could stop them.

"You ... you aren't? But you live with a fae." She pointed at my arm. "You have a fae token of debt."

I looked at my inner wrist. Almost invisible against my skin was a small, elegant rune. "Uh ... special circumstances. But yeah, not a witch."

"Oh." She waited, probably hoping I'd tell her what kind of mythic I was, but I knew how these things worked. Asking a mythic for their class was super rude.

I wished I could tell them my mythic class. If I were a mythic, I wouldn't be here right now—I'd be at the guild with the guys.

"You said you had a request," I prompted before my self-pity could take hold.

"We, well ..." Olivia winced. "We aren't very comfortable among the ... upper echelon of mythics. We find it difficult to meet with other guilds."

Odette's shoulders drooped. "And our experiences with this issue have left us even more uncertain. We'd hoped a casual, more intimate meeting would be easier."

Easier for *them*, not for me. They were here on guild business, but I wasn't a guild member and this was *way* above my pay grade—meaning it was time to end this "meeting" before I got myself into real trouble.

"Alrighty then," I declared, hopping to my feet. "It was nice meeting you, Misses Double-O's, but I'm afraid I'm the wrong person to talk to. If you want help with something, you'll need to speak with—"

"Please, Tori," Odette interrupted, her soft voice somehow cutting through mine. "Please, hear us out. You don't have to do anything. Just listen, and pass on our plea to your guild."

I hesitated. Hear them out? That didn't sound so bad …

But no. One, strange mythics were in my house and that wasn't safe. Two, I was already under MPD investigation for interfering in guildy things. And three, I was possibly drunk. Okay, probably drunk.

At the thought of my banishment, sorrow and loneliness trickled through me. Were the guys at the pub right now, drinking in their usual spot beside my station? Kai, scrolling on his laptop, looking for their next bounty to chase, while Aaron and Ezra bantered. I should have been there, serving their drinks and bantering with them.

Slowly, I sat down on my stool again. I was cut off when I so desperately wanted to be part of their world, but here was a tiny piece of it, sitting primly on my sofa. I couldn't bring myself to show them the door.

"Okay," I grumbled. "Spit it out."

"Thank you," Olivia gushed. She tucked her wavy hair behind one ear, blue eyes shining with gratitude. "You have no idea what this means to us. We have no one else to turn to."

"Yeah, sure." I waved at her to continue.

"Allow me to start at the beginning. My coven's territory, as I'm sure you know, spans the entirety of Stanley Park, as well as the downtown area, though, of course, there are few fae in the city."

"Of course," I agreed, pretending I'd known that.

"Early this spring, several fae went missing in Stanley Park. It's a large space as far as parks go, but it's a small pocket of wilderness with daily visitors, so the fae population is limited to faeries, sprites, and pixies. We searched for the missing fae, but they've vanished entirely."

"You sure they didn't just leave? Twiggy vanishes whenever he feels like it."

"Ah." Odette coughed. "You may already know this, but as semi-corporeal beings, fae can move between our reality and their own. Those without the Spiritalis gift can't detect fae who have crossed into Elysium, but we can."

"Oh. Sorry, yeah, I'm not up on all the witchery stuff."

"Many mythics aren't," she lied kindly. "Trust us when we say these smallfae have truly vanished."

Olivia straightened her skirt, her motions stiff. "Unfortunately, that was just the beginning. The fae have continued to disappear from the park. In total, eighteen smallfae have gone missing in the last four months."

Concern rose inside me, sharpening my thoughts. "That's terrible."

"We went to the other guilds, but every single one turned us away." Odette's eyes flashed. "Non-Spiritalis mythics aren't equipped for fae, they said, but really, they simply couldn't be bothered to help. They don't care about smallfae."

"That's what brought us to the Crow and Hammer," Olivia murmured. "To you."

"We've asked every other guild in the city that does bounty work. We even"—Odette gulped—"asked Odin's Eye to take the job. They refused, though in their case, it's because the bounty isn't high enough to interest them."

"Odin's Eye," I mumbled. That guild had been mentioned around the Crow and Hammer a few times, but never in a complimentary way.

"The only guild we haven't approached is the Grand Grimoire, but I'm sure you understand why we would avoid them."

I nodded, even though I had not the slightest clue.

"The Crow and Hammer is our last, desperate hope." Tears filmed Odette's eyes. "If you won't help us, we'll have no choice but to forsake the missing fae and disband our coven, since we're obviously unfit to—"

"Whoa, let's not be hasty." I rubbed my hands over my face to clear the alcohol haze. "Do you have any leads? Any idea what's happening to the fae in the park?"

Brightening at this sign of cooperation, Olivia leaned forward. "We don't have any solid theories, but our best guess is black witches."

"Black witches ..." A bad witch, I was assuming. "Humor me. What makes a witch a *black* witch?"

"Any witch who treats with darkfae," Odette answered promptly. "Or witches who lie to, trick, or betray the fae they treat with."

"Or witches who commit crimes on behalf of fae to win greater rewards," Olivia added.

I tugged on my ponytail. "Okay ... so what would a black witch want with the fae in Stanley Park?"

"Normally, I would say nothing," Olivia replied slowly. "The smallfae are too weak and inconsequential to interest a black witch. However, we've found signs of a familiar hunt."

"A familiar hunt? Familiar how?"

"A hunt *for* a familiar," she clarified, her mouth creased with distaste. "Black witches often find it cumbersome to arrange an exchange of equal value with a fae, so instead they'll hunt down a fae they think is powerful or impressive and forcefully bind it to them as their familiar."

"But as Olivia said," Odette continued, "the smallfae in the park are too weak to be worth hunting and binding. We're not sure what's going on."

"*Something* is happening there. Something dreadful."

"The black witches must be stopped."

"The lost fae must be found, even if it's too late to save them."

"We need your help. We need your guild."

"We have no one else to—"

"Stop!" I pressed a hand to my forehead, my brain sloshing from their rapid back and forth. "Just stop. I need to think."

Folding their hands, they waited.

I massaged my temples. All that energy I'd had while singing and cleaning had evaporated, and all I wanted to do was crawl into bed. Maybe throw up first, *then* go to bed.

"I can't promise anything," I finally said. "But I'll pass it on to my guild. They'll decide what they want to do and all that."

Beaming, the witches swooped down on me and shook my limp hands.

"Thank you, Tori. Thank you so much!"

"We'll eagerly await your guild's reply."

"The coven will be so relieved to hear the good news."

"You can contact us at any time through the coven. Don't hesitate to call with any questions."

"We'll help in any way we can. Just let us know when your guild is ready to begin the investigation!"

My head was spinning again. "Hold up. I never said we—"

"We won't trespass on your hospitality any longer," Odette gushed, still shaking my hand.

"Bless your heart, Tori. I'm so happy we came to speak with you. You are truly a woman of integrity and compassion."

"No, I'm not—" I stammered. "I didn't—"

Releasing me, the two witches swept toward the stairs. I scrambled off my stool and rushed after them, but by the time I got to the bottom of the steps, they were at the top, waving farewell.

"We'll speak again soon, Tori! Thank you from the bottom of our hearts!"

And with that, they vanished through the door. Grabbing the railing for balance, I careened up the stairs and onto the stoop, but the yard was dark and empty. The sisters were gone.

Well, shit. Face scrunching, I mentally reviewed our conversation, searching for the moment when I'd promised the Crow and Hammer would take the job. Hadn't I clearly said I couldn't promise anything? I *had* said that, right?

Or had I accidentally committed my guild to investigating a case of missing fae that every guild in the city had turned down?

Oh man. Kai was going to yell at me. Aaron would laugh, but Kai … yeah, he was going to yell.

5

I **WOKE** with the mother of all headaches—a mother headache nursing baby headaches inside my temples, and the throbbing family threatened to split my skull across my eye sockets. Groaning, I dragged my pathetic ass out of bed and swallowed back the foul taste in my mouth. Whiskey was the devil's drink.

I made a mental note to ask the guys if demons drank whiskey. I knew nothing about the Demonica class, except, well, *demons.*

Too bad the guys were busy pretending I didn't exist until MagiPol went away. And by then, I'd be out of a job, if not our friendships. That was assuming they didn't friend-dump me for the whole witch fiasco last night.

I tried to run my hands through my curls, but my fingers got stuck in the rat's nest. What the hell had I been thinking? I never should've answered the door, let alone invited the witches in, let alone encouraged them to dump all their problems in my lap. And how had they arrived at the conclusion that I'd promised my guild's help? I *really* didn't remember saying that.

Ideally, I would call the witches up, explain the misunderstanding, and brush the whole incident under the rug. Perfect solution—*if* I had access to the mythic database of guilds and their contact info. Which I didn't.

Locating my cell under my pillow, I pondered the screen. Aaron was one call away ... but Ezra had warned me that MagiPol liked to snoop through their phones. What if Agent Harris had Aaron's phone right now? What if calling him led the MPD right to my doorstep?

Nope, not safe. I had only one option if I wanted to speak with the guys.

As a grin spread across my face, I checked the time—quarter to eleven. Aaron, Kai, and Ezra rarely showed up at the guild before two, usually closer to four. Lazy bums slept in later than I did, but that worked in my favor today. With a little luck, I could catch them at home.

I took a bouncing step toward my bedroom door but stopped when my head gave an extra violent throb. Trying again at a more sedate pace, I swung my door open.

A stool from the kitchen was positioned directly in front of my room. And standing on the stool was Twiggy, his solid green eyes intense. Huh?

While I stared in confusion, he drew himself up. "Slap bet!"

And then he smacked me across the face.

I reeled into the doorframe. Hand pressed to my cheek, I shrieked, "What the hell is wrong with you, you piece of green shit!"

"Slap bet!" he repeated shrilly, a delighted grin stretching his cheeks. "It's funny, right? Humans like funny things like—"

I lunged for him. He leaped off the stool and I collided with it.

"Slap beeeeet!" he wailed, fleeing across the living room. "It's funny!"

"No, it's not!" I bellowed, chasing after him. "I'm going to wring your skinny neck!"

Yanking open the crawlspace door, he dove into the darkness beyond. I skidded to a stop and kicked the door shut.

"Stay in there!" I yelled. "And no more sitcoms!"

"But they're funny!" he shouted from the crawlspace.

"You wouldn't know funny if it hit you in the goddamn face!" Snarling and rubbing my cheek, I stalked into the bathroom and slammed the door. Curse past-Tori for her genius idea to let a faery who couldn't grasp the most basic of normal human interactions watch *sitcoms*.

After a shower that was too short to put a dent in my headache, I examined my cheek and decided Twiggy hadn't hit me hard. The hangover had merely made it *feel* like he'd cracked my face open. Stupid faery.

Vibrating with the need to yell at someone, I grabbed my phone and pulled up a conversation. My fingers flew over the digital keyboard as I typed a furious message.

Fae are stupid and you're stupid and if you were a decent human being you would tell me how to get out of having a faery roommate.

I sent it and waited for a count of ten. As usual, he didn't respond. Not that I could blame him since all I ever did was insult him. I couldn't help it. It was cathartic, and even if he hadn't done anything to deserve this round of abuse, karmically speaking, he still deserved it. He had a backlog of assholery to answer for.

Ten minutes and three glasses of water later—hangovers sucked, ugh—I was heading up the stairs as I adjusted the final piece of my disguise. Okay, it wasn't really a disguise, but I didn't want to walk around flashing my red hair at anyone who might be watching Aaron's house.

I'd donned a lightweight sweater, its hood pulled up, and my hair was tucked under a ball cap. A pair of oversized sunglasses completed the concealment, and I didn't even look like a weirdo since the weather had transformed from sunshine bliss to gloomy clouds. I grabbed my umbrella, just in case.

The walk to Aaron's house took just over half an hour—not because it was far, but because I had to go around the ten square blocks of train terminal and business complex between our neighborhoods. Twitchy paranoia buzzed through me as I reached his street, lined on one side with houses while the other was a barrier of old trees that hid the aforementioned business complex from view.

I checked for any vehicles with chain-smoking detective types sitting in them—no sign of anything suspicious—then walked well past the blue cottage-style house. I entered the yard through the back alley and tried the handle. Locked.

Squatting, I pulled up the loose brick at the edge of the stoop and grabbed the spare key. After unlocking the door, I replaced the key and waltzed inside.

As I'd been doing for the better part of three months, I kicked my shoes off and set my purse and umbrella on a nearby counter, then walked into the middle of the kitchen. I'd been over here plenty of times, but never this early—and never unannounced.

To my surprise, the house wasn't silent. The bass beat of music thumped through the floor, and I frowned at the door to the basement. They were up? Really? It wasn't even noon.

I tossed my sunglasses into my purse, then cracked the basement door open, letting the music—some generic rock song with a quick beat—into the kitchen. The lights were on, but all I could see was a sliver of an unfinished room.

A polite, tactful person would've called down to announce her unexpected presence, but I'd never been called tactful in my life. Smirking, I padded down the stairs, paused at the bottom, then stuck my head around the corner, prepared to be shocked or possibly scandalized.

The rumpus room stretched the length of the house. One end was full of the usual basement collection of boxes, bins, and storage shelves, but the rest had been converted into a full-service gym. Treadmills, stair master, stationary bike, weight machines, free weights, and a mirrored wall. The other side had a punching bag suspended from the ceiling and thick sparring mats forming a large square. Music poured from a stereo in the corner.

Aaron was lying on a weight bench, holding a loaded barbell a few inches above his chest. Ezra stood in the spotter position, hands hovering below the bar.

Both guys were staring at me.

Right. Sneaking up on Ezra was almost impossible, despite him being half blind. With his aeromage magic, he could sense disturbances in the air caused by people moving around.

"Uh, hi?" I stepped off the last stair. "What's up?"

"Tori, what are you doing here?" Ezra blurted.

"Oh, just … you know … passing by." The last bit came out in a distracted mutter, because Aaron's sculpted arms were beautifully displayed by his sleeveless shirt—every muscle taut and bulging under the barbell.

"Passing by?" Ezra repeated, his surprise melting into amusement. "Where—"

With a grunt that sounded kind of like Ezra's name, Aaron lifted the bar about six inches, only for it to tilt dangerously to one side.

Ezra grabbed the barbell, taking its weight, and continued without missing a beat. "—were you headed that our place was on your way?"

I gazed at him, dumbfounded. "Uh ..."

Aaron sat up, wheezing, his face red from exertion.

"Just to be clear, Tori," he panted as Ezra placed the barbell on the rack, "I was at the end of my set before you came in. I don't normally need a rescue."

"Sure," I agreed absently. Frowning, I crossed the room to the bench. The guys watched me examine the setup, then step into Ezra's spot and grasp the bar loaded with weights.

"Um, Tori—" Aaron began.

I pulled. It felt like pulling on a piece of steel embedded in concrete. Teeth gritted, I strained to shift it. The barbell didn't budge.

"What the hell?" I muttered.

"It wouldn't be exercise if it were easy," Aaron pointed out. "I'd be happy to help you start weight training, but don't yank on that or you'll hurt yourself."

"But ..." I looked from the weights to Ezra. "You ..."

He blinked. "Me?"

Yes, him. He'd lifted that immovable hunk of metal like it was made of papier-mâché. I pursed my lips at the barbell. Maybe it wasn't that difficult to move for guys as fit as them, and Aaron had only struggled because he'd been at the end of his endurance.

Aaron poked at my sweater, breaking my trance. "What's with the getup?"

"I'm in disguise. Who knows if MagiPol is scoping out your house?"

"It's a possibility, to be honest. It's not a good idea for you to be here."

Hurt cut through me. I folded my arms angrily. "Well, maybe I wouldn't have had to come by if you'd bothered to contact me. I've been sitting around for days, not knowing what's happening or if I'll ever see you again, while you've been going on like nothing is wr—"

"Tori," Ezra interrupted, his tone unexpectedly sharp. "I told you this was temporary."

His obvious displeasure surprised me. He was normally impossible to offend. I opened my mouth, then closed it.

Aaron hopped off the bench and slung an arm around me. "Well, you're here now! Damn, I've missed you."

I wrinkled my nose. "You're sweaty."

"That happens with exercise. We're two hours into our routine."

My mouth fell open. "Two *hours*? Why are you doing such a big workout so early?"

"Early? We started late today." He steered me toward the stairs. "We'd normally go for another hour, but we can cut it short today. We still need to do a cooldown, though."

I did some easy math in my head. "A *three-hour* workout? Is it a special fitness day or something?"

"We train like this almost every day."

Whoa. Seriously? How did they have time for that much exercise when—

"Wait. Is *that* why you guys never show up anywhere before mid-afternoon?"

"Did you think we slept twelve hours a day?"

Maybe. "So you're saying you work out for hours every morning?"

"Yep," he said, releasing me as we entered the kitchen. Ezra came in after us and tossed Aaron the water bottle he'd carried up. The pyromage took a long drink before continuing. "We need to be in top condition to withstand the drain of our magic. Any mage worth anything trains like an athlete."

I'd heard that before, but I had given little thought to how *much* training Elementaria required—especially to be at the top of their class.

"We need to do a cooldown, then shower," Aaron added. "Give us a few minutes."

He leaned down to kiss me. I tilted my face up and his lips brushed mine, then he was hurrying back downstairs. Ezra started to follow.

"Ezra!" His name popped from my lips against my better judgment.

He glanced back, head angled so he could see me with his right eye.

I bit my lip. Was I seeing things that weren't there? But no, awkwardness lurked in his silence. Something I'd said had upset him.

"I'm sorry," I blurted.

His eyebrows pulled together. "For what?"

"I don't know." I wrung my hands together. "But you're mad at me and I'm sorry."

His mismatched eyes softened. "I'm not angry, Tori. It's just that I promised you this was all temporary, and you didn't believe me. That sucked to hear."

"I …" I swallowed. "I didn't mean to not believe you. I just know how these things always play out."

"How do they always play out?"

My gaze dropped to the floor. "I lose my job and all my new friends forget about me."

"Do you really think we're like those other people?"

I peeked up at him, the intensity of his question catching me off guard. So fast I wondered if I'd imagined his solemn tone, he gave me a quick smile and disappeared down the stairs.

Blinking at the empty doorway, I rubbed a bewildered hand over my mouth. Morning-Ezra was full of surprises.

He was cagey about his past, but I was too, so I didn't ask questions. What I did know was that Ezra could beat anyone at video games, liked mountain scenery, read thrillers and police procedurals, watched *Game of Thrones* religiously, disliked *Harry Potter* for some reason I'd never understand, picked bell peppers out of his food, couldn't cook a meal without breaking a dish—half blind, remember?—and fell asleep partway through most movies.

I knew way more than that—the little things, the day-to-day things—but when it came to the important stuff, I was left in the dark. *None* of the guys would let me in. Even Aaron, who I was supposed to be dating, didn't talk about his childhood, his family, his future, his ambitions, or his wildest dreams.

Was I as much their friend as I thought I was?

Lost in thought, I wandered into the living room and sat on the sofa. A few minutes later, my anxious reverie was interrupted by Aaron, dressed in jeans and a t-shirt, rubbing a towel over his dripping hair. I hadn't heard the shower running in the main-level bathroom, so he must've used the downstairs bathroom—a mythical place I had never seen.

"Did you show up just because you missed us?" Aaron joked as though no time had passed. He pulled the towel off his head and smiled roguishly. "Did you miss *me?*"

"Of course I missed you."

He blinked, startled by my honesty. He must've expected a smartass comeback.

"Give me an update," I ordered. "What's happened with the MPD? Did you go to your summons? What about the charges against Ezra?"

Tossing his towel on the coffee table, Aaron flopped onto the sofa beside me. "The investigation? Let's see. Kai and I went to our summons on Monday. It was easy to rearrange the story to make it seem like the Rivers revealed Nadine's situation instead of you."

I nodded earnestly. "Speaking of Kai, where is he?"

"Took his lady-of-the-week out for lunch."

Glad to see all the chaos surrounding the guild wasn't interfering with Kai's love life. I kept forgetting he was a complete player who dated multiple women at once but never for more than a few weeks. He just didn't *seem* like a womanizer.

"How could he skip his workout?" I asked jokingly.

"He didn't. The asshole got up at six."

"Oh." I shuddered. "That sounds horrific."

"Agreed." Aaron pondered for a moment. "Back to the investigation, Darius had a meeting with the MPD and convinced them to drop the 'excessive force' charges against

Ezra since a kid's life was at stake. They're still searching for you, but Kai and Darius came up with a great cover story that's thrown the MPD off your trail."

"Nice! What's the story?"

"Probably better you don't know it, in case they ever question you." He straightened out of his slouch. "That's basically it. The investigation is ongoing, but when they can't find 'Patricia Erikson,' they'll post a bounty and be done with it. Then we'll be back to normal."

Ezra had said that too, but my doubts remained firmly entrenched.

"Now it's your turn."

I blinked. "My turn?"

"Yeah. *Something* brought you over here first thing. Spill it."

Right. Hoping to start off on a light note, I dramatically declared, "Last night, my house was invaded by witches."

As I spoke, the door to the basement stairs clacked. Then—

"Witches?"

I looked toward Ezra's voice and my mind went blank. Totally blank.

"Dude." Aaron's voice barely penetrated my daze. "Why are you naked?"

He wasn't naked. A towel was wrapped around his lean hips, but aside from that, he was clothed only in glistening droplets, the water clinging to every inch of his smooth bronze skin and hard muscles.

"I forgot to bring clean clothes down with me," Ezra said. "Tori, what do you mean witches invaded your house?"

Along with his mouthwatering musculature, his scars were on full display—three parallel white lines that raked up one hip, across his stomach, and stopped at his sternum. I'd seen them once before, but they looked more terrible than I'd remembered—the lines thicker and more jagged.

I hauled my gawking stare off him and over to Aaron. Eyes on Aaron. Yes. I was dating Aaron, and I would not be *that* girl.

"Witches!" Hearing a faint note of panic in my voice, I cleared my throat. "They asked the local fae for a friendly witch and got pointed in my direction."

"You're not a witch," Aaron observed dryly. If he'd noticed my punched-in-the-throat expression, he wasn't showing it.

"They thought I was." I stared intently into Aaron's gorgeous big blues. Ezra needed to put clothes on. *Why* was he standing there in his towel? Him being completely unaware of his good looks was clearly a problem.

Desperate to stay focused, I spoke at top speed. "They said fae have been going missing in Stanley Park for the last four months and they think it's the work of black witches but no other guild will help them so they asked me but I told them I couldn't agree to anything but they somehow misunderstood and now they think the Crow and Hammer will investigate and—" I ran out of breath and had to gasp for air. "And that's about it."

Aaron gave a slow blink. "You told them we'd investigate?"

"No. Definitely not. I said I'd tell you about it but I couldn't promise anything." I grimaced. "At least, I think that's what I said."

"You *think?*"

"I might have been a little drunk."

"Drunk?" Ezra repeated in surprise.

I almost looked at him again but resisted. Oh my god, go get some damn clothes!

"Why were you drunk?" Aaron asked.

"I did a few shots to go with my cleaning spree. I had nothing else to do."

Sympathy flickered in his expression. "We should've snuck out to see you."

Damn right they should have, but I'd already made myself seem pathetic enough. "Whatever. It's fine."

Aaron rubbed his jaw. "So, the coven expects us to investigate the fae disappearances?"

I wilted. "Sorry."

He threw his head back and laughed. "We send you home on vacation, and you turn around and sign us up for a job. Well played."

My lips quirked into a smile. I'd known Aaron would laugh—and Kai wasn't here to yell at me.

I snuck a peek at the other end of the living room, but Ezra had vanished—presumably upstairs to find clothes. About goddamn time. I'd seen him close to naked before, but not all wet and glistening and—

No, not thinking about that.

"Anyway!" I said brightly. "I did my best to handle it. Now it's your problem."

"Thanks, Tori. Appreciate your effort." His grin melted into thoughtfulness. "Everyone else turned them down, eh? That's weird. We aren't the only guild with witches on the roster."

"The O-sisters claim they even asked Odin's Eye, but they passed based on money."

"No surprise there. Odin's Eye are bounty specialists. They don't get out of bed for anything less than five figures."

Footsteps thumped quietly down the stairs, then Ezra appeared in jeans and a thin V-neck t-shirt. As he sat on the armchair, Aaron dusted his hands together.

"All right, Tori. Let's take it from the top. Tell us everything they told you."

I ran through all the details, then let the guys mull it over.

"It's strange," Ezra finally said. "That many missing fae isn't something MagiPol would ignore. There must be a posting for it, so why would the other guilds refuse to investigate?"

"There's definitely more going on here," Aaron agreed. "And I've got to wonder which cards those witches were trying to play."

"What do you mean?" I asked.

"The witches may have approached you thinking that if they could convince one guild member, a sympathetic witch, to accept the job, it would force the entire guild to follow up."

"But we have five witches." Ezra scrubbed his fingers through his damp curls. "Reaching out to them would've been easier. Why approach Tori?"

"I wondered that too," I muttered. More so after sobering up, but no need to mention that.

"Maybe they know more about Tori than they let on," Ezra continued thoughtfully. "What if they know she's inexperienced and thought she'd be easier to manipulate?"

My eyes narrowed. "Manipulate" was one of my least favorite words, especially when I was on the receiving end.

Aaron nodded. "Seems unlikely that any fae would call her a witch. They'd know better than anyone she's not."

"You think the witches know I'm human, and they came to me because I'd be easier to trick?" My hands balled into fists. "I thought witches were all sweet and nature-loving and shit."

"They're people, and all people can be assholes. It wasn't necessarily malicious. I think we need to know why the other guilds hung them out to dry."

Ezra replied in a murmur and they began discussing theories, but I wasn't listening. I was too busy seething. Those witches had put on a real good act, but they'd been way too cool about my drunken state and way too happy to explain everything to me—things a mythic should have known. It made perfect sense: they knew I was human, or at least inexperienced, and they'd *used* me.

Once again, I was the useless human. Why couldn't I have been born a mythic too? Being back with the guys was driving my desperate desire for inclusion even deeper.

As Aaron headed upstairs in search of a laptop, I tugged on a lock of hair that had escaped my hat. "Hey, Ezra?"

"Mm?"

"When did you first know you were a mage?"

He canted his head at the random topic. "Elementaria is a hereditary class, so ... I can't remember ever *not* knowing. Young mages develop magic in pre-adolescence, and I was using simple air magic by ten years old. Aaron and Kai started even earlier."

"What if you didn't *know* you were born a mage? How would that work?"

"Magic comes naturally to most mages," he replied after a moment's thought. "Making it through my teens without discovering my magic would've been all but impossible, even if I hadn't known to expect it."

Aaron traipsed down the stairs with his open laptop balanced on one palm, screen already glowing. "Known to expect what?"

"That I was an aeromage," Ezra said before I could change the subject. "Tori was asking how mages start using magic."

I suppressed a cringe, praying the guys wouldn't guess the motivation behind my ill-thought-out question.

"Oh yeah." Aaron dropped down beside me. "We don't need training to start. I was drawn to fire as a toddler and igniting everything flammable by kindergarten."

Wow, Aaron *had* started young. Having famous mage-trainer parents might've helped.

Ezra's curious gaze swung back to me. "Why do you ask, Tori?"

"Just wondering," I said lightly, thanking my lucky stars that Kai wasn't around. *He* would've immediately guessed why I was asking. "Aaron, have you found anything about the missing fae?"

His fingers were sliding across the laptop trackpad. "Gimme a minute … okay, here. There's a listing and a standard bounty, but there are no investigative notes and no one has—wait." He squinted at the screen, then swore.

"What?" Ezra and I demanded in unison.

"The Crow and Hammer is listed as the lead guild in the investigation."

"*What?*" Perfect unison again. We even used the same part confused, part outraged tone.

"Looks like the coven made the decision for us," Aaron growled. He pulled his cell out of his pocket.

"What are you doing?" I asked.

"Calling Kai and telling him to come home. I want to get to the bottom of this before the coven signs us up for anything else."

"Oh." Kai. Returning to the house to hear all about the trouble I'd caused. That sounded like something I'd rather skip.

I pushed off the sofa. "I should head home then. Don't want the MPD catching me here."

Aaron grabbed the back of my sweater and yanked me down. "Oh no you don't."

"But I'm not supposed to be here," I protested.

His thumb swiped across the screen as he pulled up Kai's number. "Doesn't matter. You have to stay now."

"Why?"

Lifting the phone to his ear, he gave me a look that said I should know *exactly* why. "Because if Kai decides to yell at someone, better you than me."

I slumped into the cushions. Goddamn it.

6

KAI YELLED AT ME.

Okay, to be fair, Kai didn't actually yell. He rarely raised his voice, but he had this stern lecture tone where disapproval oozed from every syllable and it *felt* like being yelled at. Aaron called it yelling too, so I wasn't the only one.

After his lecture—covering everything from letting strangers into my house to accidentally making promises on the guild's behalf—he and Aaron decided to investigate the coven to make sure their fae case was legit before proceeding with anything else.

And then they sent me home.

Back under house arrest, just like that. Ezra's and Aaron's reassurances that this was all temporary seemed even flimsier, and dread gathered in my chest like a blob of cold slush lodged in my lungs.

I spent two more days moping around my house and skimming job postings with zero interest. I needed to find paying work, especially now that summer was ending. It was the last Friday of August, and next Tuesday was my first day of the fall semester. With college classes to fund and bills to pay, I couldn't lounge around much longer.

Yet here I was, sprawled on my bed in my PJs with a Disney movie playing on my laptop. At nine o'clock on a Friday night. Oh yeah, living it up. Look at me, total party girl.

Grumbling, I pillowed my head on my arm and watched Mulan's musical training montage. I empathized with her misfit status so hard, but her transformation from wimp to soldier left me depressed. I wished a shirtless captain with a topknot could sing a catchy song and magically turn me into a badass mythic.

I tried to imagine Darius singing. Nope. Maybe Girard? Yeah, that was more likely.

The movie continued, but I wasn't paying much attention. Ezra's brief explanation about magery had confirmed what I already knew: there was no way I could be a mage. I hadn't honestly believed it was possible, but a desperate part of me had still hoped.

Being not-special sucked.

Rolling onto my back, I stared at the ceiling. I wasn't secretly an Elementaria mythic, but could I belong to another class? *Something* had drawn me into the mythic world … right? Little human me had been surprising mythics since day one. If I could discover what was special about me, then I would cement my place in their world.

Someone knocked on my bedroom door.

I bolted upright on my bed. It couldn't be Twiggy. He never knocked; he lurked outside my door and ambushed me when I came out. Besides, he was still avoiding my wrath after the *slap bet*.

The handle turned, then the door creaked open. I grabbed my pillow, ready to defend myself.

Tousled copper hair appeared in the gap. "Surprise!"

"Aaron!" I gasped, pressing a hand to my chest. My heart hammered against my ribs. "I thought you were an axe murderer."

"Axe murderers don't typically knock." He pushed the door all the way open. "Figured I was due for a little revenge after your unannounced visit."

Shutting my laptop on Mushu's face, I swung my legs off the bed. "What are you doing here? Do I have my job back or is the MPD about to raid my house?"

"Neither." He waltzed over to my bed. "I snuck over to see you. Or, more specifically, to spring you from prison and take you out on the town."

"Huh?"

He gave my sloppy ponytail a playful tug. "A beautiful woman shouldn't be stuck at home on a Friday night."

What a cheesy line. I couldn't help smiling anyway. "You're a dork."

"That's a terrible thing to say—but if we're stereotyping, no dork is this ripped." He flexed his biceps in emphasis. "Ready for a night out?"

"Do I look ready?"

"You look gorgeous." He appraised my baggy t-shirt and yoga shorts before his gaze settled a good bit lower than my face. "If you want to go like that, I have zero complaints."

I gasped in mock affront and covered my chest. Grinning, Aaron leaned down and captured my mouth. His hot lips sent a steamy swoop through my middle, and desire threaded through his kiss as he slid a hand into my hair.

"Or we could stay in," he murmured against my mouth. "Watch the rest of your movie together."

With one hand pressed to his warm side, his soft cotton shirt all that separated my palm from his hard, muscular body, I seriously considered it. But I also knew my ability to resist his smoldering allure was next to none. If he joined me in bed for a movie, our clothes wouldn't stay on for long.

Aaron and I had been casually dating for weeks now, but we hadn't yet made it into his bed or mine. It wasn't that I didn't want him—oh hell yes, I did—or that I had a reason to hold back. We were just so casual, and I liked it that way. Sleeping with him would take our … whatever we had going on … to the next level. I wasn't ready for that.

"I've been stuck in the house all week," I said. "Please, get me out of here."

Unfazed by the rejection, he straightened with a smile. "Late dinner, or a movie, or both?"

"Both!" I hopped up and opened my closet doors. "Start the countdown. Ten minutes to get ready."

"No woman can be ready in ten minutes. I bet fifteen."

"Eight," I countered. "And I get to pick the movie."

"Deal." He pulled out his phone to set a timer. "If I win, I get to pick the movie *and* order your dinner."

"What? That's not fair." I pulled out a sleeveless purple top, then flipped a pair of skinny jeans over my shoulder. "I get to order your meal if I win."

"Fine." He grinned. "You're having steak."

I wrinkled my nose. "*Not* rare."

"My choice." He watched me select a lacy black bra, heat sparking in his gaze.

Heading toward the bathroom with my outfit, I called over my shoulder, "You're getting a salad."

He gagged as he followed me. "I'll starve to death before the movie is over."

"I'll order extra croutons. You'll be fine." I closed the door on him, then stripped off my lounge clothes, shimmied into my jeans, put on my bra, and pulled on the top, adjusting the plunging cowl neck over the tight black underlayer. Swinging the door open again, I dug a handful of bobby pins out of the vanity drawer. "How's the investigation into the coven going?"

Aaron leaned in the doorway. "The witch sisters are legit members. Olivia and Odette O'Conner. They've—"

"Wait. *O'Conner*? Seriously? Their parents have a terrible sense of humor."

He chuckled. "They've been with the coven for two years. Kai confirmed the fae disappearances, but we're still unclear on why the other guilds are snubbing the bounty. He also talked to the matron, who swears up and down that our guild agreed to take on the job."

Grinding my teeth at the last part, I twisted my hair into a messy bun and started pinning it in place. "What next?"

"Kai arranged a meeting with the matron for tomorrow afternoon. We'll see how bold she is once we're all in the same room. Philip is coming along too. He's the unofficial leader of our five witches."

My hands paused. "Dudes can be witches?"

"Yeah. Some covens are all women, though. Discriminatory, if you ask me."

"Do they have something against male witches?"

"Nah, just an old tradition. Because Spiritalis magic is so ritualistic, witches are more superstitious than most classes."

I reached into the drawer for a final bobby pin. "Time che— huh?"

Instead of bobby pins, I pulled a handful of small pine cones from the back of the drawer. "That faery!" I chucked the cones in the garbage and located a bobby pin. "Time check?"

"One minute left," he informed me triumphantly. "You haven't even started your makeup."

Smiling smugly, I gave my frizzy bun a spritz of hairspray, then grabbed a tube of lip gloss and applied it in two swift strokes. After tossing it in the drawer, I turned to face him, hands on my hips. "Done."

"What? No mascara? No blush or that skin-colored goop … uh … foundation?"

"Meh." I arched an eyebrow. "Unless you think I need to wear makeup?"

His blue eyes skimmed my face, then followed my tight jeans from the curves of my hips down to my ankles. His smile was slow and sultry.

"No," he rumbled. "Definitely not."

He stepped into the bathroom and my heart skipped a beat. I subconsciously licked my lips, tasting the cherry gloss. His hands curled over my hips, drawing me closer, then he kissed me.

As his mouth leisurely moved across mine, I wound my arms around his neck, fingers sliding into his hair. Pressing against the hard planes of his torso, I let a soft moan slip from my throat.

He wrapped his arms around my waist and pushed me into the bathroom wall. His kiss deepened, laziness kindling into hunger. I parted my lips and his tongue flirted with mine. As heat spiraled through me, my hand crept from his neck to the top button of his shirt.

I popped it apart and slid my fingers under his shirt collar. His skin was hot. His mouth was even hotter. Arching off the wall, I pulled my mouth away to gasp in a breath. His lips slid along my jaw to my ear.

My blood was rushing and I tried to remember my reasons for keeping our clothes on. Couldn't have been that important if I'd already forgotten them. Biting my lower lip as he kissed down the side of my neck, I undid the next button of his shirt.

The blare of a ringing phone shattered the quiet.

Jerking upright, Aaron swore. "I meant to turn it off. I'm sorry."

"It's okay," I said breathlessly. "This isn't a good time for you to be unreachable. Go ahead."

With a black scowl, he dragged his phone out and lifted it to his ear.

"What?" he barked. A muffled voice replied, and his eyes widened. "No way. Right now? Well, shit."

Disappointment sank through me in a cold wave. Glumly, I looked down at my pretty top and sexy jeans.

"Yeah," Aaron muttered. "Okay. I'm on my way."

Heaving a silent sigh, I tugged an uncomfortable bobby pin out of my hair, and a curly lock sagged free from my bun. It would be a night in after all—and not the fun, naughty kind. Mushu, Mulan, and I would have to make do without a scrumptious redhead for company. Without anyone for company.

"That was Kai," Aaron told me, his brow creased as he shoved his phone in his pocket. "The O'Conner sisters just called. There's activity in Stanley Park and they think it's the black witches—or whoever the culprits behind the disappearances are."

My eyes widened. "Are you going to check it out?"

"Yeah. Kai just ditched his date. He's heading for the park, and I need to pick up Ezra." He backed out of the bathroom and hastened across the main room. "We need to grab our gear and let the on-duty officer know—who's on duty tonight? Tabitha, I think? Let her know where—"

He stopped abruptly and turned, distress creasing his forehead. "Tori ..."

I forced a smile as I joined him. "It's cool. I'm the reason you're going, right? Go catch some bad guys."

His brow furrowed even more, then he grinned. "Come with me."

"Huh?"

"Come with us!" He caught me around the waist and pulled me close. "Those O'Conner sisters are shifty, and we could use an extra pair of eyes on them."

I bit my lip uncertainly. "Darius was clear. Jobs are for guild members only."

"Rule number two." He winked. "Besides, the witches involved you first."

I considered that, debating whether he really wanted me along or if it was a pity invite. Probably both, but how much did I care? This might be my last chance to do mythic work with the guys—and maybe, if I got out there one more time, I'd figure out how I fit into their world.

"I'm in. Gimme one sec."

I darted into my bedroom and opened my nightstand drawer. In it were three sorcery artifacts: my Queen of Spades card, stolen from a rogue sorcerer in my first violent mythic encounter; a fat ruby-red crystal on a leather tie, also stolen; and a very illegal spell set in a green crystal that I probably shouldn't be hanging on to.

Weighing my options, I took the card and the ruby crystal and stuffed them in my pocket, leaving the extra taboo spell behind. I grabbed my black leather bomber jacket, then trotted back to Aaron.

"Okay, I'm ready."

He caught the loose lock of my hair and twisted it around my bun, then brushed his fingers across my cheek. "I missed that."

"Missed what?"

"Your smile. The real, happy one, not that fake one you put on." My heart tumbled over itself, but his gaze was already sharpening with mischief. "Let's kick some mythic ass."

7

"WE'RE ALL SET," Ezra announced as he ended the call on his cell. "Tabitha gave the okay, and she's putting Philip on standby as our Spiritalis backup."

We were jammed in Aaron's old sports car—Aaron driving, me in the passenger seat, and Ezra getting leg cramps in the back. Streetlights flashed by as we sped through the last Coal Harbor skyscrapers. We'd just passed the corner to Justin's apartment building, and straight ahead was Stanley Park—a huge chunk of land connected to the northwestern tip of downtown and surrounded by ocean.

"Tabitha also mentioned that MagiPol came knocking again this evening," Ezra added. "Another surprise search."

"Assholes," Aaron growled. "They know something is up and they aren't letting it go."

"Yeah," Ezra agreed. "I wonder if their persistence has anything to do with their grudge against Darius."

"What grudge?" I asked.

Ezra leaned over the center console. "Darius is always weaseling guildeds out of trouble. He knows the rule book front to back and he's found all the loopholes."

"Like last year," Aaron mused, "when I burned that building down and Darius got me off on a technicality."

This wasn't the first time Aaron had mentioned burning a building to the ground. The pyromage was a walking insurance claim.

I had to ask. "What technicality?"

Aaron flashed me a grin. "*Technically*, I was destroying evidence of werewolf activity."

"And we didn't mention that, *technically*, the fire had been an accident," Ezra added.

"I started the fire, but you blew burning debris all over the place."

"I was blowing it *at* the werewolves. It was very effective. They hate fire."

"That's what I told Darius, but he still enrolled us in a fire safety course as punishment." Aaron cast me a look of traumatic suffering. "It was full of middle-aged, corporate paper pushers. We had to do pretend evacuations."

"We did a real evacuation too," Ezra pointed out. "After you set off the smoke detector."

Aaron shrugged. "I wanted to see how they would react."

I choked on my laughter and ended up in a coughing fit. Wiping tears from my eyes, I asked, "Do you think Darius can get MagiPol off my back?"

"He'll make it happen. The guy is a genius."

"And a legend," Ezra added with obvious admiration. "Him and Alistair."

"Darius is a luminamage, right?" I asked, recalling our miraculous escape from the MPD agents. "How does that work exactly?"

"Luminamages can control light," Aaron explained, checking his mirrors before changing lanes. The car zoomed across a short bridge, and towering trees closed around the road as we entered the forested park. "He can bend light around objects to hide them, suppress all the light in a room, or even stop light from reaching someone's eyes, effectively blinding them. Lumina magic is difficult to master—it requires more finesse and control than the other elements."

I resisted the urge to glance at Ezra. He, too, had an eerie ability to make rooms go dark—and cold.

"It's an insanely effective defense," Aaron continued. "When he and Alistair work together, they're unstoppable."

"What kind of mage is Alistair?"

"Volcanomage," Aaron answered reverently. "Fire and earth. Probably the most destructive Elementaria combination."

"Think lava," Ezra suggested helpfully.

I rolled my eyes. "Thanks, Ezra. I wouldn't have guessed that from the 'volcano' part."

Dark trees leaned over the road. It was ten o'clock and the last of the dusk light had vanished while we were driving. The forested corridor went on forever, but finally, Aaron turned onto a single-lane road. No other cars exited the main thoroughfare with us, and we drove alone around another winding bend. The woods opened into a parking lot, empty except for two vehicles: a blue sedan and a black motorcycle a few spots over.

Aaron parked beside the bike and we piled out. As he opened the trunk so he and Ezra could gear up, I pulled on my leather jacket and checked that my runners were double knotted. Trip on my shoelaces? No thanks.

The guys joined me—Aaron with his big-ass sword, Sharpie, strapped to his back, the hilt jutting over one shoulder, and Ezra with his fingerless gloves running past his elbows, the knuckles shining with steel. A strap crossed his chest, holding his weapon against his back—a transformative pole-arm that could be used as a baton, twin short-swords, or a double-bladed staff.

Mages wielding weapons had taken me by surprise, but I'd learned they worked best with special tools—called switches— to channel their magic. And being combat mages, their switches were always weapons.

Aaron also carried a black bundle under one arm—Kai's gear, I figured. He set out first, and Ezra and I fell into step behind him. Across the parking lot, a sidewalk led to a cluster of buildings—a steakhouse, a small café, and a souvenir shop, all dark.

"Where are we?" I whispered.

"Prospect Point," Aaron answered over his shoulder. "Kai texted me that he's waiting with the witches at the lookout spot."

I didn't have to wonder what that meant. Ahead, the trees ended, and the sidewalk widened into several tiers perched upon a cliff edge, offering a stunning view of what lay beyond.

Dark water, moonlight reflecting off its rippling waves, stretched across a wide inlet. Orange city lights blazed along the coast at the other end, and beyond them, a backdrop of low mountains was silhouetted against the midnight blue sky. A brilliantly lit suspension bridge arched over the water, each thick cable topped by a star-like sparkle.

On the lowest tier of the lookout point, three shadowed figures waited. Kai, his arms crossed, stood a few feet away from two familiar blondes. Olivia and Odette smiled shyly at me, but I stared back coldly. Kai's expression was painfully neutral—meaning he was pissed off. But who was he irritated with?

Aaron handed the electramage's gear over, then gave the witches a grin that toed the line between friendly and sharp. "You two must be the O'Conner sisters."

"Aaron Sinclair," Odette said breathlessly. "Your reputation precedes you."

His grin was definitely sharp now. He gestured. "This is Ezra Rowe, a Crow and Hammer aeromage."

The sisters assessed Ezra, their eyes nervously tracing the scar on his face.

"How lovely to see you again, Olivia and Odette," I said with venomous sweetness. "I hope we didn't keep you waiting long."

"N-not at all," Olivia stammered. "Though we really should get moving."

"Look west," Kai instructed as he pulled on his ninja-vest, the subtly armored black garment arrayed with pockets of throwing knives and steel stars. "Someone has lights set up down on the beach."

I squinted along the coastline. Beyond a rocky outcropping, a man-made glow glimmered on the water.

"There are definitely people down there," Aaron agreed. "Let's go see who they are and what they're up to."

He strode back up the pathway with Kai beside him. Ezra and I followed, leaving the witches to trail after us. We traipsed up the sloping sidewalk and across the parking lot, then started down a paved path that wound into the thick woods.

"Excuse me," Olivia called in a low voice. "We were wondering … when is the rest of your team arriving?"

"This is the team."

She stumbled and almost fell. "Oh. I see."

I kept half an eye on her as we followed the winding trail down toward the coast. The lapping water grew louder and the odor of rotting seaweed permeated the air, overpowering the pleasant leafy smell of the forest. Light flickered through the trees, and nerves tightened my stomach. We were getting close.

Aaron and Kai slowed, then stepped off the trail into the trees. They moved carefully, barely rustling the undergrowth as they inched toward the lights. Ezra and I stopped to watch. Neither of us was any good at stealth.

"The seawall and a walking trail are just ahead," Odette murmured. "It's a steep drop from here down to the trail, though."

When Ezra and I made no effort to start a conversation, the sisters moved away from us and began whispering. The night was so silent I could almost make out their rapid words. I angled my head, trying to catch the sound.

Ezra glanced at me, then at the witches. A soft breeze kicked up, blowing their voices toward us.

"… only three mages," one was muttering. "I thought they were bringing a real team! It won't be enough."

"It might," the other whispered back. "As long as they interrupt the—"

With a rustle of foliage, Aaron and Kai stepped back onto the path. The electramage swiveled sharply toward the witches. "Care to explain what's happening down there, ladies?"

Olivia's eyes widened. "Is something happening? What did you s—"

"You know what we saw," Aaron snarled. "What game are you playing?"

"What did you see?" I demanded.

"A black magic ritual on the beach. A massive circle, a dozen mythics, portable lights, and crates of supplies. This is no small operation."

Cold spread through me, adrenaline tingling in my fingers. A dozen mythics was too many, even for three tough-as-shit combat mages.

"You were supposed to bring a *real* team," I informed them with heavy sarcasm, then jerked my thumb at the sisters. "According to them, anyway."

"You have five seconds to start explaining," Kai said flatly. "Starting now."

Olivia and Odette exchanged panicked looks, and I thought wistfully of my illegal interrogation spell.

When they didn't speak, Kai nodded curtly. "Very well. Aaron, Ezra, Tori—let's go."

"Go where?" Olivia yelped.

"Back to our guild."

He strode past them, and Ezra followed. Aaron grabbed my hand on his way by, pulling me into motion.

"We're leaving?" I whispered incredulously.

"Hell yeah. We might be reckless, but we aren't crazy. There's too many of them, and we'd be going in blind. It could be an ambush for all we—"

"Wait!" Olivia ran after us, her sister on her heels. "You can't leave! You have to stop them!"

Kai didn't slow. "No."

Ooh, someone didn't like getting played either. I felt a fresh surge of affection for Kai.

"Please!" Odette begged. "You can't let this happen."

The guys kept walking, but I hesitated. Whatever was going down on the beach sounded nasty. We should at least find out what those mythics were up to, shouldn't we? It was the responsible thing to do.

Yeah. Responsible. It had nothing to do with my burning curiosity.

I stopped, drawing Aaron to a halt, and arched an eyebrow at the sisters. "Last chance. Explain."

Olivia hesitated, then steeled herself. "Those rogues are trying to *bind a fae lord*."

She said it like she expected me to gasp loudly, lay a hand against my forehead, and contemplate fainting on the spot.

Instead, I scrunched my nose. "Huh?"

"A fae lord!" she repeated with a spark of anger. "The most elite and powerful of the wyldfae. Black witches have ways to force fae into becoming their familiars, but no one has ever bound a fae lord before. If they succeed, they'll command a power beyond—beyond anything we can comprehend!"

"You knew about this all along," I accused. "Was all that stuff about the missing fae a lie?"

"It wasn't! The smallfae *have* gone missing—those rogues have been killing them."

"If you knew it was rogues killing the fae, why didn't you say so? Why hide it?"

"Because …" Odette gulped audibly. "Because the rogues down there are from Red Rum."

Ominous silence hung over our small group, but I had no idea why. It sucked being out of the loop all the time. "Red Rum?"

"The nastiest rogue guild you'll ever have the pleasure of meeting," Aaron told me grimly. "They specialize in everything from extortion to assassination. Think 'mob boss' and add in the worst of the dark arts."

"If they bind the fae lord, they'll command his power." Olivia grasped my elbow. "Do you understand? Red Rum in control of a sea lord? It would be catastrophic."

Tugging my arm free, I brushed two fingers across my inner wrist where an almost invisible rune marked my skin. I'd met a wyldfae before, and the thought of Echo under the power of a rogue guild terrified me.

Faint heat kindled in my wrist, tingling under my skin.

"Hold up," Aaron cut in. "Sea lord? How do you know what type of wyldfae they're after?"

Olivia's eyes darted around as though she were searching for an escape. "Only one fae of any note comes here … There are legends about him—a sea spirit that once lived beneath the cliffs at Prospect Point."

"Anything else you'd like to share?" I asked nastily.

Her shoulders wilted. "The ritual will succeed or fail within the next hour. They must complete it before the tide comes back in. They can't be allowed to succeed …"

I pointed at the sisters. "You two wait there. We need to have a huddle."

"A huddle?" Aaron repeated bemusedly.

Taking his and Ezra's arms, I steered them twenty feet away. Kai followed with one eyebrow arched. Grabbing him too, I pulled them into a literal huddle, my arms around Aaron's and Kai's broad shoulders. Across from me, Ezra grinned in amusement.

"What's the game plan?" I whispered.

"Is the huddle necessary?" Kai asked grumpily.

"Absolutely. I've always wanted to be part of a superhero huddle."

"Which we're not," Aaron snorted.

"Shut up and let me have my moment." I looked between them. "We can't let Red Rum get control of an uber-fae, can we?"

"Assuming the ritual works, which I doubt it will." Kai considered our options. "We can stay and observe, but we shouldn't get involved. Red Rum isn't a guild we can afford to provoke. I'm betting they are the reason all the other guilds turned down this job. No one wants to end up with a target on their back."

"But what do we do if it looks like they might succeed?" I asked. "Don't get me wrong. I don't want you guys going up against *any* Red Rum rogues, let alone twelve, but ..."

Aaron nodded like I'd shared a complete thought instead of trailing into awkward silence. "She's got a point."

"Agreed." Kai pulled out of the huddle and withdrew his phone. "I'll text Darius."

As he sent off a quick message, I massaged my wrist and frowned toward the beach. Rhythmic sound rumbled through the trees—male voices chanting.

"They've started," Odette gasped. "They're summoning the fae lord!"

Aaron gestured for us to follow and stepped off the path. I got behind him as we crept through the trees, the sound of our movements covered by the chanting men.

Just before the hillside dropped off, I parted the branches of a shrub and peered out. Twenty-five feet below, a paved footpath hugged the coastline, and beyond that was a rocky beach. Shining puddles covered the mud exposed by the retreating tide.

Positioned on the foreshore was a cluster of men in dark clothes. Big work lights on stands surrounded them, shining bright beams on the circle they had carved deep into the mud—which must have been fifty feet across. Precise shapes had been drawn through it, and various tools and materials had been placed at specific points inside and around the outer ring.

Seven people stood back from the ritual, while four were stationed at the compass points of the circle, hands raised toward it as they chanted. The last man stood in the center, his back to the coast as he faced the ocean.

"Sorcerers," Olivia hissed. "The one in the middle is a witch. This is a foul blend of Arcana and Spiritalis."

I chewed my lip as the sorcerers continued their measured chant. The unfamiliar words vibrated through me even from this distance, making my skin itch.

"Anything from Darius?" Aaron whispered to Kai.

"Not yet. I just sent a message to Tabitha as well."

Crouched uncomfortably in the bushes, we watched for a few more minutes. The men chanted without pausing or stuttering, and I had to appreciate their perfectionism. How much had they practiced this?

"Maybe it won't work," Odette whispered hopefully. "Maybe the fae lord will resist the—"

An electronic buzz interrupted her. Kai raised his phone, the screen glowing with an incoming call. He swiped the screen and lifted it to his ear.

"Darius?"

"Under no circumstances are you to engage Red Rum." The guild master's stern words were loud enough to hear, even without switching the phone to speaker. "Withdraw immediately."

Kai's expression flickered with surprise, then hardened. "Yes, sir."

A protest bubbled up in my throat but I swallowed it back. Darius might hear me, and that would ruin the "secret" part of me joining the guys on this job.

"We'll leave immediately," Kai continued. "Should we—"

"Look!" Olivia gasped, pointing toward the ocean.

The water, which had been gently lapping against the muddy foreshore, frothed in agitation. The rogues continued chanting, and the others had spread out defensively. White-capped waves surged forward, almost reaching the ritual circle. The air shimmered and danced, and an even larger wave exploded upward like something invisible had slammed into it.

"Oh, blessings of the Mother Earth," Olivia tremored. "They have him."

Rippling like a mirage that wouldn't take form, a shadowy shape slid in and out of reality—a glimmer of scales, a flash of fins. The chanting rose in volume. Another shimmer distorted the water, then the creature solidified in a spiral of glittering light.

A gargantuan serpent writhed on the mudflats. Its body glistened with shades of deep blue, its pale underbelly protected by plates of leathery scale. A line of pointed dorsal fins ran down its back, and a fringe of fins and horns surrounded its large head, the wide brow tapering to a pointed muzzle.

Bracing its huge front fins on the ground, the beast threw its head back and loosed a horrendous shriek of primordial rage.

"A leviathan?" Aaron breathed in disbelief. "Holy shit, it's massive."

I bobbed my head dumbly. Oh yeah. Big and beautiful, just like a dragon. I'd know, having met a few.

"Kai!" Darius's voice cracked through the phone speaker, bringing the three guys to attention. "Withdraw."

The phone pressed to his ear, Kai hesitated. The fae twisted violently, as though trying to retreat, but it inched closer instead—irresistibly drawn to the circle, even as it fought with all its strength to stop.

"*Kai.*"

He sucked in a breath, then let it out. Catching Ezra's and Aaron's gazes, he said into the phone, "Yes, sir. We're leaving."

Backing away from the precarious drop-off, he got to his feet. Aaron sidled back as well, and Ezra rose into an awkward half-crouch, waiting for me to clear the way. Jaw tight, I minced backward.

"Cowards!" Olivia launched up, her hands clenched. "Get out there and stop them!"

"We're not—" Kai began.

The witch sprang forward, hands thrusting out. She slammed both palms into Ezra's chest—and shoved him backward off the bluff.

8

EZRA PITCHED DOWN the steep slope in a wave of dislodged foliage and clumps of clay. A gust of wind blasted the falling debris away as he broke his fall with a cushion of air—but he still slammed into the ground with painful force.

I hung half off the bluff, my arm outstretched in a failed attempt to grab him. Aaron held the back of my coat to keep me from falling too, and he yanked me into the cover of the trees.

On the mudflats, the leviathan writhed against the magic relentlessly dragging it toward the circle, but that distraction wasn't enough. The rogue mythics had noticed Ezra's plummet. Three of them broke away from the group and started toward the seawall.

Even with his wind magic, Ezra would never make it back up the sheer bluff. The seawall path followed the coastline, leaving nowhere to flee and nowhere to hide.

Without a word, Aaron took two running steps and jumped off the bluff.

As he plunged out of sight, Kai swore. He shoved his phone into my hand, spun on his heel, and sprang after his friends. The wind gusted as Ezra used his magic to slow Kai's fall.

And that left me alone with the two witches.

"You!" I snarled, pivoting to face them. Fury twisted through me, and my fist was flying before I knew what I was doing.

My knuckles cracked against Olivia's cheekbone and she fell back into a tree. Pain ricocheted through my hand and it felt like I'd severed my thumb—because I was still holding Kai's cell. As I yanked my hand back, the phone slipped from my grip. It bounced once, then tumbled off the bluff. A second later, a crunchy crack announced its arrival at the bottom.

I winced. Oops.

As Odette clutched her sister, babbling incoherently, Olivia cast a burning glare my way. Clambering up, she stalked to the bluff's edge, cautiously pushed off, and slid down it like a muddy waterslide—except a few feet from the bottom, her heel caught on a rock. Thrown off balance, she pitched forward and splatted on the concrete trail.

Ouch. That must've hurt. Somehow, I didn't feel too bad for her.

Olivia scrambled up and straightened her shirt, then ran toward the three mages. Ezra, Aaron, and Kai had retreated along the seawall, but the three rogues were closing in fast—and two more were on the way.

An ear-splitting cry erupted from the leviathan. It was a dozen yards from the ritual circle and twisting like a snake in agony, its pectoral fins gouging the mud.

The rogues reached the mages, and orange light erupted as Aaron unleashed the first attack. He charged in, flanked by Kai and Ezra. I expected them to split apart, one mage for each rogue, but as Aaron bowled through the first guy, Ezra slammed into the same mythic right after. Fast attacks—giving the sorcerers no time to complete an incantation.

Kai darted past them as Aaron swung his sword, unleashing a band of fire into the second rogue while Ezra blasted wind in the third's face. Kai swung around, his hands flashing in quick movements. Then he raised his fist.

Lightning leaped from him and speared the three rogues. They collapsed in convulsions and even after the crackling power had died, they didn't stir.

"Amazing," Odette whispered.

Olivia reached the guys, her mouth moving and hands gesturing emphatically toward the leviathan. Kai shook his head. Olivia pointed again, then jumped off the seawall and charged toward the mudflats. As she went, a shape formed at her heels—an orange tabby house cat. Her fae familiar?

Aaron, Kai, and Ezra exchanged looks, and I knew what they would do. They were too valiant to do anything else. They jumped onto the rocky beach, racing after Olivia as she ran straight for the oncoming rogues.

There was no way this wouldn't go badly. Growling, I grabbed Odette by the hair and hauled her toward the bluff.

"Stop!" she yelped shrilly. "What are you doing?"

"This is your fight too—so get down there and *fight!*"

"I can't!" Odette wailed, grabbing at my arm. "I don't have a familiar!"

"So?"

"Witches don't have any offensive magic! Without a familiar, we can't fight any more than you can!"

Bullshit. I was way more capable of fighting than this cupcake. "You're completely useless."

"That's why we needed a powerful guild," she whimpered. "That's why we got the Crow and Hammer to send their mages."

My gaze darted toward the bluff. Aaron, Kai, and Ezra, with Olivia behind them, were locked in combat halfway to the circle, but they weren't fighting two rogues anymore. They were battling two rogues and two shadowy beasts—one that resembled an ox on two legs, and something small that flitted around on blurry black wings.

"What the hell are those?" I demanded.

Odette tugged on her hair, still in my grip. "Red Rum's witches have enslaved familiars. They're darkfae that would normally be too powerful to … to … to …"

She kept repeating the word, her voice growing fainter. Her throat bobbed as she mumbled "to" over and over, her bugged-out eyes fixed on something in the trees behind me.

Releasing her hair, I spun around.

At first, I saw nothing. Then the air shimmered, rippled, and melted. A shape materialized from the darkness.

"Such fascinating chaos, brazen one." The otherworldly voice whispered across my senses as the creature's form solidified. It was a fae.

A fae I recognized.

Flowing garments in unfamiliar fabrics draped his lean body, but that wasn't the strangest thing about him. No, that would be the black dragon wings rising off his back, the long tail slithering along the leaf litter behind him, and the dark talons that tipped his slender fingers.

"Echo?" With effort, I closed my jaw. It had been weeks since my first and only glimpse of the dragon wyldfae's humanoid form. "What are you doing here?"

"I have answered your summons, as promised." He glided closer, silent on the forest floor. Halting beside me, he gazed toward the ocean and the dual battles—one between my mages and the rogues, and one between the leviathan and the ritual circle. "A most unpleasant night, I see."

I stared at his flawless skin, so close. I wanted to touch his delicately pointed ears and feel the texture of his braided black hair, shining with blue and purple streaks, that hung over one shoulder down to his waist. He didn't seem real, more like a dream than a living creature.

Another enraged cry from the leviathan snapped me out of my daze. "I didn't call you."

His large, dark eyes turned to me. Crystalline, pupilless, and with a hint of swirling stars in their depths. "You touched my mark upon your arm and called my name."

"No, I didn't. I touched my arm but I—I only *thought* your name. *Silently.*"

His lips curved in an unsettling smile, and I remembered a certain druid's warning to be very careful around this wyldfae.

A purplish glow blazed across the foreshore. The leviathan had reached the circle, and its lines pulsed with light. Contorting its thick, powerful body, the sea fae screamed as it was dragged toward the rogue in the center.

"Great fae!" Odette gasped, her voice shaking so badly the words were nearly incomprehensible. "Oh, noble lord, please, I beg you. Intercede in this black ritual and save your kin."

Echo didn't react to her plea. He studied the struggling leviathan, then appraised me with the same disconcerting focus. "You called, and I have answered. What aid may I give you?"

I pointed. "Can you stop that?"

"No longer." His leathery wings stretched wide, brushing the nearby trees, then folded against his back. "Llyrlethiad is already bound. All that remains is for the witch to enslave him."

My stomach dropped. Aaron, Kai, and Ezra were fighting to save the fae, but it was already too late. "There's nothing we can do?"

Echo canted his head. "Wrong question, little one."

Urgency pounded through me, and I struggled to calm myself, to think. To understand what the fae wanted me to ask.

"What can *I* do?" I blurted.

He smiled, flashing his predatory fangs. "*You* can deliver Llyrlethiad from the witch's enslavement. I will instruct you how, and the debt between us shall be met."

"Okay, yes! I agree," I added formally.

Echo's tail lashed side to side, rustling the shrubbery. "The witch holds a relic of fae power, for no human magic could enslave one such as Llyrlethiad. Part the relic from the witch's hold and you will save Llyrlethiad from his fate. This you must accomplish before the ritual is complete."

"How long until it's complete?"

Echo glanced into the sky where the full moon hung above the ocean. "Minutes."

Well, that was specific. "Anything else I need to know?"

"This you alone can do." Another fang-laden smile. "I shall offer one more small assistance."

"What's th—"

His elegant hands closed around my upper arms. Wings unfurling, he drifted weightlessly upward, and with a flick of his tail he pulled me off the bluff.

I choked on a shriek as we dropped, but his huge wings caught the air and my feet settled lightly on the ground. The pressure of his touch faded to a whisper and his soft, alien voice crooned in my ear.

"Farewell, brazen one."

I twisted around, but he was already gone. Okay then.

Facing the battlefield, I gulped down a wave of panic. I was on my own, but I could do this. I would make it work.

With my two sorcery artifacts in hand, I jumped off the seawall, landed on the rocks, and sprinted toward the mudflats. Red fire and white lightning flared, illuminating the ugly darkfae familiars—three now. The last two rogues not involved in the ritual had joined the fight.

Aaron and Kai held their tiny front line, the former with a blazing sword and the latter by whipping throwing knives into his enemies, followed by bolts of lightning. Ezra covered them from behind, his wind buffeting and blinding their opponents. Even Olivia was helping—sort of. She chucked rocks at the rogues while her nimble house cat familiar distracted the small, flying darkfae, keeping it out of the action.

My plan was simple: run *around* the scary mage/fae/rogue battle and figure out what to do about the remaining four sorcerers once I'd reached the ritual circle. No way that could go wrong, right?

I scrambled over the rocky beach and onto the sticky mud. It squished under my shoes, but at least it was flat. Running hard, I angled to zoom past the guys' fight.

But nope, not even that was going to work.

A rogue peeled away from the struggle and moved to cut me off. Gripping my Queen of Spades, I changed course—and ran right at him. His hand came up, a small object in his grasp. An artifact. He shouted an incantation.

I thrust my card out at the same time. "*Ori repercutio!*"

A swirl of gold light leaped from his artifact, hit the shimmering reflection of my spell, and rebounded. He threw himself down and the golden spell shot over his head, flashed across twenty feet of foreshore, and hit another rogue in the back.

The man crumpled face-first into the mud. In a single move, the nearest fae—an ox thing trying to smash Kai's skull in—whirled and grabbed the unconscious witch with two giant hands. Not in a nice, protective way, but with all the violence of an enslaved creature whose master had just lost control of it. The other rogues shouted in alarm, and one gestured wildly. The small, winged darkfae abandoned its attack on Olivia's familiar and flew at the ox's face.

My sorcerer opponent scrambled to his feet and pulled out another artifact. Now I was the one retreating—my Queen of Spades card needed five minutes to recharge and it was the only defense I had.

A blast of wind slammed into the sorcerer's back, throwing him off balance. Ezra charged out of the chaos and the sorcerer spun to meet him. The man bellowed an incantation, but Ezra flicked his fingers. Spiraling wind shoved the man's hand up, and the fiery light from the sorcerer's artifact shot into the sky.

Aaron broke away from the battle and swiped his sword through the air. A band of flame hit the sorcerer in the face and the man collapsed with a scream, clutching his eyes.

"Tori!" Aaron shouted. "What are you doing?"

"I need to get to the circle!"

"What? Why do you—"

The leviathan howled, drowning him out, but I was already running again. Aaron shot after me, while Ezra raced back to Kai and the three-way battle between fae, witches, and mages.

"Tori—" Aaron began in a shout as he caught up.

"I have instructions!" I bellowed cryptically. We were almost to the circle, its lines rippling with eerie purple light. "I can save the fae!"

He grunted breathlessly, then surged ahead of me. Fire coated his blade as he grasped the hilt with both hands. Detaching from the circle, the four sorcerers ran to intercept us.

Orange flames raced up Aaron's arms and across his shoulders. "Go right, Tori!"

I veered to the right. Aaron skidded to a halt, set his feet wide, and brought his sword back. With a roar of effort, he swung the blade in a broad arc. An inferno exploded out of the steel, blasting toward the approaching sorcerers.

Arms pumping, I sprinted past the fiery maelstrom, wholly focused on the black-robed witch in the circle's center. I leaped over the outer ring and my feet hit the mud within the circle. Electric power shot up my legs. Stumbling, I raced for the witch. The leviathan towered over me, its thick serpentine body thrashing against the mud.

The witch didn't move until I was almost on top of him. At the last second, he turned, his eyes widening and hands clutching a sphere of delicate silver threads woven into elaborate patterns.

I tackled him.

We crashed into the mud and I jammed my red crystal against his face as I reached for the sphere with my other hand.

"*Ori decidas!*" I shouted.

With a flash, the crystal's immobilizing spell activated. The witch went limp at the same moment my fingers closed around the sphere, and I tore it from his grip.

9

ON MY KNEES in the mud, I raised the orb triumphantly. "Aha!"

That was as far as I got before hot magic slammed into my hand and up my arm. Excruciating pain lit my nerves on fire—and the leviathan's head swung down, its blazing ivory eyes fixing on me.

Uh-oh.

I tried to drop the sphere, but my hand was clamped around it, muscles refusing to unclench. Pain spread through my body, searing every nerve until I could barely contain my scream.

The leviathan's jaws opened, revealing pointed fangs and huge curved canines. It roared in fury. The ocean frothed, forming a giant wave. The wall of water rushed toward me, hit the edge of the circle, and parted around it. The ocean raged past us toward the shore, and everything went dark as the water swept the electric lights away.

I didn't have a chance to worry about the guys as the leviathan's massive jaws snapped a foot from my face. Its head was almost as long as I was tall, its giant eyes glowing from within.

"*I will not submit.*"

The snarling voice ripped across my senses, and I cringed. Tears streamed down my face from the agonizing magic pounding through me.

"I don't want you to submit!" I yelled. "I'm trying to save you!"

"*Your treacherous tongue cannot deceive me, witch.*" Its fangs snapped again, way too close, its hot breath blasting my skin. I had no idea how it was talking—its mouth didn't move with its speech.

"I'm not a witch, you stupid blind fae!" I hunched over, shuddering with agony. No matter how hard I tried, I couldn't release the sphere. "Go back to the ocean and be free or whatever. What are you waiting for?"

The leviathan's head dropped a few inches and tilted to bring one huge eye closer. "*You are human.*"

"I know that," I gasped. "I don't want or need a familiar. I stopped the ritual, so get your scaly ass back out to sea."

A snarl rumbled from the beast, but I didn't care if I had offended it. Everything hurt and I couldn't think. My anger-fueled mouth was the only part of me still working.

"Make it stop," I groaned, my limbs trembling, but my hand remained fused to the sphere.

The leviathan's head weaved side to side, then its lips pulled up, baring its fangs. "*So be it, human.*"

Heat flashed through my body in a dizzying wave. Beneath my fingers, the silver sphere disintegrated into dust. The purple glow of the circle snuffed out—and whatever magical force had been holding the ocean back disappeared.

Icy water slammed into me. As I went under, I managed to grab the leather cord of my fall crystal off the downed witch. I tumbled beneath the surging current. Flailing, I found the muddy bottom with one hand, planted my feet, and pushed up.

My head broke the surface, and I gasped in a desperate breath. The black water crashed across my shoulders, pushing me backward as I dug my heels into the mud. I slipped and plunged under again.

Arms clamped around me and hauled me upright.

"Tori!" Aaron turned us sideways to reduce the current's drag. "Are you okay?"

"Yeah," I half spluttered, half coughed. Freezing water pulled at my clothes. Why did we live this far north? I was moving to Hawaii. Just watch me.

He towed me toward the shore. As we neared the seawall, I spotted Ezra and Kai waiting for us. Grasping my arms, they hauled me out of the water. Aaron clambered out and sat on the concrete, shoulders slumped.

I pushed my sopping hair off my face, checked all my limbs were functioning, then ensured my two artifacts were tucked safely in my pocket. Olivia sat a few yards away, coughing wetly. Sitting beside her was the orange tabby, its crystalline eyes glowing with faint yellow light. Two tiny, semi-transparent dragonfly wings sprouted from its back. As I studied it, it bared its small fangs and faded out of sight.

"I'm exhausted," Aaron wheezed. "Tori, did you free the fae?"

"Yeah," I panted, clamping my arms around myself as the shivers started. "Where are the Red Rum guys?"

"The ones who survived have fled," Kai answered. "I think they expected you to sic the leviathan on them."

I nodded, my teeth chattering. "Hey Aaron, got any fire to spare?"

"Not right now."

Kai crouched beside me. "What *was* that, Tori? Why did you go running in there?"

"Uh, well, you see …"

"Tori!" Odette ran out of the darkness, following the seawall path. She must've taken the long way down. "You did it! Amazing!"

Puffing to a stop, she knelt to check that her sister was unhurt. Olivia seemed fine—except for the purple bruise rising on her swollen cheek. Ah. Hmm. I may have gone overboard there.

Aaron pulled me up and wrapped an arm around my waist. I pressed against his side. He might be fresh out of fire, but his skin was always warm.

"Let's get back to the car," he said. "We can debrief there."

We made our tired way up the trail, the guys dragging their feet. Eventually, the impassably steep bluff gentled into a passably steep hill that we scrabbled up. Back in the parking lot, I trudged to Aaron's car, feeling as though a fifty-pound weight were fused to my shoulders.

As Aaron opened his trunk, the witches murmured their farewells—but they got all of three steps toward their blue sedan before Kai was in front of them, his dark eyes colder than the ocean waters.

"Where are you going? You have a lot of explaining to do."

"What's to explain?" Olivia said weakly. "The sea lord is free. That's what matters."

"Nice try." He pointed at Aaron's vehicle. "One of you is riding with us. The other can follow in your car."

The witches exchanged apprehensive looks.

Aaron heaved a duffle bag out of his trunk and unzipped it. "Ezra?"

The aeromage held out his arm, revealing the claw marks that raked from his wrist to elbow. Blood streaked his skin. Aaron slapped on gauze from the first aid kit, then roughly taped it over the cuts.

"That'll do until we get back." Sorting through the spare clothes, Aaron offered me a sweatshirt. "Here."

"Thanks." Taking it, I fumblingly unzipped my jacket.

"Tori," Kai said. "What did you do with my phone?"

I paused, about to pull my jacket off. "Uh … I broke it. Sorry."

"Broke it? How?"

"I punched Olivia in the face with it."

He rolled his eyes, but I swore his lips quirked into a smile.

"Mine is soaked," Aaron said as he peeled his wet shirt off. It was a testament to my exhaustion that I only ogled his muscles for a couple seconds. "Ezra, don't suppose your phone survived the …"

He trailed off. As I tossed my drenched coat in the trunk, I looked at him curiously. He was staring at me. So was Kai. So was Ezra. Their expressions were identical mixtures of confusion and dread.

I looked down at my top, soaked with stinky sea water. No surprise there. But …

Gaping in disbelief, I stretched my right arm out. A bright azure rune was emblazoned on my palm and glowing merrily. Coiling lines and spiky runes spread out from it, climbing my arm to my shoulder. Luminescent sigils spiraled over the right side of my chest above my shirt.

In a panic, I dragged the hem of my shirt up. The markings ran all the way down my side and disappeared under my pants. I shoved my jeans down a few inches. Runes wrapped across my hip.

"You!" Olivia shrieked, pointing at me with a shaking hand. "You took the familiar bond for yourself!"

I gawked at her. "But—but I freed him—"

"Those are fae runes! You're a lying—"

"Olivia!" Odette grabbed her sister's arm, forcing it down. "It must've been an accident."

"Shit, Tori," Aaron whispered. "What did you do?"

"I—I don't know." My frantic gaze flashed from the markings to him and back. "I thought the fae—he said—I didn't mean to. It was an acci … dent …" My eyes narrowed as my panic morphed into suspicion. An accident? Maybe not.

Jerking away from the car, I spun in a circle, searching. "Echo? Echo!"

"She's lost it," Aaron observed, not quite managing his usual flippant tone.

"Tori, this place doesn't echo," Kai said cautiously.

I threw my head back and bellowed, "*Echo!* Show yourself, you oversized salamander!"

Not my best insult, but I was at my wit's end here.

"Such insolence, brazen one."

The air shimmered above Aaron's car, and the wyldfae materialized out of nothing. Wings spread, he hovered a few inches above the vehicle.

Aaron swore and backpedaled, his hand shooting to the hilt of his sword. He grasped it but didn't draw. Kai made no sound but took three swift steps backward, as shocked as I'd ever seen him. Ezra didn't move, his mismatched eyes locked on the fae and his expression eerily blank.

I pointed accusingly at Echo. "You lied! You said if I took the relic from the witch, the sea lord would be saved!"

"Saved from enslavement by the witch, yes." Echo smiled, showing his fangs. "Indeed, you delivered him from a humiliating fate."

I gestured violently at the glowing marks all over my body. "Then what is *this*?"

"The bond forged between your soul and Llyrlethiad's."

"Then you *did* lie about—"

His tail lashed. The barbed end hit the car's back window and shattered the glass. Aaron twitched like he'd been electrocuted, a croak escaping his throat. My eyes darted from the casual destruction back to the fae, and a healthy dose of fear cooled my temper.

"I spoke no lies." The fae's dark eyes appraised me. "You, and not a witch, hold the vile bond. You, who have no power to command him."

My hands clenched. "You tricked me."

"I spoke no lies," he repeated in his lilting accent. "Llyrlethiad was already bound by the ensnaring spell. It could not be undone. *Someone* had to claim the magic."

So Echo had sent me, a human with "no power to command" the sea lord.

I bared my teeth. "You're a treacherous—"

His wings flared wide. He swept down from above the car and stopped with our noses almost touching, his midnight blue eyes filling my vision.

"You are but an infant to the ways of my kind," he crooned softly. "Out of respect for the druid, I will gift you with this moment of instruction. Do not disparage my name or slander my character, or I shall have no recourse but to carve my honor into your flesh."

Swallowing hard, too frightened to utter a sound, I nodded.

His fingers closed around my wrist and a spark of tingling heat imbued my skin. "My debt is paid. I will answer your call no longer."

I gave another mute nod.

His unnerving smile reappeared with a flash of fangs, then he swept his wings down. As he soared skyward, the air rippled and danced. His body darkened, lost in the shimmers. For a bare instant, the shape of the massive dragon, galaxies swirling across his dark sides, was silhouetted against the stars, then he faded from sight.

I pressed a hand to my forehead, feeling dizzy. "You know, I really don't like fae."

"How could you be so disrespectful?" Odette asked in a quavering whisper. She and her sister were clutching each other like they'd just witnessed the descension of an angel. "Do you have any idea how powerful that fae is?"

Nope. Didn't know, didn't care.

"Holy *shit*," Aaron exclaimed. He gazed despairingly at his car's broken window. "That's the same dragon fae that flies the Ghost around, isn't it?"

I said nothing. Stupid oath spell.

"Tori?"

"Can't explain," I muttered.

Aaron swore.

"Out of the frying pan, into the fire," Kai muttered dryly. "We need to call Darius."

"My phone is in my purse." I hobbled wearily toward the car. "I left it under my seat."

Aaron caught my elbow, and only then did I realize how badly I was listing to one side. "You okay?"

"I'm fine."

"You're white as a sheet."

"I'm *fine*." I pulled free and opened the car door, the simple movement causing me to stagger. The marks glowing down my arm blurred as my eyesight lost focus.

"Tori—" Aaron reached for me again and I stubbornly stepped away from him, ignoring the way the ground shifted erratically under my feet.

"She's going to faint," Kai said.

"Don't be stupid," I snapped, pulling myself together. "I've never fainted in my life."

No sooner were the words out of my mouth than my vision darkened and I pitched toward the pavement.

IO

ON THE BRIGHT SIDE, I was back at the Crow and Hammer. It felt like returning home after an unpleasant vacation, and I had the strange urge to wipe counters.

On the not-so-bright side, it was god-awful early. Six a.m.? Seven a.m.? Whatever the time, it was too early for consciousness. Also, I was still covered in fae markings. And on top of *that*, I was mostly naked in front of a bunch of people I didn't want to be naked in front of.

I stood in the center of the room, arms held away from my sides, wearing nothing but my bra and undies. And seventeen people were staring at me.

To be fair, two of them weren't paying attention to my near nudity. In one corner of the second-level workroom—filled with long tables, whiteboards, and computer desks—Ezra was sitting on a chair while Sanjana, the guild's apprentice healer, treated the gouges in his forearm.

But the *other* fifteen people were staring at me. Or, more precisely, at the markings that started on my right palm, ran up my arm, covered most of my chest, coiled down my side and hip, then petered out at my right knee.

Off to one side, Aaron was pacing while Kai leaned against a table, his open laptop beside him. He watched me and the mythics—all of whom he'd called in at this ungodly hour to examine me.

Tabitha, her porcelain skin flawless and jaw-length brown hair neatly styled, observed like a queen overseeing her court. She was only here because she was the on-duty officer, and she'd already graced us with an icy lecture on involving me in guild work. Oddly, her chilly anger was threaded with worry, which irritated me. I wanted to despise her, not consider that her resistance to my presence was partly motivated by her concern for my safety.

Then again, the other part was her elitist desire to keep the guild human-free, so I wasn't changing my opinion of her anytime soon.

Felix, the guild's third officer, was also present. Kai had called him because he specialized in the detection and dispelling of magic. The other sorcerers included Andrew, an experienced team leader, and Lyndon, a counter-magic specialist.

Weldon had also come in, but I didn't know him particularly well—mainly because I didn't care to. An old man who always wore a greasy cowboy hat and matching boots, he'd gotten on my bad side during my first shift, when he'd given his drink order to my boobs. I was especially displeased to be standing in my underwear in front of him, but to my surprise, he seemed as focused on the markings as the others.

The final two sorcerers were a pair I'd barely spoken to: Lim and Jia Chen, an elderly couple who rarely drank anything but herbal tea. With wispy white hair, wizened faces, and thick glasses, they were tiny and hunched and looked like a mild puff of wind would blow them over. But they were the first ones Kai had called.

After calling Darius, I should say. That had been a fun conversation. The guild master wasn't present, only because he was already dealing with the Red Rum angle—and the very real threat that the notorious rogue guild would retaliate against the Crow and Hammer.

Rounding out the group of voyeurs were all five of the guild's witches. Chewing her lip worriedly, Kaveri finally broke the silence. "I can't detect the fae. Can anyone else?"

Sitting beside her, Kier—her boyfriend—shook his head. With a beefy build, rugged features, and longish hair tied up in a man-bun, he reminded me of a super-Zen Jason Mamoa.

Philip, the middle-aged leader of our witches, rubbed his stubbly jaw. "The fae must have withdrawn as far as possible. Perhaps the binding magic exhausted him."

"It's disgusting." Delta tossed her braided hair over her shoulder, their decorative beads clattering noisily. "Stealing a fae's will is utterly profane."

"Can we worry about morality later?" Aaron cut in, halting to glare at the witch. "We're here to break the connection between Tori and this fae."

"Lim and Jia," Kai said quietly, "what do you think?"

Jia took her glasses off and folded them, her dark eyes nearly lost in wrinkles. "It's a complex amalgamation. I suspect elements of Arcana, Spiritalis, and Demonica."

"Demonica?" I repeated nervously.

"The binding elements are related to the contracts that subjugate demons," she explained. "When a demon is summoned, its contractor gains near full control over its power."

"You'd need something equally binding to control a fae like this," Lyndon said, drumming his fingers on the tabletop. "I'd bet this fae is even more powerful than a demon."

Jia levered herself out of her chair and hobbled over, scanning the markings. "Arcana and Demonica are not what concern me. They are simple in their complexity. Two plus two always equals four."

She poked a big rune that spanned most of my right hip. "What worries me are the Spiritalis elements. These are not as simple to unravel."

Philip joined the ancient sorceress. "It's not just Spiritalis. The sphere relic Tori described was fae-created. Even witches don't understand fae magic. It follows rules we can't grasp."

Jia tapped another rune on my side. "Fae magic combined with a dark Arcana ritual. This is beyond my knowledge."

"Mine as well," Lim agreed in his gravelly voice.

Around the room, every mythic agreed that they didn't know enough to undo the bond. Sick dread sank through me and I wrapped my arms around myself.

Aaron appeared at my side and handed me an oversized sweater. I pulled it on gratefully, then put on the sweatpants he offered next.

"Don't worry," he told me. "This doesn't mean we're giving up."

"We will begin researching immediately," Jia announced. "Lim and I will visit our friends at Arcana Historia. They are very knowledgeable."

"I'll put out feelers among my old comrades," Lyndon offered, rising from his chair. "They've done their fair share of dabbling on the edge of illegal magic. They might have a few ideas."

"Be careful what you ask," Kai warned. "We don't want to reveal too much."

"I will." He headed to the stairs.

Andrew stretched, stifling a yawn. "I know you were hoping I'd seen something like this before, but I'm sorry to say I haven't. I'll ask around too and see what I can find out." He left, followed by Jia and Lim.

Philip rubbed his hands together, the gesture more nervous than thoughtful. "Those O'Conner sisters are downstairs, correct? I'll speak to them before I leave." He offered me a reassuring smile. "We'll sort this out, Tori."

Keeping my doubts about the O-sisters' usefulness to myself, I nodded as he and the other witches headed off. Olivia and Odette were waiting in the guild's basement, presumably too scared of Kai to leave without permission.

Weldon, the sometimes-creep, got up. "The others can ask around all they want, but this ain't your next-door conjurer's type of magic. You need a dark-arts master."

"We don't have one of those on speed dial," Aaron snapped.

Weldon held his wide hands up placatingly. "I'm just sayin', boy. Without a fae-magic expert or a dark-arts practitioner, you won't get far."

"You'd know something about dark-arts practitioners, though, wouldn't you?" Kai asked sharply. "That's why I called you."

"So would you, eh, Yamada?" Weldon shot back. "I don't know nothin' about this fae crap. Good try, though."

With a farewell shrug, he slouched down the stairs and out of sight.

"I can't think of a single time Weldon has been useful," Aaron growled. "I don't even know why he's a member."

"He's useful, I promise." Felix scrubbed a hand through his short blond hair. "There are a few dispelling techniques I could try on Tori, but I'm not keen to start experimenting right off the bat. She seems safe enough for now, so let's see what the others come back with. Kai, make sure Tori isn't left alone."

"Of course."

Once he was gone, Tabitha also headed toward the stairs. She paused at the top, her cool eyes sweeping over us. "Not here, however. Miss Dawson can't be at the guild while the MPD investigation is ongoing."

"I'm aware," Kai replied, his voice even chillier.

She left. I sneered at the spot where she'd vanished, then asked, "Do I need to leave right now?"

"Not yet," Aaron answered. "Ramsey should arrive soon. I want to see if he knows of any artifacts that might be helpful." He fought back a yawn. "I need caffeine. I'll go put on a pot of coffee."

His departure left just me and Kai in the large room, plus Ezra and Sanjana in the corner. She'd drawn fancy sigils all around his injured arm and was chanting quietly.

I slumped into the chair near Kai's laptop. Sitting as well, he tapped a key to wake the machine and turned it toward me.

"Does Llyr Llediaith sound like the fae's name?"

Echo had spoken the fae lord's name several times, but with all the chaos and adrenaline, we couldn't quite remember it. I peered at the short Wikipedia article on the laptop screen.

"It was Llyr-something, but that doesn't sound quite right." I scanned the article, anxiety clenching my stomach. A Welsh sea deity from ancient legends, and the name was close enough that I had to assume it was the same being. "I really screwed this up, didn't I?"

Kai braced his elbow on the table and rested his chin on his palm. "Actually, this is probably the best outcome we could have hoped for. If the fae was already caught in the binding and had to be tied to someone, better you than a Red Rum witch."

"Why do they want this fae so badly?"

"I have a few theories. Red Rum is so difficult for MagiPol to fight because they run their operations from international waters. Their highest-ranking members live on luxury yachts, plus they command a veritable fleet of smaller vessels. Controlling a sea god would make their ships unassailable."

Oh, yay. Didn't that sound like a fun guild to piss off? I glanced at my palm glowing with runes. "I'm glad Red Rum didn't get the fae, but I'm not feeling so great about me getting it instead."

"We'll figure it out." He pulled me close to his side. "Together, there isn't much we can't handle."

I leaned my head against his shoulder and closed my eyes wearily. Keeping me tucked under his arm, he clicked on his laptop with his other hand. I listened to Sanjana's quiet incantation, trying to calm the twisting dread lodged under my heart.

Kai's arm was warm and comforting. He wasn't really the affectionate type, which made me all the more grateful. After too few minutes, his shoulder shifted under my cheek.

"Looks like Sanjana is almost done. We'll head out soon. Why don't you find Aaron and Ramsey?"

"Sure." Sliding out of my seat, I trudged down the stairs to the bar. The sight of scattered chairs and dirty glasses stacked on the back counter should have been irritating, but longing rolled over me instead.

Male voices rumbled out of the kitchen, so I circled behind the bar and reached for the saloon doors.

"… worried about Tori."

I paused at the sound of my name.

"Philip is concerned about what the fae bond might do to her," Aaron continued in a low voice. "She's human, not Spiritalis."

Why did everyone keep rubbing that in? I scowled silently.

"How is she?" The other voice belonged to Ramsey, the weekday cook and our in-house artifact expert.

"Pale and tired, but I don't know if that's from lack of sleep or what." He made a low, unhappy sound. "I shouldn't have brought her with us. What was I thinking?"

"Don't beat yourself up, Aaron. She wanted to go, didn't she?"

"Yeah," he mumbled. "She did."

"It's a damn shame she isn't a mythic," Ramsey mused. "She'd make a great combat sorcerer."

Emotion flashed through me, but Aaron replied before I could examine it.

"She would, and that's why I keep forgetting she *isn't* one." His voice hoarsened in a way I rarely heard from him. "I'm going to get her killed."

Standing with my hand on the saloon doors, I didn't move, unsure what to do. Walk in? Back away?

"What's the deal with you two?" Ramsey asked after a moment. "Are you a couple or …?"

"Hell if I know." Aaron sighed. "I really like her. She's smart, funny, hot, brave as a damn lion. I know we have chemistry, but ..."

Ramsey was quiet, maybe waiting for Aaron to continue. "But what?"

"But there's something missing," he answered softly. "Half the time I think she just wants to be friends, but she's never suggested we shouldn't date. It's like she's holding back or ... or she's just not that into me. I don't know."

"Damn," Ramsey muttered. "That's rough."

"Tell me about it. I haven't got a clue what to do, so I'm just going with the flow."

Ramsey said something in response, but I was backing away, my heart banging sickeningly against my ribs. I retreated to the farthest end of the bar, a hand pressed to my chest.

Eavesdropping was bad and I was a bad person. I was also a self-centered twit.

Here I was, happily doing the casual dating thing with Aaron, oblivious to the fact he didn't want to be casual. Justin had questioned whether Aaron was stringing me along with unspoken promises of something more, but I was the one doing that to *him*. And he, being the good-natured guy he was, was rolling with the punches, hoping I'd give him a clear signal.

Well, I felt like a royal piece of shit.

Swallowing hard, I called, "Aaron?"

Their voices paused, then Aaron replied, "In the kitchen."

I walked back along the bar and pushed through the doors. Forcing a smile, I waved at Ramsey.

Tall, lean, and goth—though less goth than usual with no eyeliner and his hair hidden under a ball cap—he gave me a quick smile in return. "Heard you got yourself a shiny new fae lord for a familiar."

"I don't think that's quite how it worked." I showed him my rune-marked palm, the only part of the intricate pattern visible now that I was dressed. "Don't suppose you have an anti-fae-magic artifact tucked away somewhere?"

"Not precisely."

I sighed.

We talked to Ramsey until Kai, Ezra, and Sanjana joined us. The healer dragged me into the pub, sat me in a chair, and gave me a basic checkup. Declaring that I was exhausted but otherwise healthy, she turned me over to the guys.

A few minutes later, I was settling into Aaron's drafty car as he started the engine. Ezra had climbed onto the back of Kai's bike—the car's back seat was full of broken glass and unfit for passengers—and the motorcycle zoomed out of the small lot ahead of us.

Aaron drove out after them. A few blocks down, Kai turned off the main road, but we continued toward my apartment. I stared moodily out the window at the early morning gloom, shivering as wind swirled through the car. So nice of Echo to break the back window.

"Sin is on her way," Aaron told me. "Kaveri will join you too, in case you have issues with the fae. Since we don't know what to expect from this sea lord, having a witch nearby is the best we can do. She's swinging by her apartment to pack an overnight bag first."

Since I needed mythic supervision, I would rather have stayed at Aaron's house, but thanks to MagiPol's stupid investigation, that wasn't an option.

He stifled a yawn with one hand. "I'm beat. Once I've gotten some sleep, I'll pick up a burner phone to replace my regular one and text you the number so you can call me if you need me."

"Sure." I rubbed his shoulder. "You guys need to rest. The fae bond isn't going anywhere."

"You need rest too. You look even tireder than I feel."

"Tireder?" I repeated in amusement.

"You can't expect me to English properly on this little sleep. Especially after that fight." The car rolled to a stop in front of my bungalow and he cut the engine. "I'll wait with you until Sin arrives."

"That's okay." I unbuckled my seat belt. "She's on her way. I'll be fine on my own for a few minutes."

He hesitated, worry shadowing his blue eyes. "I should probably ..."

"I'll be *fine*," I reassured him. Leaning across the center console, I planted a kiss on his frown. "You're exhausted. Go home and get some sleep."

Heaving a sigh, he gave in. "Okay. But have Sin text me— wait, no, my phone is fried. Email. Have her email me when she arrives."

"I will." I hesitated, then leaned in again and brought our mouths together.

My kiss was slow and deep, full of emotion I hadn't had time to process. My hand found his stubbly cheek, fingers stroking his warm skin. I pressed my mouth harder against his, an inexplicable surge of desperation rising through me.

When I pulled back, a hint of confusion lurked in his gaze, but he smiled. "Have a good nap. I'll call you when I'm up again."

"I'll be waiting." With a final wave, I got out of the car and shut the door. The engine grumbled to life, and he leaned sideways to search my face through the window. Then the vehicle rolled away, and I waited on the sidewalk until the red sports car was out of sight.

Turning on my heel, I hastened toward the house. My messed-up relationship with Aaron would have to wait. I had ten minutes before Sin arrived and I couldn't waste it. As I strode into the backyard, I pulled out my phone and dialed a number. It rang while I unlocked the door and stepped into the vestibule.

Ten rings. Twelve. I growled, loping down the stairs. Pick up, pick up, *pick up*. I let it keep ringing. Fourteen. Fifteen.

The line clicked, and a deep, husky voice rumbled in my ear. "You've never called before. This better be good."

"Hello, *dah*ling," I purred dramatically. "Tell me how desperately you've been longing to hear my voice again."

A long, heavy pause, then the line went dead.

Swearing, I called right back, a hand on my hip as I let it ring another million times. Finally, the line clicked.

"You have no sense of humor at all," I complained before he could speak. "I *am* calling for an actual reason, you know."

"And what reason is that?"

I scrunched my face, nose wrinkling. The words were difficult for me to say, but I didn't really have a choice. Weldon had said only a fae-magic expert or a dark-arts practitioner possessed the skill to deal with my problem.

Conveniently, I happened to know someone who was both—assuming he didn't hang up on me again.

I sighed. "Zak, I need your help."

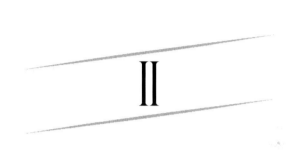

II

"TELL ME AGAIN," I said, my brow furrowed, as Sin sorted through miniature bottles filled with bright colors, "why we need to paint our nails."

"Because," she replied like it was the most obvious thing in the world, "it's a traditional sleepover activity. I haven't done a sleepover since I was twelve, and I'm milking it for all it's worth."

She selected a bottle of hot pink lacquer from her tub of nail polishes and held it up. "How about this one?"

I couldn't think of a more revolting color. "Sure, why not."

"Kaveri, what color do you want?"

The dark-haired witch looked up. She'd constructed a small circle out of nature-y things in the middle of my living room, and Twiggy was sitting in front of it, looking as delighted as I'd ever seen him.

This was the weirdest sleepover ever.

"Nail polish is full of harsh chemicals." Kaveri added another leaf to her circle. "It isn't environmentally responsible."

"Commercial nail polishes aren't." Sin uncapped the pink bottle and held it out to me. "Mine are all natural. Smell it."

I cautiously sniffed. Instead of harsh paint odors assaulting my senses, all I detected was a hint of lavender. "Ooh nice. How permanent is it?"

"Without my remover potion, it won't so much as chip unless you tear your nail off."

Hmm. "Can I choose a different color?"

She passed me the container and I examined the bright shades. Choosing a fire-engine red, I handed it back. "So, what other traditional sleepover activities do you have planned?"

"Watching rom-coms, eating popcorn, and a pillow fight."

"You're basing this entirely on nineties chick flicks, aren't you?"

"Pretty much," she confirmed shamelessly, selecting a shade of turquoise that matched her wavy hair.

I squinted at Kaveri. "What exactly are you doing?"

"This?" She added another dried leaf to the circle. "It's a woodland balance rite. Human technology and activity disrupt natural forces. Through this ritual, I can bring the nearby energies into balance. It doesn't last long, but it's rejuvenating for fae."

Twiggy nodded rapturously. "It feels good. Bright and clear."

"Mmm," I murmured noncommittally. "Arcana uses circles too, doesn't it?"

"Yes, circles are present in most magic constructions. They define boundaries. Arcana and Spiritalis share some basic concepts, but the execution is very different." She pondered her circle, then lifted a pouch from her bag and sprinkled dirt in the center. "All witches can sense the flow of power within nature, and we can tell when it's out of balance."

I frowned at the dirt she was dumping on my floor. "You can *sense* it?"

"Oh yes. The urge to correct the balance is inherent, and many young witches will teach themselves basic rites through trial and error. It's the primary ministration we offer fae— balancing the energies they depend on for survival."

I stifled a sigh. If I'd had the slightest doubt, here was the final nail in the coffin—no way was I a Spiritalis mythic. I scarcely tolerated outdoorsy activities, let alone felt the urge to arrange leaves and dirt for esoteric purposes. Not to mention I lacked that special ability to perceive fae that the O-sisters had described. I could see fae only when they wanted to be seen.

"With Spiritalis rites, you can't simply follow a recipe," Kaveri added with a smug smile in Sin's direction. "We must adapt every rite to the current state of the natural world in which we're working, and only through our unique senses can we do that."

Sin snorted. "Yeah, but *balancing* is about all you witches can do unless a fae trades over its magic. Arcaners *harness* energies into potions and artifacts."

My phone chimed, and I tuned out their snippy debate while I surreptitiously checked the message. Nerves flitted through my stomach. I'd slept most of the day, but in the several hours since I'd woken, my top priority had been to devise a plan. So far, I had nothing—and now my time was up.

I jumped to my feet and hurried into the kitchen to check my pantry. "I don't have any popcorn! I'm fresh out of soft drinks too."

"Damn," Sin grumbled as she uncapped her turquoise polish.

"Hey, Kaveri," I said brightly, "why don't you make a snack run? The grocery store is open for another forty-five minutes."

Rising to her feet, she brushed leaves off her yoga pants and I tried not to let the mess annoy me. Twiggy was humming and crooning at the nature circle. At least he was happy.

No sooner had I thought it than he cut off his discordant tune. His head tilted to one side—and he faded out of sight. Little weirdo.

"I'm supposed to stay with you," Kaveri said uncertainly.

I refocused on my mission.

"It'll only be a few minutes," I told her breezily, hoping I wasn't laying it on too thick. "And you wanted me to try chai tea, right? You could get some of that too."

Her face brightened. I'd have no choice but to drink the tea now. The sacrifices I was making …

"Okay," she agreed. "The store isn't far, right?"

"You'll be back in no time!" Except the closest store was already closed and she'd have to drive to a different one. Keeping my smile in place, I ushered her up the stairs and out the door.

When I came back down, Sin had turned around on the sofa and was leaning against the back, squinting suspiciously at me.

"You're acting weird," she accused.

No point in denying it. "*Everything* is weird," I hedged, waving at the glowing marks all over me, displayed by my shorts and tank top. "Sin, I need to ask …"

I trailed off as Twiggy appeared behind her. His body language set off my alarm bells—the faery was up to something. I *knew* that look.

Before I could warn Sin, Twiggy pressed a green leaf against her bare arm. Surprise flickered across her face, then she slumped into the cushions, limp as a corpse.

"Sin!" I sprinted to the sofa. "Twiggy, *what did you do?*"

He widened his eyes innocently and waved the leaf. "I did what he told me!"

"What who—" I cut myself off as Twiggy's gaze moved past me and worshipful awe blanked his waxy features.

I spun around.

A man stood at the bottom of the stairs, leaning against the door jamb. His long black coat hung to his knees, the hood pulled up and casting deep shadows over his face. Tall, broad-shouldered, oozing menace.

"Ever hear of knocking?" I demanded, gulping down my racing heart. "And what did Twiggy do to Sin?"

He pushed his hood off. The shadows slid away from his face, revealing unnaturally bright green eyes set in one of the most gorgeous faces I'd ever had the pleasure of ogling. I sighed wistfully.

"Leaf of yarnroot," he replied.

I sighed again. That voice. Raspy, rumbly, and sinfully deep. Damn. I'd forgotten the man was sex appeal incarnate. It just wasn't fair.

"You're a dickhead," I declared to remind myself of that important fact. "What did the leaf do to her?"

He rolled his spectacular eyes at my unprompted insult. "The touch of a single leaf will render an adult unconscious. Its effect lasts about an hour and"—a dangerous smile touched his lips—"it leaves no trace."

I shook my head in disbelief. "It won't hurt her?"

"Not unless she eats it."

Twiggy grinned and stuffed the leaf in his mouth, chewing loudly and humming like he'd taken a bite of the sweetest cake.

I waved at Zak. "Help me move her over to my bed."

He crossed the room, simultaneously pulling off his coat to reveal a soft black t-shirt and muscular arms darkened by tattoos. I reminded myself not to drool. He tossed his coat on the sofa, then lifted Sin into his arms. Guess my help wasn't needed.

After depositing my unconscious friend on my bed, he returned to the main room and looked me up and down. "You're glowing like a Christmas display. Let's see what we've got."

I approached him at a cautious mince. Losing patience, he whisked me over to the open space behind my lonely sofa, positioned my arm out to my side, and began examining the fae markings.

"Hi Zak," I murmured into the silence. "It's been so long, hasn't it? I'm doing well, thanks for asking. This fae nonsense has been quite tiring, though. I appreciate your concern. It's very thoughtful."

"You're tired because the fae's magic is hammering your body like an invisible surf."

When he pulled my shirt up, I flinched but didn't stop him. He knew how to behave himself, plus he'd already seen more of my skin than this.

"You'll grow more and more fatigued," he continued, "until you can barely stay awake, and sleep won't help. You'll scarcely be able to function."

"Uh." Alarm clanged through me. "That sounds ominous."

"It is." Kneeling to study my leg, he pushed the edge of my cotton shorts up. "The Red Rum witches are fools. Even I couldn't handle a bond with this fae for more than a few months."

I blinked at the top of his head. "You're talkative today."

He looked up at me, exasperation written across his unsmiling face.

It was a long story how I'd come to have the phone number of the city's most notorious rogue. The Ghost, as he'd been dubbed, was a mystery to almost everyone in the mythic community—a secretive criminal known for dealing in the darkest arts and kidnapping teenagers. No one knew his name, his face, or what magic he wielded … except me.

And the cold bastard had forced me to swear a black-magic oath that prevented me from revealing anything about him, even by accident. Hence why I'd sent Kaveri away and why he'd ensured Sin couldn't see or hear anything that would trigger the oath spell, at which point I would gruesomely perish.

How I'd perish I didn't know. Zak hadn't said, and I was too chicken to ask.

Crossing to the stairs, where a black duffle bag sat on the floor, he unzipped it and withdrew a pad of paper and a pencil. "I'm going to sketch the markings. Hold your clothes out of the way."

I pulled my shirt up, baring my midriff. "Can't you take a photo?"

His pencil scratched across the page. "Magic doesn't photograph well."

That was inconvenient. "Tell me more about how the fae's magic is turning me into a blob of fatigue. Don't you have a similar bond with your familiar?"

"Not even close. *Your* bond isn't a true familiar relationship. It's enslavement." He stepped sideways to draw the runes that curved around my back. "You have a real talent for getting yourself into trouble."

"Well, this is probably the last time. MagiPol is investigating my guild, so I'll be getting the boot back to the regular world any day now."

His hand stilled, and I grimaced. My voice might have quavered on that last bit. He resumed drawing without comment.

"How's Nadine?" I asked.

"Well enough. Angry with me."

"Angry? Why?"

"She doesn't want to leave."

"Leave?" I yelped, stepping toward him. "You promised to take care of her!"

His mouth pressed into a thin line. He spun me around and poked my back with his pencil eraser. "Don't move. And I *will* make sure she's safe, but she can't stay with me anymore. None of them can."

"Why not?"

"Because I'm shutting down the farm."

Gasping, I started to spin but he caught my shoulder, holding me still. His statement burned my ears. Somewhere in the nearby mountains, Zak owned an entire valley where he sheltered a rotating dozen or so homeless teens and young adults who needed a safe place to get back on their feet. For all that his reputation was terrifying—and his morals allowed ruthless murder—he was a decent guy.

"Why are you shutting it down?" I demanded.

"It's not safe. That bitch sorceress found me. She knows too much, and she's already spreading the information around. I sent the older ones on their way within a week, and Terrance took all his apprentices except Nadine. She needs better protection than he can give her."

My hands balled into fists. "How much of this is my fault?"

"None. I took in Nadine. Varvara would've found me sooner or later based on that alone, and if not for you, I wouldn't have known I'd been discovered—or by whom." With the sound of tearing paper, he added, "I'm finished."

Turning, I glanced over his work—all the runes marking my body were drawn in 2D as though he'd skinned me and laid out my hide to tan.

"So?" I prompted as he studied the drawing.

"Not great." He pointed to a few gaps in the design. "There are missing pieces—parts of the ritual that weren't completed properly. Probably steps you were supposed to take when you bound the fae."

"I'm not so worried about whether it's working properly," I admitted. "I'm way more concerned with how to break it."

"Yeah," he muttered, frowning at the page. "That might be a problem."

"What do you mean?"

"These things are usually for life. Like a demon contract, it only ends when the contractor dies."

I swallowed. Why did I get myself involved in these things?

A warm hand closed around my elbow. "Tori? Don't faint."

"I never faint." Except for that one time. Very recently. It didn't count.

He steered me around the sofa and nudged me onto the cushions, then sat beside me. "Our main problem is that fae relic you told me about on the phone. If this was dark-arts Arcana alone, I could break it, but a fae created the magic. The Arcana merely gave it shape and rules."

"Are you saying it's unbreakable?"

"I'm saying it won't be simple. But it needs to be broken." His solemn green irises slid over me. "You won't survive it for more than a few weeks."

My stomach dropped out of me. I pressed a hand to my spinning head. "Shit, Zak."

His gaze snapped to the stairs. "Someone just parked out front. A woman."

"How do you know?"

"I left a varg to keep watch."

I shuddered at the memory of his loyal fae wolves. "It's Kaveri. I sent her to the store." Panic rose through me. "If she sees you, will I die on the spot?"

Confusion flickered over his features, then he grunted. "No. The oath doesn't work that way. I'd be revealing myself—which I'm not planning to do. Taenerpatninarkin?"

For a second, I thought he was having a stroke, then I realized that was Twiggy's real name. Wow, Zak had remembered it?

Twiggy peeked out from behind the sofa. "Crystal Druid," he squeaked reverently.

"Can you keep the woman from entering the house?"

"Yes. Yes, I can!"

"Without hurting her," I added sharply. "Just distract her or something."

Twiggy nodded so fast his whole body rocked. "I can do that!"

"Then do it," Zak ordered. "Tori will let you know when you can come back in."

Beaming, Twiggy vanished on the spot.

"Now what?" I asked.

Zak rose to his feet. "Now it's time to talk to the fae lord. We might need extra space."

When he crouched to take hold of my sofa, I hopped up and grabbed the other end. We pulled it out of the way. Luckily, that was it for furniture.

"What's the fae's name?" he asked.

"Uh … Llyr-something."

His eyes went out of focus. "Llyrlethiad, then. This will be interesting."

He flexed his arms and the dark feather tattoos that swept down from his shoulders shifted. The black design blurred, then shadowy wings lifted away from his skin. An ebony eagle emerged from his back, shadows rippling off her feathers.

His familiar swept to the breakfast bar and perched on the counter. I was still gawking at her appearance—not that I hadn't seen Lallakai before, just that she was magnificently beautiful—when two shaggy vargs materialized on either side of the druid.

"Uh …" I muttered.

Zak rolled his shoulders like he was warming up for a boxing match. "I've never met Llyrlethiad before. He might try to kill me."

Not comforting. "What about me?"

"He can't kill you, or he'd have already done it. The magic prevents him from harming you."

I remembered the leviathan's massive jaws snapping inches from my body. Then I pictured the beast and looked around my apartment. "Zak, he won't fit."

"He will." His eyes lost focus again.

"No, really, he's too—Zak?" I stepped closer, weirded out by his blank stare. "Hello, Zak?"

"Shut up, Tori," he growled. "I'm trying to call the fae."

"Oh."

His eyes went vacant again, and I realized he was looking at something I couldn't see—or listening to something I couldn't hear.

Tingles rushed through the fae markings on my skin.

"Here he comes."

I didn't need Zak's warning—I could feel the fae's approach like a rising tide inside my body. Foreign power surged through my flesh.

The air in the apartment blurred as the humidity shot up. Water coalesced out of nowhere and a wave of salty liquid plunged down on us.

Pouring over our heads, the icy wave flooded the floor. Water swirled and spun, and out of it, massive coils emerged, filling the entire room. The serpentine body writhed, smashing into the walls.

The leviathan's head burst out of the water, massive jaws gaping, and it lunged for Zak.

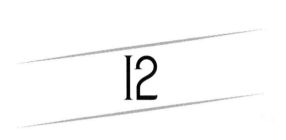

12

LALLAKAI DOVE in front of her master, wings spread wide. The wolfish vargs flanked her, hackles raised and teeth bared. Shadows roiled around the eagle and she whipped them at the leviathan. It recoiled with a snarl.

Zak sprang through her dark magic and pressed both hands to the leviathan's scaled muzzle. The creature went still, its pearly eyes shining with outrage. The fae was maybe a third the size it had been on the beach, but it was still a lethal giant.

Cowering in the corner, I crouched in a foot of cold salt water, arms wrapped protectively around my head. My body pulsed strangely, as though everything inside me were trying to expand through my flesh. I could scarcely breathe, my head spinning and lurching. The world had detached from my senses, my mind overwhelmed by a thousand zinging barbs of alien power driving through my skin over and over with each passing second.

"Tori?"

I didn't realize I'd squeezed my eyes shut. I cracked them open.

Zak crouched in front of me, and the leviathan's thick coils no longer filled the room. The serpent had shrunk again; now it was merely the size of a monster anaconda. With its pectoral fins braced on the floor, its horned head almost touched the ceiling. Its long body snaked through the water that filled my apartment, pointed dorsal fins lining its back.

Zak helped me up. I wobbled to my feet, disoriented and unsteady. The disconnected feeling between my mind and body had mostly faded, but fae power still shuddered through my limbs.

Ivory eyes gleaming murderously, Llyrlethiad waited with unnerving stillness reminiscent of a hunting reptile. Lallakai was back on the kitchen counter, and the two vargs stood on my sofa to keep out of the water.

"Are you okay, Tori?" Zak murmured.

I stretched my arm out. The fae markings were blazing as bright as the moon. "I can handle it."

He nodded and guided me toward the serpent, which was large enough to bite my limbs clean off. I resisted the urge to flee. Or curl up in a terrified ball and cry like a baby. That was an appealing option too.

"All right," Zak said in a businesslike tone. "Llyrlethiad, our goals align—to free you and Tori from this bond."

"*Kill her*," the fae commanded. His mouth didn't move—it wasn't even open—but I could hear his snarling voice nonetheless. "*I will reward you handsomely.*"

"Don't insult me," Zak snapped.

The serpent bared his carnivorous teeth. "*I will see you destroyed, druid.*"

"*You* will retract your threats. Or would you prefer I claim a debt for helping you?"

The serpent snarled. I stared at Zak, goggle-eyed.

"Let's be clear," he continued impatiently. "Tori intervened in the ritual to save you from enslavement. She wasn't aware she would be taking the witch's place. You know this, because she didn't complete the ritual."

Llyrlethiad's scaled lips curled in disdain.

"You may loathe being bound to a human, but this human wants to see you returned to your rightful autonomy. That is our goal, and with your cooperation, we can accomplish it all the faster."

"*She will perish in a matter of weeks,*" the fae growled. "*I will wait.*"

"So you lack all honor. I'll make sure to inform the Gardall'kin fae."

The serpent reared back, its head rising to the ceiling, and its powerful body thrashed. My furniture rocked in the current and a wave crashed into my TV. It wobbled, then fell off its stand, belly-flopping on the water before sinking out of sight.

"Why are we playing this game, Llyrlethiad?" Zak asked in a steely, measured tone. "We both know you owe Tori a steep debt, and you can't repay it by letting her die. If not for her, you'd be doing a black witch's bidding."

"I don't want to do any bidding," I whispered vaguely. "Let's not do that."

Zak glanced at me, his brow pinched with worry. I could understand why. My head was spinning and I was almost too exhausted to stand.

"Can you suppress your magic any further?" he asked the fae.

Llyrlethiad's cold stare whisked across me. "*No more than I am.*"

Zak curled his arm around me and I leaned gratefully against his sturdy—and soaking wet—side. I was drenched too.

"What can you tell me about the binding?" Zak asked the fae.

"*A being I am loath to call kin created it. Tuned to my power, it drew me to their circle and bound me.*" His pale eyes turned to my face. "*When she claimed the spell, she forced no commands upon me, therefore I accepted the magic before I could be thrust anew into a battle of wills.*"

"How do we break the spell?"

"*I do not know. Never have I been bound in such a way.*"

I cleared my throat. "What about Echo? He seemed to know what was going on."

Zak made an irritated noise in his throat. "I called for him before coming here. He isn't answering."

"Why not? I thought you two were pals."

"Fae aren't anyone's 'pal.' They're your ally only until they decide not to be. Echo will show up when he's good and ready, which won't be in time to be useful." Still holding me against his side so I didn't tip over, Zak rubbed his jaw. "Llyrlethiad, what can you tell me about the fae who created the relic?"

"*A foul creature who prefers the worship of humans to any honor among his kind. We call him the Rat, but I know not where to find him.*"

"Guess that's where I'll start. He's the likeliest source for magic that can break the bond."

The serpent dipped his large head in a nod. "*If you locate him, I will ensure his cooperation.*"

"Can you, without hurting Tori?"

The fae didn't reply, his silence a clear answer.

Zak straightened. "Llyrlethiad, I would have you vow to protect Tori from harm."

An instant snarl. "*I will not—*" He broke off, then hissed angrily at me. *That* sound had definitely come from his fanged mouth. "*For as long as we are bound, I will do all in my power to preserve your life. By this pledge, I pay the debt between us.*"

Zak squeezed my side. "Agree, Tori."

"I agree," I said faintly.

Apparently, that counted as a farewell, because the serpent began to fade from sight.

"Llyrlethiad," Zak barked. He pointed at the submerged floor. "The water."

The power buzzing in my bones flared and my skin felt like it was splitting open. The water covering the floor steamed, then boiled away in seconds. A moment later, the discomfort faded and I sagged in relief. Llyrlethiad was gone.

Zak pulled me over to my one bar stool. Twenty minutes ago, I'd owned two bar stools, but the other one was in pieces. Poor stool. So much life to live, snatched away too soon by an angry sea serpent.

I glanced guiltily at my TV, lying face down on the floor. Aaron wouldn't be happy. Twiggy would have a total meltdown.

Zak tipped my head back and checked my eyes, then held my wrist and counted my pulse. Lallakai perched on the counter, staring at me with her green, laser-beam eyes.

Fetching his bag, Zak set it on the counter beside me. As he opened it, a scowl pulled at his mouth. "Everything that wasn't sealed is ruined. Damn fae."

"He ruined my TV."

"He put a hole in your wall too."

Craning my neck, I saw what he meant: the crawlspace door no longer existed. In its place was a hole with two broken studs, gaping like a toothy smile. Bye-bye, damage deposit.

Zak pulled out two vials and uncorked the one full of silvery-green liquid. "Drink it."

Taking the vial, I cautiously sniffed. "What is it?"

"It'll temporarily bolster you against the fae's power. You won't feel as tired."

"You carry stuff like this around everywhere?"

"No." He rolled his eyes. "I made it for you before I came. I knew you'd need it."

I blinked at him, then at the vial, and mumbled, "Thanks."

"Thank me by drinking it."

Obediently, I poured it into my mouth and swallowed. It tasted the way pinecones smell. He handed me the second vial, this one filled with purple liquid, and I drank it too. Tasted like pure sweetness.

"What was that one?"

"A vitality potion. It'll boost your strength and help you recover from your exposure to fae magic."

"Wow. You're pretty amazing, Zak."

He snorted. "I prefer it when you insult me."

"Do you?" My lips quirked up as I handed the empty vial back. "Then you've been enjoying all my texts?"

"They've been delightful."

I giggled, then realized I was giggling. Choking it back, I arranged my expression into a stern glower. "What now?"

"Now you'll stay right here and try not to exert yourself. Don't call the fae back, and don't use his name in case he thinks you're summoning him. I'm not sure how long that first potion will last, so let me know when you feel fatigued again. You'll need to keep taking it."

"What will you do?"

"Track down the Rat fae." He eyed me, then gave my shoulder a hesitant pat. "Just hold on until then."

I smiled at his awkwardness. "Thanks, Zak. You're really not an evil bastard."

He zipped his bag. "Don't get the wrong idea about me."

"Fine, you're an evil bastard. But you're still a good friend."

His mouth twisted. "We're not friends, Tori."

"Yes, we are."

"No, we're not."

I folded my arms. "Well, we sure as hell aren't acquaintances. We got drunk together, remember?"

"We were poisoned, not drunk."

"I saw you naked."

"I wasn't naked."

"We slept in the same bed."

He opened his mouth, then closed it, unable to dispute that claim. "Friends are dangerous when you're a wanted rogue. Look what protecting one girl has cost me." He slung his bag over his shoulder. "Don't forget your oath."

"Never," I murmured, sobered more by the reminder that he was about to lose his home—a farm I was sure he loved more than any human being—than the reminder that my life was hanging by a magical thread. "Let me know if you need help finding a safe place for Nadine."

He nodded, stepping away. "I'll be in touch."

I caught his arm. "Zak ... thank you. I mean it."

He met my eyes, saying nothing, then pulled away from my hand. As he grabbed his coat and strode toward the stairs, Lallakai took off, cuffing me in the head with her wing. I scowled after her. Sweeping across the room, the eagle blurred into shadows and merged into Zak's back. Tattoos reappeared down his arms a moment before he pulled on his coat.

He drew up the hood and shadows shrouded his face. Then they swirled outward until the stairway was filled with darkness. He melted out of sight, and I didn't hear the door open or close. Chances Kaveri would spot him on his way out? Zilch.

Heaving myself to my feet, I glanced around my disgustingly damp and trashed apartment, then faced my bedroom door with a wince. How would I explain this to Sin?

13

LIAR, LIAR, PANTS ON FIRE.

I chanted the words like they would somehow alleviate my guilt. I'd lied to Sin, lied to Kaveri, and when Aaron and Kai had shown up, I'd lied to them too. Sin had called them the moment she saw the state of my apartment.

Kaveri, Aaron, and Kai knew nothing of my druid visitor. I'd told them the fae had appeared on his own, sabotaged my apartment, then left again. Sin, however, was suspicious. She'd noticed I was up to something before Twiggy knocked her out, and though I'd insisted it was all the fae lord's doing, she wasn't buying it.

Curled up on my bed, I held my glowing phone in front of my nose, idly scrolling through news articles, web comics, and silly memes. My alarm clock declared the time to be 6:03 in the morning, and no one was up yet. Kaveri and Sin were sleeping on air mattresses in the living room.

I should've been sleeping like the dead, but between the two potions Zak had fed me, I was feeling damn spritely. I could run a marathon right now.

Actually, no, I couldn't. I'd never run a marathon in my life.

Tucked under my arm was a warm sphere. Smooth bumps and ridges covered the silvery-blue orb, its surface streaked with aquamarine and fuchsia. Zak had given it to me weeks ago. According to him, it was a dormant fae and he wasn't suited to care for it. So now it was mine.

With no idea how to take care of it—and no instructions from the stupid druid—I'd been keeping it in the top drawer of my nightstand, nestled in an old sweater. At some point, I'd gotten in the habit of holding it while reading in bed, occasionally sharing random thoughts about my day. Why? No idea. Either I was crazy or lonely. Or a bit of both.

I scrolled through a few more dumb internet things, my mind wandering to Aaron's and Kai's concerned questions about the fae lord's visit. Had it only been six hours ago? My fingers tapped across my screen, closing one app and opening another. Photos filled the small display.

As I flipped through them, a smile tugged at my lips. Aaron and me at a farmer's market, pointing dramatically at a stand of oddly shaped watermelons. The three guys and me at the guild, toasting over a job they'd smashed. Sin and me at an outdoor concert last week, making faces at the camera.

I stopped at a photo of Aaron and me grinning at the selfie camera as we brandished big plastic guns. Behind us, Kai and Ezra stood at attention, faces grim, holding their own plastic firearms.

Two-on-two laser tag. Aaron and I goofed off from the start, but Kai and Ezra got hardcore into character—bleak and barking commands at each other, quipping military lines from movies, feigning injuries, and acting like they were in the middle of a war zone.

Aaron and I might have won the match if we hadn't been debilitated by laughter. Kai and Ezra kept escalating their soldier game until even Kai couldn't keep a straight face, but Ezra didn't crack once, the sparkle in his mismatched eyes the only sign that he was fighting not to laugh. He finished the match with an Oscar-worthy death scene and Kai gallantly swore to avenge him. I almost peed myself laughing.

I swiped through a few more photos from that day and stopped on the final one. I stood between Aaron and Ezra, my arms over their shoulders, a pout on my face. Aaron's head was thrown back in laughter—he'd gotten off a perfect zinger at my expense—and a huge grin lit Ezra's face, his curly hair tousled in the breeze. Kai was taking the picture with my phone, his presence as palpable as the two visible mages.

Were these photos all I'd have once this was over?

A damn shame she isn't a mythic. Ramsey's words were burned into my memory. I wanted to be a mythic, to be *one of them.* I wanted it so badly it hurt my soul. I wanted to be part of their world, so entrenched that not even the MPD could banish me.

"Tori?"

Twiggy's high-pitched whisper came from the foot of my bed. I sat up, hastily wiping at my eyes.

He faded into sight, huge green eyes gleaming in the darkness. "The witch is awake. She is making hot leaf water."

I canted my head, listening. A quiet clank drifted into my bedroom, followed by the sound of running water in the kitchen sink.

Twiggy inched along the bed, then sat a few feet from my legs. "She is angry."

Yes, yes she was. While Zak and I had been speaking with Llyrlethiad, Twiggy had stolen Kaveri's purse and led her on a merry chase up and down the street. All things considered, his efforts to distract her had been harmlessly funny. She didn't see the humor in it, though.

"You did an excellent job," I told the faery. "The druid is impressed."

Twiggy perked up. "The Crystal Druid is impressed?"

"Very much so. You did great." I held my hand up. When he stared, I added, "High five!"

More blank staring.

"Human thing," I told him, wiggling my fingers. "Hit your hand against my hand. It means, 'Good job.'"

His whole face brightened and he enthusiastically slapped my palm with his branchy fingers. "High five!"

"Yeah!" I readjusted the fae orb in my lap. It seemed warmer than usual. "Kaveri will like you again in no time."

He folded his spindly arms and sniffed. "I don't care if the witch likes me."

"Of course," I agreed, hiding my amusement. "You're just like the sea lord. You don't need no humans."

Twiggy shrank, giving the glowing marks on my arm an askance look. "The sea lord is a powerful fae."

"Yeah, I noticed."

"So is Lallakai, lady of shadow. The vargs of Gardall'kin are strong too. You know many powerful fae."

Correction: I knew one powerful druid, and he came with a bunch of scary fae minions.

"You're the best fae I know," I told Twiggy. "You're my movie buddy. That makes you better than any of them."

He blinked slowly, then a beaming smile overtook his face. "The other smallfae say humans are stupid and selfish, but you are good."

"Thanks, Twiggy."

"Tori ..." He inched closer. "Are we ... friends?"

I chuckled at his desperately hopeful expression. "Yes, Twiggy, we're friends. Just don't slap me anymore."

He nodded fanatically. "No slapping. Only high fives."

Really, Twiggy wasn't that bad. He was cute when he wanted to be, helpful when it suited him, a low-maintenance roommate, and an exceptional visitor deterrent. Last time my landlord tried to inspect my unit when I wasn't home, Twiggy had treated him to an impressive rendition of the Frankenstein monster. The faery had told me all about it.

I hugged the fae orb to my chest. I didn't want to lose all this. I couldn't go back to living like a mundane human in the mundane world. Somehow, I had to find a way to keep hold of *this* world.

But first, I needed to survive the bond with the fae lord. Priorities.

TWELVE HOURS LATER, I was ready to die, if for no other reason than the solitude. My apartment was like the start of a bad joke. A human, a faery, a witch, and an alchemist walk into a basement—actually, that sounded more like the start of a horror flick.

I liked Kaveri well enough and I adored Sin, but after twenty-four hours cooped up in my apartment with them, I was done. Thankfully, Kaveri had left ten minutes ago, but a new witch was on the way to replace her—Delta, a thirty-year-old woman with beads in her hair and an aversion to bras. I wasn't looking forward to it.

"I need to get out of this house," I moaned to Sin, flopped on my sofa with my legs hanging over one arm.

Absently tugging on a lock of her blue hair, she looked up from her phone. "I don't know ..."

"Let's walk over to that sushi place near Chinatown," I suggested. "It's twenty-five minutes away. We'll be back by the time Delta gets here."

Her frown deepened.

"Why should I be under house arrest?" I demanded. "MagiPol doesn't know where I live. They aren't watching me, and the fae lord is sulking in Never Never Land."

Zak had told me not to exert myself, but walking hardly counted as exertion. At the thought of the druid, I checked my phone in the vain hope he'd texted me. Aaron had called around noon with an update—"nothing yet"—along with news of more MPD snooping. He, Kai, and Ezra were researching fae relics and black magic while dodging Agent Harris and his female sidekick.

"All right." Sin's hesitation morphed into a grin. "I'm sick of this too. And I love sushi."

"Gimme a minute to change."

I skipped into my bedroom, stripped down, and redressed in jeans, a turtleneck, and my bomber jacket, now dry. The clothes covered all the markings, except the rune on my palm, but that's what pockets were for.

Swinging by my nightstand, I pulled it open to grab my Queen of Spades and fall-spell crystal. Huh. The nest for the fae orb was empty.

Oh right, I'd left it on the bed. I flipped my blankets back, searching, but it wasn't there. Had it fallen onto the floor? Before I could crouch to look under the bed, Sin called for me to hurry up.

Deciding to sort it out later, I shoved the sorcery artifacts in my pocket and joined Sin at the stairs.

"Hold the fort, Twiggy!" I called as I grabbed my bright purple umbrella—a gift from Aaron to replace the hot pink umbrella he'd given me before this one. I was going through umbrellas at an alarming rate.

Twiggy squeaked an affirmative, and I locked the door behind us.

The streets shone with recent rain, and I inhaled the crisp, damp breeze. Aw, man. Fresh air. I walked with a bounce in my step, rejuvenated by the sight of something besides my apartment walls.

Sin and I chatted about nothing important as we walked. A few times she directed the conversation toward Aaron and our relationship, but I steered it right off that track. Swinging my umbrella from one hand, my purse tucked under the opposite elbow, I smiled at the brick-faced buildings that lined Main Street. My neighborhood was nothing special, but it bordered some of the oldest parts of the city, which was pretty cool.

As we neared the transition from generic businesses to colorful storefronts, I paused my story about shopping for tempura ingredients with Kai and Ezra. Three police cruisers were parked along the curb. No lights or officers inside, but still weird.

"Anyway," I continued, banishing my frown once we'd passed the cars, "there we are, standing in this hole-in-the-wall shop full of Chinese herbs and pickled animal parts, and Kai is repeating the name of the sauce while the old man behind the counter is babbling in Mandarin. Then Ezra bumps into a display and …" I trailed off. "What's with that look?"

Sin blinked, the disbelieving twist to her lips fading. "Sorry. It's just so strange."

"What's strange?"

"Hearing your stories about them. Aaron, Kai, and Ezra, I mean." She shook her head as we turned down a street lined with restaurants. "Everyone at the guild has stories about them, but yours are different."

My steps slowed, my mouth turning down. "What do you mean?"

"I'm not sure how to explain it." Sin thought for a moment. "Well, for starters, I don't know of them inviting anyone to their house on a regular basis like they do with you."

That couldn't be right. Aaron, Kai, and Ezra were among the most popular guys at the guild—everyone liked them. But thinking back, I'd never seen another guest at Aaron's place.

"And Ezra—I can't recall him ever doing something without Aaron or Kai. He's *always* with them. Not that that's a bad thing," she added hastily. "It's just … he's sort of overly attached to the other two. Have you noticed?"

My frown deepened and I slowed to a stop, again trying to remember an occasion that would contradict her assessment. Nothing came to mind.

Flummoxed, I blindly turned to keep walking. A shop door swung open right in front of me, the metal edge just missing my face.

"Watch it, dipshit!" I barked at the man stepping onto the sidewalk. "Unless you're blind, you should—oh."

My brain registered the man's appearance: dark blue uniform, badge on the chest, emblem on the shoulder, gun holstered on his belt. I'd just called a cop a dipshit. I jerked my gaze up to the officer's astonished face—but it wasn't my rudeness that had shocked him.

"Tori?"

"Justin?"

He moved aside as a second officer—older with a thick beard—walked out. His radio crackled with a woman's voice.

"Sorry I called you a dipshit," I said quickly.

Justin waved his partner on, then pulled me into a quick hug. "Hey, Tor. What are you doing out here?"

"We're getting sushi." Tucking my fae-marked hand into my pocket, I tugged Sin over with my other hand. "This is Sin. Sin, this is my brother, Justin."

"Hi," Sin said in a tiny voice, her cheeks flushing pink. Justin offered his hand and she took it gingerly.

"Nice to meet you, Sin." He smiled amicably. "Is it rude of me to say your name is really interesting? I've never heard it before."

"Not rude," she mumbled, her face going redder. She seemed to have forgotten how to speak.

Burying a smirk, I jumped in to rescue her. "What's got you out here, Justin?"

"There are a few of us out this evening." He glanced around, then lowered his voice. "Bizarre complaints have been coming in since yesterday. Figures in black lurking in alleys, 'gangsters' casing businesses, men accosting women on the streets."

"Whoa. Here in Chinatown, you mean?"

"Chinatown, Strathcona, and Mount Pleasant." He gave me a significant look—Mount Pleasant was my neighborhood. "It's the kind of thing we expect in the Eastside, not around here."

"No kidding." A wet drop hit my nose and I glanced suspiciously at the sky.

"It isn't a good night to be out. Did you two walk?"

"Yeah," I answered. "We're almost to the sushi place, though, then we'll head straight back."

"I'll walk you to the restaurant, then you should take the bus home." He frowned. "Actually, I'll drive you back. They can spare me for a few minutes."

"You don't need to do that." I scrutinized his expression—full of familiar stubbornness. "But thanks."

We got three steps down the sidewalk before the rain started in earnest. I popped my umbrella open, handed it to Justin, then stepped under its plastic dome. Sin took the spot at his opposite elbow, her cheeks still flushed. Justin, the ol' smoothie, made small talk with her, and she stumblingly responded.

Shy Sin was so cute! I giggled to myself, then a flash of something pale caught my eye. When I turned, I saw nothing but shops with glowing OPEN signs and colorful awnings above the doors. A few people trailed along the sidewalk a ways back, looking at a window display.

We made it to the sushi shop and Justin waited outside with the umbrella while Sin and I went in to order. The moment the door shut behind us, Sin swung toward me.

"You never told me your brother was hot!" she hissed accusingly.

"What did you expect?" I flipped my curls with mock arrogance. "We have good genes."

She snorted, then glanced at Justin's silhouette outside the glass door. Her expression crumpled. "I'm such a loser. This is why I don't have a boyfriend."

"Because you go mute the moment a cute, single guy smiles at you? Yeah, that doesn't help."

She perked up. "He's single?"

"Newly single. *Very* newly. And possibly rebounding."

Chewing her lower lip in thought, she turned to the counter to order.

Laden with bags of delicious sushi, we exited the shop. Justin asked Sin what her favorite dish was, but I missed her answer as another pale flicker caught my eye. I glanced sharply along the street but saw only the same window-shopping trio. They'd passed the sushi place and were a dozen yards down the sidewalk.

Huddled under my umbrella, we started back. As Sin attempted to flirt with my brother—poorly—I glanced around, searching for the pale thing I kept seeing. Was I losing my mind? Sheesh.

I scanned the trio, checked the nearest dark alley—then did a double take. The three people had reversed direction and were following us again.

Déjà vu sparked through me. I'd been followed once before by strangers in black, and it hadn't ended well. I looped my arm through Justin's and picked up the pace, hurrying him and Sin along. Was I paranoid? Or were they stalking us?

Footsteps scuffed behind us—the trio increasing their pace. My neck prickled. I twisted to look back—and light gleamed off the shiny black pistol the middlemost man had pulled from his coat.

Shouting in alarm, I tore the umbrella out of Justin's hand and swung the plastic dome down.

The gun popped. Yellow paintballs burst against my umbrella shield, and I almost cheered in relief that the gun wasn't the bullet-firing kind. But the yellow splatter dripping off the plastic—I'd bet my paycheck it wasn't paint.

These weren't your average hooligans. They were mythics.

Justin pulled his *actual* bullet-firing gun from its holster and leveled it at our attackers. "Drop your weapon!"

The black-clad mythics exchanged perplexed glances, like they hadn't expected this. Really? Had they thought Justin was dressed in costume?

I stood frozen, umbrella positioned in front of me. Mythics were attacking us—bad. My very human brother who knew an unknown amount about mythics was defending us—also bad.

"Drop your weapon!" Justin ordered again. "I *will* open fire on you."

The man with the paintball pistol glanced at his buddies, then slowly lowered the gun.

"I said *drop*—" Justin began.

Twitching his wrist, the leftmost goon produced a short, fat stick from his sleeve. Three things happened at once:

The sorcerer shouted, "*Ori impello plurimos!*" and runes flashed up his wand.

Paintball Guy swung his pistol up.

And Justin fired his gun.

The bang of the gun burst my eardrums as a band of force struck my chest like a battering ram. I flew backward and crashed down on the sidewalk, the umbrella tumbling from my hand. Justin and Sin hit the ground beside me, blasted off their feet by the spell.

Paintball Guy swore, blood shining on his arm from Justin's shot. Teeth bared, the rogue pointed his weapon at me and pulled the trigger.

Wind gusted wildly, blowing the yellow potion-ball off course. It missed me, and for an instant I thought Ezra was here, protecting me with his wind magic.

With a pale flash, a sinuous shape appeared above the three men. Glowing faintly in shades of bluish silver, aquamarine, and pink, the creature swooped down and plucked the gun from the man's hand. The weapon somersaulted through the air and clattered in the middle of the road. The creature shimmered out of sight again.

The pause gave me time to launch up, Sin and Justin following a second behind—but the sorcerer was faster.

"*Ori amethystino mergere ponto!*"

Purple light ballooned out from his wand's tip. Rippling violently, the distortion of air shot toward me, expanding as it came.

"Tori!"

Sin shoved me out of the way and the weird purple orb hit her. It whooshed outward, engulfing her entire body, and she flailed helplessly from within it—suspended inside a magical bubble.

My mouth hung open. What *the hell* was that?

I wasn't the only one stunned speechless. Gun clutched in his hands like he'd forgotten about it, Justin stared at the rippling bubble that held Sin like a science-lab specimen suspended in goo.

Paintball Guy was gripping his arm, which was leaking an alarming amount of blood, but the sorcerer was aiming his wand at me again. This time I was ready.

I whipped my Queen of Spades card out and pointed it at the sorcerer. "*Ori—*"

"*Ori percunctari!*"

I'd gotten used to the Queen saving my butt, and until now, I'd managed to get its mouthful of an incantation out fast enough to repel attacks. But as the green flash of the sorcerer's spell hit me in the face, it occurred to me that maybe, all those times before, I'd just gotten lucky. That, or I'd been fighting shitty sorcerers.

Cold magic washed over me in a bone-chilling wave, and I stepped back sharply.

Or I tried to.

My limbs felt like they were moving through thick sludge. In ultra-slow-motion, my left leg started to bend. My brain flew ahead of the movement, trying to jerk my body forward, to raise my arms, to finish my incantation as the sorcerer flipped a new wand into his hand.

But nope, my foot continued to travel in its backward trajectory at the speed of about an inch per minute. The sorcerer pointed his new wand—thicker and carved with runes—at me and opened his mouth.

Gunshots shattered my eardrums for a second time.

Pistol held in a textbook cop grip, Justin fired at the sorcerer. The man lurched backward, shock splashing across his face before he toppled over. Paintball Guy stumbled and fell too, his skin white.

The third mythic raised her hands in surrender—and the air behind her rippled. A shadowy form materialized out of the darkness and rain. The beastly creature towered over her, ten feet tall and covered in thick black fur, with lantern-orange eyes that glowed in a skull-like face framed by curling ram horns.

A fae. A nasty fae.

Bigfoot loosed a horrific roar. Oh shiiiit. Even if I could use it—which I couldn't, since I was stuck in magical slo-mo—my little Queen of Spades card was no match against this thing.

Justin went rigid at the sight of the monster, but no brother of mine was coward enough to flee, even when facing a giant, shaggy, skull-faced beast with monstrous yellow teeth. He swung his gun toward it and emptied his magazine into the creature's chest.

The fae didn't even notice. It lumbered forward, snarling.

All at once, my movements snapped back to normal—and my body tried to complete every order my brain had sent, all at once. I flailed like a wacky inflatable tube man and fell over, landing on my butt—but at least the spell had worn off.

Just in time for Bigfoot to charge us.

"Llyrlethiad!" I screamed.

Justin's final shot drowned out my voice, and for a second, I feared the fae lord might not have heard me.

Alien power rushed through my body—and the drizzling rain morphed into a torrential downpour. As the world turned into a silver blur of plunging water, a shape coalesced out of the liquid.

Gargantuan serpent coils twisted through the sheeting rain, looping around me, Justin, and Sin—still trapped in the purple bubble. The leviathan's horned head, fifteen feet above the sidewalk, glistened as it looked down on the puny witch and her Bigfoot familiar.

I stayed parked on my butt in the rapidly deepening puddles. What was the point in moving? First off, Llyrlethiad's power was flooding through me in dizzying waves, and my soul felt like it was being pushed out of my body by the magical force buzzing under my skin.

And second, I'd summoned a giant-ass sea god into a downtown street, and that felt like a much bigger deal than when the fae had been breaking walls in my apartment.

Witch lady took a good long look at said sea god, then did the only reasonable thing she could do—she turned tail and ran like her life depended on it.

Her familiar, however, didn't flee. It bared its teeny yellow fangs at the leviathan—yes, I'd recently called those fangs humongous, but it's all a matter of perspective.

Llyrlethiad pondered his opponent, then lunged. Whatever Bigfoot had been planning to do, it never got a chance. The serpent's massive jaws engulfed the other fae's head and shoulders, and the sea god lifted the struggling beast into the air. He chomped a few times, bones popping and crunching, then spat the mangled body onto the pavement.

My stomach crawled into my throat and I clapped a hand over my mouth to keep it down.

While the serpent had been chewing on his opponent, Paintball Guy had dragged the wounded sorcerer to his feet, and the two of them hobbled into an alley. I had zero desire to chase them down.

The torrential rain continued, flooding the street. Llyrlethiad's pale eyes turned back to his fallen fae opponent, and the deepening water began to spin around Bigfoot. More water pulled into the spiral, and the fae's body disappeared into the whirlpool.

With a splash, the maelstrom dispersed and the water settled. Bigfoot had vanished, gone without a trace.

Despite my dizziness, I pushed to my feet. My mental approximation of Llyrlethiad's power readjusted from red-zone ultra-boss to … I didn't even know, but it was scary as hell.

Over the sound of pouring rain, the wail of police sirens reached my ears. Oh hell. How was I supposed to explain a giant sea serpent to a bunch of coppers?

As though hearing my thoughts, Llyrlethiad's ivory gaze moved across me, then fell on Sin in her spell bubble. Power surged through me, heating the hidden fae runes on my skin. The weird purple bubble popped, and Sin landed on her feet, wobbled, then fell on her knees.

A sudden increase in the deluge turned everything to sheeting water, then the rain lightened to a gentle shower. The serpent had vanished too.

My knees trembled but I stubbornly locked them. I was cool. I was good. Dizzy, but good. No fainting from this girl— not again.

The sirens were rapidly drawing closer. Justin holstered his gun, then extended a hand to Sin. She grasped it and lurched to her feet, her face bleached of color. Justin was even paler, his eyes huge and white all the way around.

"Are you two okay?" he asked, his voice only a little unsteady. My brother was tough as shit. *My* first magic experience had been way tamer. One little fireball. Nothing compared to all-out mythic warfare and a sea god.

Before he could say anything else, two cruisers skidded around the corner. They slid to a halt beside us, splashing water over my calves, and four officers leaped out.

"What happened?" one of them barked. "Dawson, are you injured?"

"I'm fine," Justin answered. With a warning look I understood to mean, "Say nothing," he hastened to the officers and spoke in a low, rushed voice. Two cops pulled their guns and started down the alley where the injured rogues had fled, while another got on his radio to call for backup.

I gulped down that sickly post-adrenaline feeling. "Are you all right, Sin?"

She heaved a deep breath. "Yeah. That spell wasn't pleasant ..." She glanced at Justin. "What should we tell him?"

"Nothing," I muttered, watching my brother. He knew about magic from his police work, but he didn't know *I* knew. Safer to keep it that way. "We were in the wrong place at the wrong time. We don't know anything about what happened."

Her eyebrows rose, and she lowered her voice. "Even though the rogues were obviously targeting you?"

I nodded. All the more reason not to involve Justin. I was already in over my head in mythic business, and I didn't want to put his life—or his job—at risk.

As blaring sirens announced the approach of more cops, Justin returned to us. "I need to take your statements, then I'll drive you home."

My statement? Sure, no problem. I'd just make sure not to mention that I'd summoned the giant sea serpent, that those people had been targeting me, that they were rogue mythics ... or that I suspected they were members of the notorious Red Rum guild.

Red Rum knew I had their fae lord—and they wanted him back.

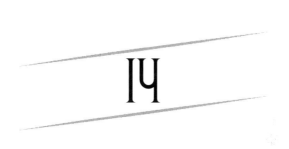

14

I STIRRED OUT OF A DAZE when the car door slammed. Blearily, I realized we were parked at the curb of a familiar street. Aaron's house. Right. That was the address I'd given Justin after he'd loaded Sin and me into the back of his cruiser.

Justin circled the car and opened my door. I dragged my exhausted limbs out, relieved to see lights glowing inside the house. As I wobbled upright, Sin skooched across the seat toward the open door.

"Justin, will you take Sin home?" I asked before she could get out.

"I thought this was Sin's place?"

"No, this is Aaron's house." I shrugged. "I'm sure Sin would rather go home than …"

"Than hang out at your boyfriend's?" he finished for me, missing my flinch at the word "boyfriend." He ducked to look into the car. "Want a ride, Sin? Where do you live?"

Her face reddened at his smile and she mumbled a weak protest. I nudged Justin with my elbow and winked. Pulling a face, he closed the door on Sin, trapping her in the cruiser. She glared at me through the glass.

"You okay, Tori?" he asked as I stepped toward Aaron's front walk.

I shrugged. Honestly not the scariest thing I'd faced these last few months.

His brow furrowed, and I remembered I was supposed to be ignorant of the existence of magic. I hadn't brought up the attack or the fantastical occurrences beyond vaguely describing the encounter in my statement, so I didn't know what he thought of it all.

"Uh," I blurted, backtracking. "I mean, that was all … really terrifying. And I thought I saw some, uh … some really weird shit."

Frown deepening, he squinted at my face. I tried to hold my expression of bewildered anxiety, but he wasn't falling for it. Why did my brother have to be intelligent?

"We can talk about it later," he muttered. "I need to get back and finish my report. Will you be okay? Would you rather stay at my place?"

"I'll be safe here. Aaron and his roommates are big tough guys."

Justin glanced at the house. "Call me if you need anything."

"Yep. And thanks for chauffeuring Sin." I arched an eyebrow. "By the way, she thinks you're hot."

He choked, a faint blush creeping above his neatly trimmed beard. Muttering something under his breath—all I caught was "inappropriate" and "timing"—he got into his cruiser. Starting the engine, he waited for me to go into the house.

Purse over my shoulder and umbrella in hand, I trudged to the front stoop. The door was unlocked, so I threw it open and stepped inside, waving at Justin. The car rolled away. At least I didn't have to worry about Justin freaking out about Sin being a mythic. When the officers were completing our statements, she'd produced a normal driver's license, sans MID number. Handy trick, that.

"Tori?"

I turned.

Ezra stood in the hallway that led past the living room, his brow furrowed over mismatched eyes. "What happened? Are you okay?"

His meltingly smooth voice washed over me like sinking into a hot bath after a bad day. I took three long steps, arms already reaching. He swept me into his embrace and I pressed my cheek against his soft blue t-shirt. Our first hug, shared in an apartment building hallway, had been phenomenally awkward, but it had somehow evolved into something special between us.

"I'm okay," I said into his chest. "Sin and I went to get sushi and we were attacked by mythics. Red Rum rogues, I think."

"What? Shit." Hands shifting to my upper arms, he stepped back to scrutinize me for injuries. Seeing none, he pulled me into the living room and urged me onto the sofa. "Aaron and Kai won't be back for a few more hours. They made a last-minute trip to Victoria to investigate a grimoire that might include the fae-binding ritual."

Noticing how quiet it was, I glanced around the cluttered room. The TV was off and no music played on the speakers, but the acoustic guitar from Ezra's bedroom was leaning against the sofa. Shrugging my purse off, I set it and my umbrella on the coffee table, knocking a stack of vintage car magazines onto the floor.

Ezra perched on a cushion beside me. "What happened?"

I described the encounter. Halfway through, I remembered my sushi and fished it out of my oversized purse. Skipping over the silvery fae creature—I wanted to run that particular weirdness past Zak first—I told him the rest as I cracked open the container and offered it to him. He picked out a California roll and stuffed it in his mouth.

"Do you think they were searching for you?" he asked after I'd finished. "Your brother mentioned suspicious activity in the area. I wonder if Red Rum had a way of detecting the fae lord's visit last night."

"The timing fits. Do you think they can track me because of the fae magic?"

"It's possible. I don't know much about Spiritalis." He patted the pockets of his loose black sweats, then rooted around the coffee table until he uncovered his phone. "I'll fill Kai and Aaron in on what happened."

Munching sushi, I watched him bring the phone to his ear. His dark curls were messier than usual, the sexy scruff on his jaw thicker than his normal barely-more-than-a-five-o'clock-shadow. His t-shirt was the kind of old, worn, ultra-soft cotton I saved for PJs, and he was barefoot. Lounge-Ezra. I wasn't sure I'd ever seen him this casual before.

Remembering what Sin had said, I thought back and realized this might be the first time I'd been alone in the house with him.

He finished the call, his forehead creased. "They're coming back as soon as they can, but the ferry ride is an hour and a half."

"It's fine." I stifled a yawn. "No one followed us, and as long as I stay indoors—" Another yawn interrupted me.

Ezra caught the empty sushi container as it tipped out of my limp hand.

"Sorry," I mumbled. "I'm so tired. The fae's magic completely wipes me out."

"I can imagine." Still radiating worry, he collected the garbage and carried it into the kitchen. Returning, he tugged a throw blanket free from between two cushions and draped it over me. "Your clothes are damp. Do you want something dry?"

"I'm good." I snuggled into the blanket, thinking longingly of his bed upstairs. My first time sleeping over, he'd offered me his room—mainly to prevent an argument between Aaron and Kai—and since then it had become my standard bed-away-from-home.

Realizing Ezra was still standing, I tugged a pinch of his pants. "Sit down. Don't just hover like an anxious mother hen."

He sheepishly dropped onto the sofa. "Do you want to watch a movie?"

"Too tired." I yawned again, then slid the tie out of my hair, loosing my curls to let them dry. "Did I interrupt you? What were you doing before I barged in?"

He glanced at the guitar. "Nothing."

"Do you play?"

A shrug.

I flopped more comfortably into the cushions. "That's fine. Collecting instruments you don't play just to carry them around the house is perfectly normal."

He gazed at me seriously. "I thought about collecting pianos instead."

My mouth twitched. I frowned to keep from smiling.

"That seemed too challenging," he added somberly. "Even a piano with wheels is awkward to move around."

"Why not harmonicas?" I suggested, my voice cracking from the effort not to laugh. "Easy to carry."

"They don't look as cool."

"Of course not."

"Maybe I should collect tubas. Tubas are cool, right?"

The mental image of him waltzing around the house with a tuba was too much. A snort escaped me and I tried to suck it back in—and burst into snickers instead. His grave expression cracked into a grin, and I vowed that someday I would make him laugh first.

I nudged his ankle with my toes. "Play something."

Hesitatingly, he picked up the guitar and settled it on his lap. Plucking a few strings, he tilted his head shyly. "I don't usually play for people."

A flutter danced through my middle. "Will you play for me?"

He looked down at the instrument. The frets squeaked under his left hand, and he plucked a few strings with his right. A melody emerged, then stuttered. Beginning again, he skimmed through a few tunes—playing a familiar chorus, then the solo from a popular song, then a snippet of a recent radio hit.

Not bad, but having an audience was making him uncomfortable. Pulling the blanket closer, I closed my eyes so he might feel less like he was performing.

He paused, and I could feel his gaze on me. The strings squeaked again as he repositioned his hand. A moment of silence.

A soft waterfall of notes poured from the strings in a delicate melody. As more notes joined the measured rhythm, I cracked my eyes open, unable to believe he could coax that much music from a single instrument.

One hand slid up and down the guitar's neck, his strong fingers flexing as he pressed into the frets, sharp tendons running from his knuckles to wrist. His right hand hovered in front of the wooden body, his fingers dancing over the strings. As the haunting melody built, he thumped the heel of his hand against the guitar body, adding a hollow drumbeat to the strumming cascades of notes both sharp and soft.

"Beautiful," I breathed, utterly mesmerized.

He ducked his head, embarrassed, and the notes trailed into silence.

"How long have you been playing?"

"A long time." Cradling the instrument on his lap, he plucked through a swift scale. "I enjoy it. It's calming. Like meditation."

"Thank you for playing for me," I whispered.

He moved his head in a slow nod. Now I understood why his first attempt had been so stilted; he'd played popular music, something impersonal. I didn't know why he'd chosen to share a piece he truly enjoyed, but I was touched he had.

"Ezra …" His name came out in a strange croak.

He shifted on the sofa to look at me. "What's wrong?"

I coughed, not sure what I'd intended to say, and asked a different question instead. "Do you really think everything will go back to normal?"

"What do you mean?"

"The MPD investigation … my job …" I bit my lip. "I don't see how it could work."

"Even if you can't work at the guild, it won't change anything with us. You're our friend, Tori."

"Right." I smiled wanly. "Of course."

He twisted further to see my face. His mismatched eyes, one warm brown like melted chocolate, the other pale as ice and ringed in black, swept over me. "You can't believe it, can you?"

My hands tightened around fistfuls of the blanket.

Facing forward, he strummed a few chords. "I didn't believe it, either. Not at first. It took a long time for me to trust Aaron and Kai ... to trust they wouldn't give up on me."

I fought the urge to tense. Ezra, more so than the other two, never spoke of the past.

"I didn't get it until a year after I first met them." His voice dropped to a murmur. "I'd assumed our friendship was temporary, that sooner or later they'd come to their senses, wonder what they'd seen in me, and that'd be it."

My chest constricted. That was exactly how I felt now.

"Then ..." His hand clenched around the guitar neck. "I hurt Aaron."

I'd never heard such a rough rasp come from his butter-smooth voice before.

"I lost control ... really lost it ... and I hurt him badly." He paused, the silence throbbing with pain and regret. "I knew that was it, that I should've left a long time ago. While Kai rushed Aaron to a healer, I packed my things."

My eyes widened. When he'd said "hurt," I thought he'd meant feelings, not that he'd *wounded* Aaron. What had Ezra done that would require an emergency magical healing?

Kai's voice, words he'd gasped weeks ago, echoed in my ears. *Stop them before Ezra kills Aaron.*

Ezra stared at nothing for a long minute. "Kai caught up to me at the bus station. He dragged me back, shoved me into a chair at the healer's house, and sat beside me. He said there was no way in hell he was letting me ditch them. He said …"

When he didn't continue, I dared to whisper, "What did he say?"

"He …" Ezra drew in a slow breath, then shook his head. "We sat there all night. After the healer discharged him, Aaron never said a word about what I'd done. He's never mentioned it, not once."

His gaze flicked to mine, too quick for me to hide my horrified disbelief. Just how badly had he injured Aaron? The guys had warned me about Ezra's temper, but I couldn't imagine him lashing out at his friends with that degree of violence.

Weariness and bleak humor blended in his expression. "Second worst night of my life."

"You've had a *worse* night?" I asked incredulously.

He nodded and touched the bottom of the scar that cut down his face.

"Oh. Right."

"So, you see, Tori? An MPD investigation is nothing to them. Aaron and Kai will stick by you through everything— through the worst of anything. They'll never let you down."

I nodded, comforted if not convinced. Aaron and Kai's loyalty to Ezra didn't necessarily extend to me, but a girl could hope.

Ezra's eyes slid away from mine. "Tori, nobody knows I'm the one who hurt Aaron."

My breath hitched. I swallowed soundlessly, understanding what he was asking. "I'll never tell a soul."

He started to play again, a soft, soothing melody that verged on a lullaby. My eyes drifted closed. For the first time, Ezra had revealed one of his secrets—a frightening one, but I suspected all his secrets were scary. I wished I could ask more about those early days of his friendship with Aaron and Kai.

My fatigue had grown unbearable. The world grew fuzzy, and dark dreams, woven through with sweet notes, overtook my mind.

I didn't stir until the music stopped. Rustling movements, footsteps retreating, then returning. Careful hands slid under me, then Ezra lifted me off the sofa and into his arms. I tucked my face against his warm neck, sleepily inhaling.

His swaying steps moved across the room, heading for the stairs, but the clatter of the back door opening brought him to a halt. More footsteps approached, but caught on the edge of sleep, I was too weary to open my eyes.

"How is she?" Aaron whispered.

"Tired. She fell asleep on the sofa."

"We got the grimoire," Kai said in a low voice. "I'm almost positive it has the ritual. Now we need someone who can figure out a counter spell."

"One step closer," Aaron murmured. "We'll get her through this."

Ezra adjusted his hold on me. "I'll put her to bed."

My senses whirled as he climbed the stairs. A door creaked open. He shifted me into one arm, bearing my weight like I was no more cumbersome than a doll. He leaned over the bed, blankets rustling, then laid me down.

I sank into the mattress, my head on the pillow and my nose clouded with his delicious scent. He pulled the blankets over me and tucked them up to my chin.

Silence fell over the room, and I sleepily wondered if I'd missed the sound of him leaving.

The slight creak of a floorboard beside the bed. A whisper-soft touch on my hair, his thumb brushing my cheek. Then quick, quiet footsteps, followed by the snick of the door latch.

I opened my eyes and stared at the closed door, my skin tingling in the wake of Ezra's gentle touch.

15

FACE BURIED IN THE PILLOW, I wondered if it was possible to be alive while this exhausted. Maybe I'd died at some point and was now a zombie.

I'd slept through the night and gotten up for breakfast like a normal person, then fallen asleep on the sofa. I'd woken up in Ezra's bed again with no clue which guy had carried me upstairs. It was now—I squinted at the alarm clock on Ezra's nightstand—eight o'clock in the evening. I'd done nothing but nap all day, and I didn't feel any less tired. Clearly, Zak's fancy potion had already worn off.

Anxiety rolled through me. I'd texted Zak every time I'd been awake enough to pilot my phone, but he hadn't responded. What a jerk. I might literally be dying here and he didn't care.

Voices rumbled from the lower level—Aaron and Ezra, and it sounded like Kai was home now too. He and Aaron had been in and out all day, carting their newly acquired black-magic grimoire to various guild members, hoping someone could decipher it.

Sighing wearily, I checked my phone for notifications. No responses from Zak, but my battery was at twenty-six percent. Great. I flopped toward the bed's edge and leaned over it, scanning the floor. Aha, my purse. Stretching out an arm, I grabbed the bag, heaved it onto the bed, and dug in, searching for a phone charger. I didn't *think* I had one, but the contents of my oversized handbag had surprised me before.

Wallet, sunglasses, crumpled receipts. I pulled out a knitted winter hat—why was I carrying that around in the summer?— and froze at the gleam of something pale.

A silvery-blue orb was nestled in the bottom of my bag. Hadn't I left the dormant fae at home? I had no recollection of putting it in my purse. I lifted it out and weighed its smooth warmth in my palms.

The ridged texture heated under my skin—then the whole thing moved. It unraveled and expanded, spiky wings lifting off its back, a sinuous neck uncoiling, pink eyes shining. My empty hands hung in place.

A fae hovered in front of me: the silvery creature that had saved me last night.

Its serpentine body undulated like a Chinese dragon, weightless and immune to gravity. More aquamarine-blue than silver, its reptilian face was shaped like a gecko's, with giant pink eyes and a matching crystal in the center of its wide forehead. It had two small front arms but no hind legs, and its body morphed into a thick tail at least five feet long. Small wings, like a cross between bat wings and butterfly wings, rose off its back.

Two pairs of long antennae protruded from its head, ending in glowing blue crystals. They bobbed as the creature brought its blunt muzzle close to my nose, those huge eyes fixed on mine expectantly.

"Um." I swallowed repeatedly. "Hello?"

Its tail snaked back and forth through the air, filling half the room. Wings flicking open and closed like a folding fan, the creature drifted backward. Its jaw opened, displaying needle-sharp teeth in a wide yawn. Ducking its head, it rapidly curled its body inward. Its long tail wound into the ball, the whole shape tightened and shrank, then the bluish-silver sphere dropped into my lap.

I gawked like a simpleton. How dense was I? I should have recognized the fae's color scheme last night. Rubbing a bewildered hand over my face, I hesitantly patted the fae orb. It didn't react to my touch.

"You're supposed to be dormant," I muttered.

Not that I was unhappy the fae had woken up—and saved my ass—but it was one more thing I'd have to deal with. Why had Zak given it to me? He still hadn't replied to my messages, and now I *really* wanted to talk to him.

Setting the fae aside, I minced to the door and cracked it open. The guys' muffled voices carried up the stairs, and I waited until I'd picked out all three before closing the door and dialing Zak's number.

Once again, it rang for half an eternity before he answered with a friendly, "I'm busy."

"I'm half dead," I retorted with a growl. "I can hardly stay awake. I need more of that potion."

"Already?" he muttered. The distinct sound of voices in low conversation trickled through the phone. "That was fast."

"The fae lord had to make an appearance last night to obliterate some Red Rum assholes, so that probably contributed. Where are you? It sounds like a conference hall." Or a wedding before everyone got drunk.

"The art gallery."

"You're not answering my messages because you're at an *art gallery?*"

"There's an event tonight with several attendees who might have useful information related to your fae problem."

My *fae problem.* What a nice way to put it. "I didn't know black-magic felons appreciated fine art."

A quiet snort. "The location makes them feel classy. I'm ruining the mood with my lack of penguin suit and monocle."

"Okay, well, I'd tell you to have fun, but I really need that potion."

"I have another dose with me, but you'll have to hang on until morning."

"But—"

"You won't die, Tori. Just be patient." The line went dead.

He had no phone manners. Or any manners, really.

Gazing at the fae orb—which he hadn't given me a chance to mention—I considered my options. Sleep another twelve hours and hope I didn't slip into a coma. Or … I bit my lip. Or go get my potion.

It wouldn't be difficult. Pop over to the art gallery and tell him to duck out for a minute to give me the potion. He could return to schmoozing with barely a blip in his night.

As a yawn cracked my jaw, I gave myself a "wake the hell up" pep talk. *The* art gallery could only be one place, and I pulled it up on my phone. A thirty-five-minute walk through most of downtown, but by car, it was only ten minutes away.

There and back in no time. I tapped my lower lip. One of the guys could take me. I'd make them wait around the corner or something while I met with Zak.

Ezra didn't drive, so he was out. Aaron could drive, but he was kind of excitable. I needed someone calm and coolheaded. Someone who wouldn't get worked up over a strange request.

Footsteps creaked on the stairs, and I could tell by the sound who it was. Huffing nervously, I opened the door.

Kai paused with his hand on his bedroom doorknob, laptop tucked under one arm.

"Hey Kai!" I said brightly.

His eyes narrowed immediately.

"What?" I demanded, wounded by his wariness.

Faint amusement touched his features. "Tori, if you don't want to seem suspicious, don't act so sweet and sugary."

"Oh, come on. Why is me being cheerful suspicious?"

Leaning against his door, he looked me up and down like I might be carrying concealed weapons. "What do you want?

I smiled hesitantly. "Wanna take me for a ride on your motorcycle?"

His guardedness returned in full force. "A ride where?"

No matter how I answered that, he'd be suspicious, so I batted my eyelashes and chirped with all the sweet sugar I could muster, "It's a surprise!"

He stared at me—then threw his head back in a laugh.

FIFTEEN MINUTES LATER, I was gripping Kai's leather-jacket-clad waist as his motorcycle rocketed down Dunsmuir Street. Yellow streetlamps and red tail lights flashed past as we weaved through traffic. I pointed over his shoulder and he careened through a left turn, cutting it way too close to an oncoming car.

Ahead, the skyscrapers opened up. Squatting among the giants was an old-fashioned building with a stone exterior, four-story-tall columns marking the dramatic entrance, and a domed roof. The structure, once a courthouse, was over a hundred years old.

I looked around for a parking spot, but dozens of sleek cars and SUVs, most of them black with the occasional silver or gunmetal gray, were parallel parked bumper to bumper. Kai slowed the bike, and I gestured helplessly toward the gallery as we passed it.

"*Here?*" he shouted in disbelief over the road noise.

"Yeah."

His helmet swiveled as he scanned the street. The engine revved, then he spun a one-eighty into the opposing traffic and shot back down the road. With a squeal of tires, he cut across the pavement and onto the sidewalk. Slowing to trolling speed, we passed a grand three-sided staircase that looked like it had spilled off the second-level terrace. The gallery entrance was tucked into the inner corner of the L-shaped building.

Stopping the motorcycle beside a row of trees in concrete planters, Kai killed the engine. I loosened my death grip on him and looked around. Yeah, this wasn't a parking space, but who would complain? The felonious rogue we were about to meet?

Kai pulled his helmet off to take in the pillared front entrance and even grander next level. When his gaze came back down, his dark eyes squinted with familiar suspicion.

Tugging off my helmet, I hunched my shoulders guiltily. "Umm ..."

"We're not meeting Sin to pick up a potion, are we?"

We *were* here to get a potion, but not from Sin. I'd had no choice but to lie; revealing the true nature of my errand could trigger the deadly oath spell.

"I need to pick something up, and I swear it's important," I told him, pleading for forgiveness with my eyes.

Hooking my helmet on the saddlebag behind me, I dug my phone out of my pocket. Zak hadn't answered my message warning him that I was on my way. I shot off another text telling him I was waiting outside and that I had a friend with me. If he wanted to meet in private, he could tell me where.

Kai rolled his shoulders. "The art gallery," he muttered. Judging by his growling undertone, he was immensely displeased that I'd tricked him. "Looks like there's an event tonight. I wonder what it is?"

He shot me a pointed look, and I shrank in my seat. "I don't know. That's not why I'm here."

Grumbling something I was glad I couldn't make out, he surveyed our surroundings like a scout searching for enemy soldiers. Jiggling my phone impatiently, I stifled another yawn and fought the urge to slump. Zero energy. It was ridiculous.

"You okay, Tori?" Kai asked, his tone gentling.

"Yeah." Silence fell between us. Giving in, I leaned against his back and pillowed my cheek on his cold leather shoulder blade. "This sucks."

"Philip warned us the link with the fae would tire you, but I didn't expect it to be this extreme."

"I can survive being tired." Probably. I shot off three back-to-back messages, hoping to catch the distracted druid's attention. "How's it going with the grimoire?"

"We've gone from ninety-five percent sure it contains the correct ritual to ninety-nine percent sure. If it's not the exact ritual they used, it's very close. We gave copies to several witches and sorcerers. They're working on a counter spell that could break the link."

"How long will it take?"

"No way to know. This isn't a common area of expertise."

I considered that. "Do you have any extra copies?"

"Not on me," he replied cautiously.

"Never mind then."

"Tori …" His back shifted under my cheek as he tried to look at me. "You know we'll keep your secrets, right?"

"I know," I whispered.

I felt him nod. Quiet settled over us.

After a minute, he asked, "So why did you ask me to drive you and not Aaron?"

Squirming from the question, I muttered, "No reason."

"Hmm."

A hundred thoughts crowded my head at once, including the memory of the conversation I'd overheard between Aaron and Ramsey. But no, that had nothing to do with my choice of chauffeur. Kai was the better option for a covert mission. Way more suited to it. Definitely.

Okay, *fine*. I'd been avoiding Aaron, and not very subtly either, since Kai had noticed. Meaning Aaron had probably noticed too.

"I don't think I can date Aaron anymore," I blurted.

Kai twitched like I'd poked him. "Oh?"

"Great." My shoulders hunched. "If it surprises *you*, how will Aaron react?"

"I'm not surprised by what you said," Kai corrected, his tone dry. "I'm surprised you admitted it."

"Huh?"

"It's not really a shock." He shifted on the bike seat. "You've shown none of the classic 'falling in love' signs."

"But why not?" I pressed my forehead against his back. "I really like Aaron. We get along great. We always have fun, and we have amazing chemistry. It's been three months. Why am I not in love with him already?"

"Maybe you're trying too hard."

"Eh? What do you mean?"

"I don't know." He huffed. "Why are you asking me?"

I rubbed my temples as though I could massage some sense into my brain. "I don't understand what's wrong with me."

"Maybe nothing is wrong. Maybe he isn't right for you. Just because a man asks you out doesn't mean he's destined to be your one true love." He shrugged, jostling me. "Two fiery personalities probably aren't a good match anyway. You two never relax when you're together."

"But ..." My backbone shriveled, feeling as sturdy as a stalk of grass. "How do I tell Aaron?"

"Just tell him. He already suspects, Tori. He won't hate you."

"But it'll be awkward."

"He'll get over it." Kai patted my knee—the only part of me he could easily reach. "Trust me, Tori. Aaron is ..." He paused thoughtfully. "Adaptation is one of Aaron's defining strengths. He doesn't hold grudges or dwell on the past. He's always moving forward, searching for the next adventure."

I nodded slowly, recognizing the truth in Kai's assessment of Aaron. Still, ending things with him wouldn't be easy.

Distracting myself from the thought, I checked my phone. No notifications.

Growling impatiently, I gave up on texting and dialed the stupid druid. Kai twisted to watch as I held the phone to my ear. It rang twice, then a computerized female voice informed me that the number I'd dialed was unavailable.

That dickhead had *turned off his phone*? I would strangle him.

Furious, I swung off the bike. "Screw it. We're going in."

"Going *in*?" Kai slid off too and set the kickstand. "You said you weren't here for the gallery event."

Thanks to a lethal oath spell, I couldn't explain. Hissing curses under my breath, I stalked to the entrance, Kai following me. Light blazed through the glass doors and I threw them open. A spacious but empty lobby greeted me, the ticket counter dark and quiet. A second set of doors straight ahead offered a glimpse of a large space scattered with people in dressy clothes.

I'd gotten two steps through the second doorway when a pair of burly men in black suits stepped into my path.

"Excuse me, ma'am. May I see your invitation?"

I bristled. "Ma'am? Do I look like a *ma'am* to you?"

His expression didn't change. "Your invitation, please."

Shit. Zak hadn't mentioned that this was an invitation-only event. "Uh … I just need to have a word with someone who's here."

"I'm afraid that won't be possible unless you have an—"

A delighted female shriek echoed off the walls. A petite young woman with long black hair came running—as much as she could run in five-inch heels.

"*OhmygodisthatKaisukaaaaaay?*" she squealed, all as one word.

Rushing up to us, she threw her tiny arms around Kai's waist, a diamond-encrusted purse bouncing on her wrist.

"Oh my *god*," she exclaimed again, beaming up at him. "Kaisuke, I had *no idea* you were coming. It's been so long! Everyone will be *so* delighted to see you."

Hugging his arm to her chest, she forced him deeper into the room.

A bouncer stepped toward them. "Invita—"

"Get lost," she barked, her cutesy squeal replaced with imperious command. "Don't you know who this is? He doesn't need an invitation."

The man scowled and fell back into position. Dragging my jaw along the polished floor, I trailed two steps behind as the woman hauled a silent, expressionless Kai across the grand hall. A few well-dressed loiterers glanced toward us curiously.

"Oh, Kaisuke," the young woman gushed. "I thought you'd *never* be back. It's been, what? Five years?"

"Seven," he corrected stiffly.

"So long!" she cooed, giving him a once-over. "My, you've really filled out. You're so tall! You were only, hmm, seventeen when we last saw each other?" She squeezed his bicep through his leather jacket. "Mm, I approve. You could have dressed up, though. This is a formal auction."

As she planted her hands on her hips in a playful reprimand, I scanned her sheath dress, the black fabric glittering with every movement. The men moving through the hall or standing at the cocktail bar wore suits and ties, and the women were done up in dark, sexy dresses.

Thank god I'd put some effort into my appearance before leaving the house. I wore the same outfit I'd donned last night—a snug turtleneck that covered the fae markings, gunmetal-gray skinny jeans, and my trusty bomber jacket—and I'd tamed my bed-head curls into a braid. Still, Kai and I were conspicuously underdressed. At least we matched.

The woman finally noticed me, her rosebud lips quirking. "Who is this?"

Kai pulled me to his side—clamping me tight against him. Every muscle in his body was hard with tension. "She's with me."

The woman's eyes squinched irately, then her smile flashed. "He forgot to tell you it was formal dress, didn't he?"

"No, I knew," I said, not letting Kai take the blame. "I just didn't care."

She blinked, half smiling as she glanced at Kai for a clue as to whether I was joking. When he remained stone-faced, she cleared her throat. "Well, the auction begins in a few minutes, so everyone is up in the second-level gallery. Shall we join them?"

Kai looked at me, silently asking what to do. Frantic thoughts buzzed through my head, pulling me in different directions. Whatever this was, neither Kai nor I was prepared for it, but Zak had to be nearby. If "everyone" was on the second level, that's where I'd find the druid.

"Shall we head up?" I asked Kai, giving him a chance to back out if that's what he needed to do.

A muscle jumped in his cheek, but he nodded.

"Lovely!" the woman exclaimed. She offered her hand to me. "I'm Hisaya—Yamada Hisaya. It's a pleasure."

Yamada? Oh shit.

"You're related," I said weakly as I shook her teeny hand, keeping my palm tilted down so she wouldn't spot the glowing fae rune.

"Oh, of course!" she giggled. "Distantly, though. I'm married to his third cousin. It's a huge family, as you know."

"Yeah …" I muttered, afraid to look at Kai. What had I dragged him into?

She slid her fingers into the crook of Kai's elbow like he'd offered his arm and pulled us deeper into the building. He kept his other arm locked around my waist, his white-knuckled grip on my jacket hidden by my sleeve.

"It's so *wonderful* that you've come back into the fold, Kaisuke! And don't worry, no one will hold it against you. We're just too delighted!" Hisaya chattered on without drawing breath, tossing out name after name—who was here, who hadn't made it, who would be most pleased to see him. All people Kai must know, judging by the casual ease with which Hisaya mentioned each person.

"But Kaisuke," she said as we walked into a spacious rotunda with twin staircases rising to the second floor, "you've hardly said a word! How is darling Makiko?"

He said nothing.

"Oh," she pouted. "*Surely* she's forgiven you?"

Silence. Kai was doing a great impression of Zak's impregnable caginess.

Hisaya stopped, forcing me and Kai to halt, and wagged a chiding finger under his nose. "You can't pretend she doesn't exist, Kaisuke. She's your fiancée!"

If we hadn't already stopped, I would've fallen on my face. His arm tightened painfully around me, his fingers digging into my side. Hisaya frowned at our closeness.

"Makiko and I haven't spoken in years," he said flatly.

Hisaya barely hesitated. "Well, you're back now, so you two can make up right away. I can't wait for the wedding. It'll be grand!"

"So grand!" I chirped. "Hisaya, honeycake, could you give us a moment? We'll be right up."

She blinked at "honeycake" and glanced questioningly at Kai. "Yes, of course. The auction starts shortly, so don't dawdle. I'll let everyone know you've arrived."

Smiling over her shoulder, she sashayed up the steps. I drew Kai under the curving staircase and out of the way of the final guests heading to the next level.

"Kai," I whispered, prying his fingers off my side before he left bruises. "What on earth is going on?"

"That's my line," he retorted in a low growl. "Why are we at a black-magic auction?"

"I had no idea it was an auction until she said so. How do you know it's black magic?" I wasn't surprised—why else would Zak get invited?—but what had made Kai jump to that conclusion?

"Because my family wouldn't be present otherwise."

A chill washed over me. "Oh."

"Why are we here, Tori?"

"I need to get something from someone."

"And that *someone* is upstairs at the auction?"

I nodded.

His jaw flexed, then he clamped his arm around me again. "Let's get it done."

"Are you sure?" I whispered as we strode for the stairs. "We can wait outside or try something el—"

"Hisaya is already spreading the word. It's too late for me to leave."

On the second level, we followed the other stragglers into a dimly lit gallery room, filled with at least a hundred people. Mythics, actually. Rogues, most likely. The white walls featured huge canvases of abstract compositions, soft spotlights illuminating the bright colors and thick strokes of the artist's brush.

A dais had been set up at the far end, where an elderly man at a podium spoke into a mic. He was gesturing at the thick leather tome displayed on a table beside him. Bouncers and assistants hovered around the dais.

Hisaya stood with a group of Japanese men and women, the only smiling face. She gestured for me and Kai to join them.

A sharp breath hissed through his clenched teeth, but he didn't hesitate. The moment he was close enough, Hisaya burst into rapid Japanese. Kai bent in a shallow bow for the oldest man, who nodded and said something. Kai answered in Japanese.

Why was I surprised he could speak the language? I'd realized months ago that he was part Japanese—not that anyone could guess by looking at him. His strikingly handsome features were unique, concealing his heritage, and he stood a head taller than anyone else in the group.

The Yamadas were ignoring me, so I returned the favor. I scanned the gathered mythics for Zak, then checked my phone, half listening to the family reunion. Identifying the tone of the conversation was difficult, but it didn't sound pleasant. I shot a pointed look at Hisaya, commanding her to referee this shit. She'd started it.

Her whole face pulled into a condescending sneer that communicated her exact feelings about my presence. I drew myself up, and her ugly expression shifted to alarm as she realized I intended to intervene.

"Ahaha!" she burst out before I could speak. "Kikue-san, did you hear that? The grimoire just sold for two million."

My expression froze and I involuntarily glanced at the book on display. I hadn't been listening to the auctioneer's rapid-fire babble. Two *million*? Wow, no wonder we were underdressed.

"We're interested in several items," Hisaya told Kai, terrified I might open my uncouth mouth and offend everyone present. "Do you have your eye on anything? There's a magnificent caduceus coming up later this evening."

The woman called Kikue-san said something in Japanese.

"Ah, well," Hisaya answered in English, "we can only hope he won't interfere."

"Who?" Kai asked with obvious reluctance.

"Ugh." Hisaya tossed her hair over her shoulder. "You know. The *Ghost*."

Kai stiffened.

"Half the room is afraid to bid against him," she continued with a prim sniff, "but a low-life criminal like that could never intimidate *us*."

She cast a disdainful look across the room. I followed her gaze—and there he was.

I'd missed him because he wasn't in the main group. Instead, he leaned against the wall in his own personal cloud of shadow, as underdressed as me in dark pants and his long villain-coat, the hood drawn up.

In a room of rogues and black-magic buyers, the Ghost was too scary to approach.

I almost crowed in victory at finding him. Hiding the motion from the Yamadas, I tentatively waved my hand, hoping to catch his eye.

"Three hundred thousand, from the young lady with red hair!" the auctioneer called into his mic.

I started so violently I banged into Kai. Heads swiveled our way as buyers checked out their competition, and the blood drained out of my head. No, no, no! I wasn't *bidding*. I was waving at an oblivious druid!

"Four hundred thousand. Can I get four hundred—ah, four hundred thousand to the gentleman in the front."

I sagged in relief. That had been close.

"Tori," Kai snarled under his breath.

Dragging my head up, I saw my accidental bid had achieved one thing—it had gotten Zak's attention. He'd straightened off the wall, his shadow-filled hood turned my way.

I waggled my phone and pointed at it. His hand shot to his pocket and he pulled out his cell, the screen lighting up as he turned it on.

"*Tori.*" Kai sounded like a rabid dog. He leaned down, his mouth by my ear as he hissed furiously, "*Him? That's* who you're here to meet? You have his *phone number?*"

My cell vibrated in my hand and I held it under my nose. Kai shifted to read over my shoulder.

Zak's message glowed angrily: *What THE HELL are you doing here???*

Kai half snorted, half choked. "You put him in your contacts under *Dickhead?*"

"That's what he is," I muttered. My thumbs flew across the keyboard. *Read the messages I sent you, dumbass!*

To punctuate my instructions, I glared at Zak until he looked down at his phone again. His thumb moved as he scrolled through the half a million texts I'd sent over the course of the evening. His hood jerked angrily, then he turned on his heel and strode toward the exit. People moved swiftly out of his path, pretending they weren't cowards.

As he disappeared, I turned to Kai. "You can just wait here, okay?"

Instead of replying, he brushed past me, following Zak's invisible trail. Ah, crap. I raced after him and took the lead.

Zak hadn't gone far. He waited in a shadowed side hall—of course, everywhere he went was shadowy, thanks to his "lady of the night" eagle familiar—arms folded and invisible glower scorching me. I stormed toward him, debating all possible greetings.

In the end, I kept it simple. I balled my hand up and swung at his face.

He caught my fist in a gloved palm.

"You turned off your phone, you moron! Why'd you do that?"

"Because I didn't need you pestering me every ten minutes," he snapped. "I told you to wait until morning."

"I can't wait that long! You're the one who told me—" I cut myself off, glancing nervously at Kai. As per my oath, I wasn't allowed to reveal anything about the Ghost, including things he'd said to me.

His hood shifting, Zak also looked at Kai, presumably recognizing him from our shared battle with a nasty old sorceress a month ago. Kai's expression had morphed back into stone, though wariness radiated from his terse stance.

"I told you the fae bond will kill you," the druid finished for me.

"What?" Kai said sharply. "How do you—"

Zak turned to me. "You're not on death's doorstep yet. You could have waited until morning."

"Well, I'm here now, so give it to me." I extended my hand expectantly.

"I don't have it *on* me, idiot."

"What?" I resisted the urge to shove his hood off and throttle him. "But you said—"

"I said I had it *with me*. I'm not carrying it around everywhere."

"Go get it, then!"

His hand disappeared into the shadows of his hood as he rubbed his face. "You are more aggravating than any mythic I know."

A sharp cough escaped Kai—what might have been a furiously suppressed bark of laughter. I shot him a glare.

Zak dropped his hand. "I can't leave yet. There's one more mythic I want to drill about fae enslavement magic, and I can't get to him outside this event. Approaching him requires finesse."

"Who?" Kai asked.

Zak paused as though weighing Kai's usefulness. "Carmelo Mancini. He was an officer in Red Rum before going solo. A sorcerer, but rumor has it he dabbles in hybrid magic."

"I've heard of him." Kai's jaw flexed. "You're trying to get this information for Tori's sake?"

"Obviously."

"Why are you helping her?"

Zak snorted. "I don't do charity, mage. I'm paying back a debt."

I blinked. "You are? What debt?"

"You're denser than a brick wall, Tori."

I smacked his shoulder. "You're the biggest dickhead on the planet."

Brow furrowing with disbelief, Kai looked between us. He gave his head a slight shake, then asked Zak, "Do you have an in with Mancini?"

"No. That's why I'm taking my time approaching him."

Kai glanced toward the auction hall where his relatives waited. Something close to terror flitted across his face, then he pushed his shoulders back. "I do. I can approach him, but I don't know what to ask."

Zak's hood twitched and I imagined him tilting his head in surprised consideration. "Can you convince him to step outside with you?"

"Probably."

"Then do that. Once he's outside, *I* can ask the questions—and ensure we get answers."

16

"STOP FIDGETING."

I shoved my hands in my jacket pockets and glared at Zak's hidden face. "Stop being so *bossy*."

We'd climbed up the wide steps to the second-level terrace to get a better view of the gallery entrance, Kai's bike parked a dozen yards away. Wide, paved sidewalks surrounded the building, and a big sunken square in the center was filled with structures I couldn't identify in the dark. Everything was abandoned—too late on a Monday night for random passersby, and the auction attendees were mingling inside.

After consolidating our dastardly plans, Kai and I had returned to the Yamada group while Zak skulked around the auction room, frightening people. Once the auction concluded, he left, and I slipped out a few minutes later, leaving Kai with his relatives. How he intended to lure this Mancini person outside was beyond me, but if he thought he could do it …

"I hope he's okay," I muttered.

Zak snorted dismissively. "Why are you worried?"

"Why wouldn't I be worried?"

"He's a Yamada." The druid leaned against the wall. "And here I thought I was the only black smear on your record."

I bit the inside of my cheek, then sighed. "Zak, you have to explain this one to me. I have no clue who the Yamadas are."

He pushed his hood back enough for me to glimpse his bright green eyes. "The Yamada family runs the largest international crime syndicate in the mythic community."

I tried to say something but my voice had disappeared.

"They're a legitimate guild and keep their illicit activities well hidden, but the MPD is all over them like bees on a hive. They can only crack down so hard, though, or else they risk driving the entire operation underground." He crossed his arms. "They're a thorn in my side. Impossible to intimidate and extremely well connected."

Seven years, Kai had said. He must have broken ties with his family before joining the Crow and Hammer. According to Aaron, Kai hadn't cared which guild he joined—probably because his only concern had been escaping his family's business. Now, thanks to me, he was involved again.

"I'm a terrible friend," I muttered.

"You don't say."

"You're a shitty friend too."

"Last time you said I was a good friend."

"That was before you ignored me all day while I was dying."

"Fickle," he remarked dryly, tugging his hood low again.

I tiredly chewed my fingernails. I should've been vibrating with tension, but I'd used up all my energy over the last few hours. Yawns pulled at my jaw every couple of minutes. Too weary to stay on my feet, I sank down on the top step, the cold of the concrete seeping through my jeans.

After a moment, Zak crouched so he wasn't towering over me. "What happened with Red Rum? You said the fae lord had to defend you."

I mumbled my way through an explanation.

He made a thoughtful sound. "Gifted Spiritalis mythics can sense the fae lord's presence. I didn't see any Red Rum mythics in there, at least. It would be a hassle if they spotted you."

"Mm," I agreed wearily.

"What's the point in targeting you, though? Killing you would free the fae lord, but it doesn't sound like they were using lethal force."

"I don't get it either," I muttered, scarcely keeping my eyes open.

We sat quietly for another minute, and my sluggish thoughts wandered from Kai's family situation to my uncertain future.

"Hey Zak," I mumbled. "What makes a sorcerer a sorcerer?"

"Huh?"

"Well, anyone can use artifacts, right?"

He braced his arms on his knees. "Yes, but only Arcana mythics can *create* artifacts."

"But ... why?"

"Why can Arcaners imbue power into their spells and no one else can?"

"Yeah."

He gazed at the dark sky. "The world is full of power—energies of the earth, of nature, the stars and cosmos, the sun and moon, and who knows what else. It's an electric ocean that flows through everything, immense and maybe even sentient. Each magical race and class uses that power differently."

"But humans can't use it," I whispered.

"Humans can't even detect it. Sorcerers can, and they channel that power into their spells when they build them. Alchemists do the same with their transmutations."

Months ago, Ramsey had told me my Queen of Spades artifact threw off major arcane vibes—magic I couldn't sense because I had no Arcana ability. Why was I even asking Zak about it? I already knew I wasn't a sorcerer.

Gloom settled over me. "What about psychics? They don't use the same kind of magic, do they?"

"It all comes from the same reservoir of natural energies, they just use it in a different way—most without even realizing where their power comes from."

"How does a psychic learn they're psychic?"

"Abilities typically manifest around puberty."

I was well past the joys of puberty. My head drooped forward, too heavy to hold up. I'd known all along I had no magic, but a question still lingered in the back of my mind: If I wasn't a mythic, how had I ended up this deep in their world? Was it all dumb luck? Was this feeling that I belonged among mythics all in my head?

Zak's attention weighed on me, and I didn't want him to read any more into my questions than he already had. Time to change the topic. "What will you do without your farm?"

"I don't know yet."

He went silent, and I thought that was all he planned to say. When he spoke again, his rumbly rasp surprised me.

"Everything I've built relies on my anonymity, but that's rapidly falling apart. Varvara is spreading rumors about me.

Enemies are sniffing around my property for the first time. Your guild tricked me into bringing you to my home, and I can't risk taking in anyone else."

Guilt deadened my heartbeat. "I'm sorry."

"Don't be. If I hadn't picked you up, I might have fallen into another guild's trap." His head turned, the light gleaming faintly against one cheek. "I'm not as clever as I like to think, and my arrogance has caught up with me."

A faint inkling of what he'd meant about owing me a debt sparked, but I was too exhausted to make sense of the feeling. "Will you be okay, Zak?"

"I don't know. I'm a bit lost right now."

I fumbled down his sleeve until I found his gloved hand. Entwining our fingers, I squeezed in wordless comfort.

His hood shifted as he looked down at our hands. "Why am I telling you any of this?"

Sympathy welled in my chest, and I whispered, "Because you don't have anyone else to tell."

He went very still, then sighed. "Yeah."

Light flared as the gallery doors swung open. A short, sturdy man around fifty strode out, his suit jacket unbuttoned and tie loosened. Kai walked beside him, murmuring something. Two beefy bodyguards followed them across the stone square.

"Is that him?" I asked almost soundlessly.

Zak gave a short nod.

A small light sparked as Mancini lit a cigarette. He held the lighter out and Kai leaned forward, igniting the cig pinched between his lips. With the ease of a chain smoker, he blew a gray cloud into the cool air. The bodyguard guys waited a few long paces away.

"I have to say, Kaisuke," Mancini said, mispronouncing Kai's full name as *kigh-soo-kee* instead of the *kigh-s'kay* his relatives had used. The man's gravelly voice, amplified in the quiet, echoed off the building walls. "I always thought it a shame you left the family. You had so much potential, even as a teenager."

"They weren't interested in my potential," Kai replied smoothly, inhaling through his cigarette. "I was always an outcast within the family. I think you can understand that feeling, Carmelo."

An agreeable grunt. "What brought you back?"

"I'm not *back*, not the way you're thinking. I'm here to … explore my options."

Mancini straightened. "How so?"

"I have no interest in rejoining either the family or the guild as a second-class member. I'm considering a different venture: an independent one. Another concept you're familiar with."

Mancini puffed on his cigarette, the glow illuminating his sharp grin. "I think I see where you're going with this, Kaisuke."

"You've gone independent and made yourself into a force to be reckoned with. I know several others who work well alone, but I also know it's a vulnerable position without the right connections."

"You can be independent of a guild and still have powerful allies," Mancini agreed conspiratorially.

"So, obviously, you're the first person I thought to approach."

A gruff, blustering sound. "Flattered, most flattered. I'd be interested in exploring how we can profit from each other's endeavors."

Zak made a quiet, impressed sound. "Damn. Your friend is good."

"I'm delighted to hear it," Kai replied easily. "I'm working on something, and I think you have expertise in the area—if you're willing to share it."

"That depends on what you want to know and what you're offering in return."

"My offer first, then. I'll introduce you to another independent mythic—one only an exclusive few can claim to know, let alone call an ally."

Zak's muted laugh hissed with dark amusement.

"Forging a relationship with him won't be easy," Kai added, "but I'll make the introduction."

"That's my cue," Zak whispered. "Wait here, Tori."

As he rose to his full height, Lallakai's shadowy wings unfurled from his back, then swept around him like an embrace—and his whole body faded out of sight. I clapped a hand over my mouth to stifle my gasp. He'd disappeared like a fae!

"Who?" Mancini asked sharply. "Who will you introduce?"

"You should know him by reputation alone," Kai answered dryly.

Mancini pulled his cigarette out of his mouth, face contorted with annoyance—then the air beside Kai shimmered. Zak materialized in a swirl of fading shadows, his coat fluttering, hood pulled low over his face. Dripping menace, he loomed beside Kai, taller by several inches.

I rolled my eyes. Him and his dramatic entrances.

Mancini's cigarette fell out of his limp fingers. He quickly waved at his bodyguards to stand down. "The Ghost! I—I had no idea …"

"Kaisuke and I are pursuing a joint venture," Zak rumbled, pronouncing Kai's full name perfectly. "Based on your contribution, should you make one, we might have a future as business partners."

Kai flicked ash off his cigarette, looking as comfortable as could be next to the notorious druid.

Mancini looked between them. "And what do you require from me?"

"Knowledge, assuming you have it," Zak crooned evilly. "I'm not convinced you do."

The older man stiffened. "Ask, Ghost."

"Fae enslavement. Are you familiar with the rituals?"

"There are many."

"One that could bind a high-ranking wyldfae."

"I know a few. They require rare resources."

"Such as fae relics?"

A jerky nod. "You seem well-informed already, Ghost."

Kai canted his head in a subtle invitation. Zak leaned down a few inches and Kai whispered something to him.

Zak straightened. "We don't require any assistance with the Arcana. I want to know about the relics and the fae who provides them."

"The fae … I'm not sure what you mean."

"Don't play games with me, Carmelo. How do you contact the fae who makes the relics?"

"How do you know—" Mancini bit off the question. "That's expensive information, Ghost."

"I'm an expensive partner."

"Why would I want you as a partner?"

Shadows coiled around Zak's legs. "Would you prefer me as an enemy?"

I heard Mancini's wet swallow from where I crouched. He shot Kai a furious look, but the electramage merely blew a puff of smoke.

Tugging his suit jacket straight, Mancini forced a smile. "The fae answers to the name Bhardudlin. Use any of the blood summoning arrays."

"And?" Zak prompted.

"And what?"

"How does the fae deal?"

Mancini grunted. "The usual way. Bring expendable underlings."

"That is all I require." A pause where I could imagine Zak smiling malevolently. "It would be unfortunate if your information were to produce poor results."

"And if the results are good?" Mancini demanded.

"We'll be in touch."

"Well …" Mancini shrugged stiffly. "It was a pleasure, Kaisuke. Contact me if you wish to continue our earlier discussion."

"Of course. Have a lovely night, Carmelo."

Gesturing at his men to follow, Mancini strode back into the art gallery. The moment the doors closed, Kai dropped his half-finished cigarette on the concrete and stepped on it. Renewed by a spark of energy, I ran down the stairs.

"You did it!" I stumbled to Kai's side and leaned against him, then recoiled. "Blah. You stink."

"He's a notorious smoker. It was the easiest way to get him outside." He grimaced at the ground-up cigarette.

"It worked perfectly. You were amazing." I looked between him and Zak. "You two work well together."

Kai's glare was instant, and it was *mean*. I could feel Zak's equally nasty glower singeing my face.

I flapped a hand in placation. "Sorry, sorry. Did you get the info you need? I thought you would ask way more questions."

"I'd planned to," Zak replied. "But Yamada says—"

"Don't call me that."

"*Kai*," he amended irritably, "says he's already acquired the ritual. The only thing left is the fae relic. Tori, send me a copy of the ritual from the grimoire, and I'll—"

Pop-pop-pop!

Yellow paintballs exploded against Zak's and Kai's backs. Kai shielded his head with his arms and I ducked as another volley flew past, half the shots bursting against Zak's leather coat.

Even as panicked urgency rushed through me, I had an *aha!* moment: leather clothes were resistant to potions. *That's* why Zak dressed like a supervillain.

The druid straightened, his hidden face angling toward the street.

"Looks like I was wrong," he growled. "Red Rum is here after all."

17

RED RUM WAS BACK—but this time, I had allies of a different caliber.

Deep animal snarls erupted from behind the parked cars on the nearest street, followed by yelps of surprise—and pain. Sounded like Zak had brought his vargs along. Lights blazed as our attackers unleashed defensive magic.

Zak flexed his arms and yellow magic spiraled around his wrists. "Well, Kai? Care to cover me, or should I watch my own back?"

Short throwing knives appeared in Kai's hands from under his jacket. "I'll cover you."

With no more discussion than that, they strode toward the parked cars where the rogues were hiding—and now pinned between snarling vargs and two highly displeased mythics.

I stayed right where I was, breathing hard. Useless little human. Slipping my Queen of Spades out of my pocket, I glanced at the painted royal's mysterious smile and hoped Zak didn't kill anyone. MagiPol discouraged dead bodies in the streets.

The thought had scarcely crossed my mind when metal screeched. A parked car flipped onto its side, then rolled onto its roof, forcing Kai and Zak to dive out of the way.

A man the size of a Viking on steroids stood in the new gap, flexing his huge arms. What looked like two bowling balls floated on either side of him.

Gulping, I scrapped my opposition to corpses. Whatever Kai and Zak needed to do to survive a Hulk-mode telekinetic was fine by me.

Silver flashed—a scaled underbelly filling my vision. The not-an-orb-anymore fae hovered in the air, facing me with its undersized wings spread. I blinked. Where had the fae come from? I'd left the orb in my purse, and I'd left my purse in Aaron's living room before Kai and I had departed on our errand.

The fae's fuchsia eyes fixed on something behind me.

I whirled toward the steps that descended into the sunken square. Two figures were crouched in the shadows, their guns aimed at my chest.

The fae's small paws touched my shoulders, cool and tingling, then its long tail spun around me like the coils of a snake. It squeezed and chilly magic surged through me. My vision blurred into wild ripples.

Pop-pop-pop!

The guns fired, but I only felt the fae's power sizzling inside my body. The men emptied their weapons—but nothing touched me.

The fae's tail loosened, then the creature faded out of sight. My vision steadied.

The men holstered their empty guns, then marched up the steps. I looked around sharply. The fae creature was gone, and Zak and Kai were busy fighting Telekinetic Hulk, plus an unknown number of goons. Crap. I was on my own.

I spun on my heel, ran toward the gallery entrance, and ducked behind a wide concrete column. Clutching the Queen of Spades, I waited. Footsteps approached, and I heard the two rogues split up to flank me. Scarcely breathing, I listened.

A footstep scuffed close on my left.

I jumped out, card extended. "*Ori—*"

The smirking rogue ducked, no spell in hand or magic underway. Shit, wrong guy! I whirled in the other direction—

"*Ori tacitus esto!*"

A white flash blinded me and I stumbled backward, swearing furiously—or trying to.

My lips moved, but no sound came out of my mouth. Panicking, I tried to scream—not a peep. That spell had muted my voice!

The stocky sorcerer, bulky artifacts clipped to his belt, walked around the pillar. I retreated unsteadily, clutching my useless card. I couldn't even call for help. Leering, the two rogues followed me.

"Surrender and you won't get hurt," one suggested.

Yeah, right. Since I couldn't say that, I flipped him the bird.

"Can you restrain her?" the sorcerer asked the other guy.

"Probably, but she looks like she might bite. Just use a spell."

Damn right I would bite them. I'd punch 'em too. Maybe I should start with that.

The sorcerer snapped a narrow metal talisman off his belt. "*Ori decidas in—*"

A smart person would run. Or dodge. Or duck.

I lunged at him and grabbed his wrist. His eyes widened, but he couldn't stop the last of his incantation as I wrenched the artifact toward the second rogue.

"*—astris.*"

The air rippled, and the sorcerer's unlucky accomplice pitched over backward with sparkles covering his body like he'd rolled in a glitter bath. Whoa. Neat.

"You—" the sorcerer snarled.

I punched him in the nose. His head snapped back, a pained grunt escaping him. Yeah, take that! Also, *ow*. My poor knuckles.

He shoved me backward and yanked out another artifact. "*Impello!*"

I jerked away and the invisible spell caught my shoulder, sending me spinning. A bang and a loud metallic crunch warned that the rest of the magical force had struck something besides my breakable flesh. I landed on my ass, jarring my teeth and almost biting my tongue off.

"*Ori—*" the sorcerer began.

I leaned back and pistoned my foot into his groin. Wheezing, he staggered out of my reach and thrust his new artifact toward me again.

"*Ori—*" he gasped.

A gloved hand clamped over his mouth. Appearing out of nowhere, Zak pulled the sorcerer forward, then smashed him into the nearest column. The rogue crumpled to the ground, unused talisman clattering against the concrete.

"Are you hurt?" Zak asked me.

I tried to say no but couldn't make a sound. Miming speech, I gestured helplessly at my mouth.

"Silencing spell?" he guessed. "It'll wear off in a couple minutes."

Could he sound any less concerned? I was voiceless here! It was awful!

On the street, the carnage was impressive—two flipped cars, several smoking craters, and three shattered streetlamps. The villains were nowhere in sight, so I assumed the druid and electramage had successfully driven them off. As always, Zak looked unscathed, minus the big yellow splatters on his back.

Kai joined us, his potion-smeared jacket hanging from one hand and dripping yellow goo on the ground. "Are you okay, Tori?"

I nodded. Silently.

"We should leave before—oh."

I blinked at his frozen expression, then followed his gaze. He was staring at his sleek black motorcycle, lying on its side. Ah. That metallic crunch sound. His bike.

With the pain of a bereft father in his eyes, Kai heaved his motorcycle up, while Zak and I waited at a respectful distance. A gory puddle gleamed beneath the tires, and I could smell the gasoline. Our first casualty.

Kai sighed sorrowfully. "The edge of the planter punctured the gas tank."

So … that meant we wouldn't be riding it home. I cautiously cleared my throat—and actual noise rasped from my vocal cords. I could speak again!

Suppressing the urge to whoop, I murmured gravely, "I'm sorry, Kai. You can get it fixed, right?"

Zak's hood turned toward me. "Your voice is back."

"Don't sound so disappointed." I poked his arm. "Did you drive? Can we catch a ride with you?"

His sigh was as pained as Kai's. "Fine."

"Thanks. You're the best."

"I thought I was a shitty friend? Make up your mind." He turned toward the street. "Bring the bike. You don't want to leave it here."

The druid, the human, the mage, and the motorcycle made their ragtag way onto the sidewalk, the latter leaving a gruesome trail of bodily fluid in its wake. We walked in an odd silence, passing endless lines of shiny BMWs and Mercedes.

Zak led us through a stinky alley and onto a quiet one-way street with metered parking. Stuffing a hand in his coat pocket, he pulled out a set of keys. The fob beeped, and a pair of taillights flashed in answer.

Stopping dead, I looked at the vehicle, then at the druid, then back at the vehicle. "This is yours? *This?*"

He kept walking. "Why are you so offended?"

I pointed like he couldn't see it. The lifted pickup truck towered over the nearby cars, its big, deep-tread tires hungry to flatten inferior vehicles. Mud around the wheel wells splattered the dark blue paint.

"But that's a *truck*." I rushed to catch up with him, Kai trailing behind with his bike. "I figured you'd drive a Prius or something. You know, a *non*-gas-guzzling monstrosity."

"It's diesel, not gas." He lowered the tailgate. "Tori, think about where I live."

I scrunched my face, picturing the mountain valley. "Okay."

"Now imagine trying to drive a car there. In the winter."

My face contorted further, then relaxed in defeat. "Fine. The truck makes sense."

Zak climbed onto the tailgate, and between him and Kai, they wrestled the motorcycle up onto the lined bed. Zak laid it on its side, then opened the metal box behind the cab and pulled out ratcheting straps to tie it down.

"This feels disturbingly normal," I commented to no one as he worked, "and also very not normal."

Kai shook his head and tossed his potion-stained jacket into the truck bed beside his bike.

Zak jumped down and shut the tailgate, then held out a rag to me. "Can you wipe this shit off my back?"

I took the cloth, stepped behind him, and started mopping up the potion drying on the black leather.

"You could just take your coat off," I suggested, knowing he never would. "Or is it hiding all your scary potions?"

With my free hand, I patted a clean patch of leather to see if I could feel his belt of vials.

"I know you like my ass, Tori, but could you restrain yourself?"

I choked, my face flushing, and refused to look in Kai's direction. "This yellow stuff is just smearing around and I don't want to get it on my hands."

"Fine. Toss the cloth in the box."

As I pitched the rag over the tailgate, I heard a zipper and whirled back around. Zak had undone his coat, and I gasped as he pushed his hood off and shrugged out of the leather. The nearby streetlamp cast lovely shadows across his unfairly gorgeous face.

His unnaturally bright green eyes turned to Kai's slack-jawed stare, silently daring the mage to comment, and tension thickened the air until I could barely breathe. Kai, wisely, said nothing.

Zak threw his coat into the box, then stripped his gloves off. I scanned his newly revealed outfit. To my surprise, he was wearing a different belt. The wide leather circled his hips, sporting built-in slots that held six test-tube vials just above his butt. I pursed my lips. He really did have a nice ass.

Four rough-cut crystals hung on ties around his neck, resting on a dark t-shirt. His muscular arms displayed feather tattoos that ran down from his shoulders, and circles marked his inner forearms, each one filled with a colorful rune—gifts of power from the fae he knew. A month ago, one circle had been empty, but now ...

I pointed. "You got a new one."

"Get in the truck, Tori." He walked to the driver's side, climbed in, and slammed the door.

Grimacing, I peeked at Kai. His stunned expression made me feel better about my initial meltdown at the sight of Zak's face. Though, to be fair, Kai was probably feeling faint for different reasons.

"His eyes are freaky, right?" I mock-whispered.

"Tori ..." Laser-like focus overtook Kai's shock. He opened his mouth, then seemed to rethink whatever he'd been about to say. "Let's go."

He opened the passenger door and I heaved myself up—no step rail on this truck. The cab was spacious but it had no back seat, just one long bench. I crammed into the middle spot as Kai swung into the passenger seat and shut the door.

Zak inserted the key in the ignition. "Buckle up."

I rolled my eyes. "Don't want a traffic ticket?"

"Don't want your thick head going through my windshield. Where to?"

As I gave directions to Aaron's house, I grappled with my seatbelt. The bench would've been comfortable for two large men, but it was a tight fit for three people. The engine started with a rumble, and I pressed close to Kai to keep clear of Zak's elbow as he steered the monster truck onto the road.

More awkward silence. I bit my lip, fighting the urge to speak. I couldn't ask. Not yet. Not here. Must wait. Must … be … patient.

"You have a *fiancée*?" I burst out.

"Tori," Kai growled warningly.

"I'm sorry. I just couldn't keep it in." I clasped my hands together. "*Please* explain before I die of curiosity."

"Die of unsated snoopiness," Zak muttered as the truck rolled to a stop at a red light.

"Butt out," I snapped, then turned back to Kai. "How can you date so many women and be *engaged*? How can you be engaged if you haven't spoken to her in years?"

Kai folded his arms and held his silence. I groaned.

"Arranged marriage," Zak said matter-of-factly. "Common practice in the family."

"How do you know that?"

He smirked. "A few years ago, I was offered the hand of one Fumi Yamada if I joined their guild and stopped messing up their business dealings. She was lovely, but I had to decline."

"Huh." I peered at Kai. "Is that what it is for you?"

He didn't so much as twitch for a full minute, then gave a short nod. "Arranged at birth. I left the family seven years ago, but the engagement still stands."

"But … you wouldn't actually marry …?"

"No. Never." His jaw flexed and I swore I heard his teeth grind. "But until *she* marries someone else, I'm technically spoken for."

Spoken for. Kai, who dated an endless horde of beautiful women but never progressed to a relationship with any of them, considered himself unavailable. I didn't understand how an engagement arranged by a family he'd ditched years ago could affect his romantic decisions now, but his fiancée had to be the reason he never dated anyone seriously.

Though why he didn't just not date at all, like Ezra, confused me. Was it a distraction? A big middle finger to his family? Easy sex?

Who knew, but that wasn't a question I could ask in front of Zak. I did have *some* concept of boundaries.

I randomly clapped my hands. "This is just like a road trip! We should stop at a drive-through."

"Have you lost your mind?" Zak demanded.

"Possibly. Have you ever been so tired that you *surpassed* tired and went giddy instead?"

He pressed his sexy mouth into a flat line. "The potions are in my bag behind the seat. I'll get them out as soon as we stop."

"What have you been giving her?" Kai asked sharply.

"I dosed her with a magic buffer potion, targeted to block fae magic, and a vitality potion altered for a human's stamina. I might need to adjust the potency. The fae lord is burning through her strength."

"You *are* an alchemist," Kai muttered. "We weren't sure."

"He's the best alchemist on the west coast." Was I slurring? When they both looked at me, I figured I must be. I poked Zak in the arm. "Eyes on the road."

"I'll be frank, Kai," Zak said as he returned his attention to driving. "She won't survive this for long. I don't know how anyone could. I can only assume the part of the ritual that would've protected the link's recipient is missing. Otherwise, Red Rum's witch would've been a dead man too."

Kai absorbed that in silence. "Park here."

Zak pulled up beside Aaron's cottage-style house and executed a flawless parallel park between two sedans. I wasn't jealous. No way.

Kai leaned around me to study the druid. "Tori can send you copies of the ritual, but I think it would be more efficient for you to examine the grimoire." A long pause. "You should come inside."

"Whoa," I breathed. "You just invited the big bad Ghost into your *house*."

"So your mage friends can ambush me?" Zak said, ignoring my babbling. He propped an elbow on the steering wheel. "I'll pass."

"Let me handle them." Kai's dark gaze flicked to me. "We don't have time to waste. If I've learned anything from my family, it's that enemies with the same goal make the best allies."

"Only until the goal is met." Zak rubbed the back of his neck. "Seeing the grimoire in person would be more useful."

Kai nodded. I goggled in silence, unable to believe it.

"Don't make the mistake of thinking I can't protect myself against mages," Zak warned. "You can't see my familiars, but they can see you."

"I'll keep that in mind." Kai threw his door open and slid out.

Zak frowned at me, then opened his door and jumped out too.

I sat alone on the seat, blinking dumbly at the glowing windows of Aaron's house. Then I scrambled into motion, hauling my exhausted ass out of the truck.

My mages and my biggest secret were about to clash, and I *knew* it was gonna get ugly.

18

DID I SAY UGLY? I should've said *gorgeous*.

On one side of the living room, Zak and his godly face, supernaturally green irises, and short black hair contrasting with his fair skin. Beside him, Kai with his striking features, dark-as-sin eyes, and badass biker pants.

Across from them, Aaron with his copper hair mussed, a reddish shadow along his rugged jaw, and his intense blue eyes blazing. Ezra beside him, feet braced in a fighting stance, well-worn jeans hugging his strong legs, his brown curls teasing his mismatched eyes.

And me, leaning against the wall halfway between them, trying not to pant too obviously.

Was this a normal reaction to witnessing a confrontation so tense it was liable to break into violence at any moment? Probably not, but I was out of my mind with exhaustion and this much hot maleness in one room was too much to handle. My stupid brain refused to focus on anything else.

"So," Kai said cautiously, having just finished a brief explanation about how Zak was helping me, "we're going to play nice until Tori is safe."

Oh yeah, baby. I wanted them all to play nice. Mm-hmm.

Realizing the direction of my thoughts, I gave myself a mental slap and focused properly on the threat of impending violence. A crystal around Zak's neck was glowing. I didn't remember him uttering an incantation, but he wasn't taking any chances. His vargs were probably lurking nearby, invisible to all us non-Spiritalis people.

"I won't tolerate a dark-arts-dealing, piece-of-shit rogue in my house for even a minute," Aaron spat.

"You tolerate me," Kai retorted.

"You gave that up years ago. Totally different."

"Zak isn't completely terrible," I said dreamily, my attention diverted by Aaron's eyes and the way they sparked like hot blue flames when he was angry. "He only murders bad people."

All their gazes jerked toward me and Zak looked furious, but I didn't know why.

"He's a liar, Tori. Don't believe anything he tells you." Aaron's lip curled. "I'm surprised you're buying his act, Kai."

"Have you ever known me to be gullible?" Kai barked. "Use your brain, Aaron. We have a dark-arts *and* fae-magic expert standing here, offering to save Tori. He can read the grimoire."

Aaron bared his teeth. "He's more likely to steal it than—"

"This isn't about your ego—this is about Tori. Look at her! She's practically delirious. The fae bond is killing her."

They all looked at me again.

I smiled hesitantly. "Hi."

Aaron shifted his weight. "No. It's too risky. We found the grimoire and we'll find someone we trust to read it."

"You're an idiot," Zak snapped.

"You'll regret ever laying a hand on Tori," Aaron snarled. "Now that we've seen your face, and know your classes, and know your *name*, your date with the MPD is set."

A slow, fierce smile curved Zak's lips. "I think you'll protect my identity, Sinclair."

"Why the hell would I do that?"

I knew that look in Zak's eyes. The same merciless, arctic anger had filled him when I'd revealed I worked at a guild—moments before he hit me with back-to-back spells.

His chilling gaze lingered ominously on Ezra. "You keep my secrets ... and I'll keep yours."

A pulse of silence, then Kai swung away from Zak. Realigning. Changing sides. Now, instead of two against two, it was three against one.

"Oh?" Zak's arms lifted away from his sides, limbs loosening as he readied himself. "You'd rather kill me?"

The terse truce was over. Battle was about to commence.

"*Wait!*" I shrieked, and all four men jumped. I lurched away from the wall, waving my hands. "Don't fight, don't fight! It's fine! We'll just—we can all swear super-magic oaths, okay? Everyone's secrets will be safe."

"Swear *what?*" Kai demanded.

"Magic oaths," I babbled desperately, still waving as though the faint breeze could keep them apart. "Like the one he made me swear so I wouldn't reveal anything about him and his ..."

I trailed off, the rest of my sentence forgotten. My fatigue-logged brain caught up to what I'd said—and panic exploded through me.

"Oh god!" I gasped and clapped my hands to my mouth. "Oh, no no *no*, I didn't mean it! I didn't say that!" My wild eyes shot to Zak, who was staring at me with growing horror. "Zak, I'm sorry! I'm sorry!"

"Tori—" he rasped.

The oath forbade me from revealing it. I'd just blurted out everything in front of the guys—and now I would die.

My knees gave out. I crumpled to the floor, wailing in terror. "Zak, don't let me die! I'm sorry, I'm sorry!"

Kai was at my side, arms wrapping around me. "Tori, what's wrong?"

"I'm going to die," I cried, my panic so intense it hurt, my chest bursting with terror—or was that the spell? Was the oath killing me already? "*Zak!*"

"What did you do to her?" Aaron roared, jumping between me and the druid.

"I didn't—"

I wept hysterically, clutching my ribs. I couldn't breathe. My heart was racing out of my chest. "I'm dying, it's the oath, I broke it and it's killing me and I—"

"Tori!" Zak bellowed over Aaron's shouts and my wails. "The oath isn't real!"

My shrill cries cut off. Not breathing, I lifted my tear-blurred gaze to him. He stood a foot away from Aaron, the pyromage blocking his approach.

"The oath isn't real," he repeated into the silence. "I faked it so you'd keep your mouth shut."

"You ... fake?"

"Fake." He stepped back from Aaron and folded his arms. "No spell like that exists. But you believed it did, and I figured that would be enough to keep you quiet."

I sat motionless on the floor, Kai's arm around my shoulders. "Fake?"

Zak sighed. "That's why I made you swear not to reveal it. Any sorcerer would have told you it's impossible."

I couldn't move. My head swam as the panic attack faded … and something else built in its place.

"You bastard," Aaron spat. "You terrified her with a fake spell?"

"What choice did I have?" Zak snarled back. "It was that or kill her."

Aaron got in Zak's face. "What kind of sick, twisted—"

"It was a harmless trick that allowed me to let her go."

"*Harmless?*"

I stared blankly at nothing. A trick. He had tricked me.

Zak and Aaron snarled at each other, their voices spiraling around me. Weeks of fear, of guilt, of nightmares about saying the wrong thing and dying—it had all been a trick?

I pulled away from Kai and stumbled to my feet. Zak and Aaron were shouting, and as I lurched toward them, flames sparked up Aaron's arms. Zak's hands clenched and fae magic lit up the runes on his inner wrists.

As I reached them in a stumbling run, their heads snapped toward me, but this time, Zak wasn't ready.

This time, my fist slammed into his jaw.

As he staggered, I pulled my arm back and flung another punch. Zak jerked out of the way, my knuckles grazing his nose. I fell forward—

Aaron grabbed me and pinned my arms to my sides. Zak's eyes were huge with shock as he backed away, blood trickling from his split lip. Straining against Aaron's hold, I screamed obscenities at the druid. That lying, conniving, heartless son of a—

The crash of splintering wood cut through my screeching.

Kai appeared beside me, his hand clamping over my mouth. "Tori, be quiet. Please, be quiet."

The fear in his voice silenced me. I strained my eyes toward the other side of the room.

Ezra stood at the entryway to the dining room, his back to us. The unexpected sound had been him punching the doorframe. His fist was still buried in the wood, the frame splintered and crooked.

He didn't move except for his heaving shoulders, his harsh breathing loud in the sudden silence.

And then I realized the room was freezing cold. The lights had dimmed to pinpricks. Our breaths puffed white in the wintry air.

Motions slow, Kai removed his hand from my mouth. Aaron drew me out of the living room and into the front landing. He turned the knob carefully, silently opened the door, and pushed me outside. The evening air felt warm compared to the temperature in the living room.

Aaron and Kai stepped out after me, followed by Zak, who noiselessly closed the door like he knew exactly what he was supposed to do.

Sitting heavily on the steps, Aaron exhaled a heartfelt curse.

"What's wrong with Ezra?" I whispered.

Kai leaned against the porch railing and pressed a hand over his eyes. "Everyone screaming pushed him over the edge."

"You two are playing with fire," Zak said, but the words lacked any heat or power. He just sounded tired.

Kai lowered his hand to study the druid. "What do you plan to do about it?"

"Nothing. It's none of my business."

Aaron chuffed in angry disbelief, then waved at me. "Sit, Tori. You look like you're about to fall over."

I glanced at the front door, then sank down beside Aaron. I had to swallow twice before I could speak. "I'm sorry."

"Not your fault." His glare locked on a certain druid, indicating who he preferred to blame.

Zak leaned against the siding beside the door, blood dripping off his chin from his lower lip. He didn't even have enough decency to look guilty.

"What was the whole ritual thing you did, if it wasn't a real black-magic oath?" I demanded. "What did you make me drink?"

He lifted one shoulder in a shrug. "A vitality potion. It was good for your health."

I stared at him. The purple "black magic" potion had been sweet—just like the purple vitality potion he'd given me two days ago. I was a dumbass.

Resting my head on Aaron's shoulder, I closed my eyes. "I don't ever want to see your stupid face again."

"You'll have to see it a few more times, but I'll be gone for good once you're fae-free."

That got my eyes open. "What do you mean?"

He folded his arms. "Your mage pals will make my life hell. You really think I'd hang around?"

Fair point, but I wasn't bound by an imaginary oath anymore, so maybe I could do something about my mage pals making his life hell.

I turned to Aaron. "I met his alleged victims. He doesn't abduct teens. Kids who want a new life find him, and he takes them to a safe place, trains them up in their magic, and sends them off into the world with new identities. They all adore him."

"You can't be serious."

"I am. I mean, he's a huge dickhead and he's killed some people, but they all deserved it. I think."

Zak made a disgusted sound. "This, Tori, is why I made you swear that oath."

I shot him a glare, then asked Aaron, "Can you please keep Zak's secrets? He's protecting vulnerable kids. He destroys most of the black magic he buys. He's a shitty, immoral rogue, but he terrifies even worse rogues."

Aaron's gaze darted between us, then he slumped. "This is bullshit. Fine."

"Tori," Zak said darkly. "I don't care what he promises. I'm not taking any chances. Besides that, Varvara has most of her minions hunting me. I have no choice but to drop off their radar."

"If you go into hiding," Kai remarked thoughtfully, "they'll know you're vulnerable. With a reputation like yours, why back down?"

Zak's expression went even colder. "I'll worry about my own skin."

Shrugging, Kai pushed off the porch railing. "I'm going to check on Ezra."

He disappeared into the house, and the rest of us waited in silence.

Kai returned a moment later. "He's upstairs. You can come back in."

I followed Aaron and Zak inside and collapsed onto the sofa. Fatigue rolled through me in waves, and my giddy spurt of energy had crumbled into listless depression. Zak had to go into hiding, and it was probably my fault. Ezra was alone upstairs in who knew what state, and that was probably my fault too. Could I screw things up any worse?

Zak's scorching green eyes appeared in front of me. He'd cleaned the blood off his face and a salve gleamed on his cut lip. How long had I been sitting here feeling sorry for myself?

"Potion time, Tori."

I took the vial he offered and tossed it back without looking at it. He handed me the purple vitality potion next, and as sugary sweetness flooded my tongue, I couldn't believe I hadn't recognized the taste.

Kai joined us with a heavy leather tome under his arm, and Zak followed him into the dining room. I slouched on the sofa, listening to the creak of leather, the rustle of pages, and the low murmur of their voices.

The cushions dipped as Aaron sat beside me. Without thinking, I skooched over and curled up against his warm side, my head pillowed on his chest.

"So, you don't hate me," he murmured, stroking my hair. "I was starting to wonder if I'd upset you."

Guilt slashed me. "No, it's nothing like that."

"Mm." His hand moved to my shoulder, lightly massaging tense muscles. "There's something I really need to know."

I stiffened anxiously. "What?"

"Now that you can talk about it, *how* did you lose your shoes?"

A laugh burst from me, and I quickly stifled it. The mystery of how I'd ended up at the guild barefoot following my imprisonment with the evil Ghost had been bugging Aaron for weeks.

I snuggled up to him again. "They were ruined by dragon blood. Did you know dragon blood is poisonous?"

"Had no idea. What's the whole story? I've been dying to know."

I opened my mouth, then closed it, thinking carefully. Zak's reputation was part of what protected him. Aaron knew Zak didn't kidnap kids, and that was enough. He didn't need to know all the private things I'd learned about the secretive druid. It wasn't that I didn't trust Aaron's word, just that … it felt too personal to reveal.

"I lived with the other teens for two weeks," I said simply. "When Varvara took Nadine, I revealed why I was there. He made me swear the fake oath, and a dragon flew me home."

"A dragon?"

"Echo. That's how I know him." I closed my eyes, enjoying the slow press of his strong fingers into the tight muscles of my shoulder. "I called Zak on Saturday after you dropped me off. Sorry I had to lie about everything."

"You didn't have a choice." His hand caressed my neck and tangled in my hair. "You've been under a lot of stress these last few days."

I resisted the urge to raise my head and look at the broken doorframe. At the moment, *my* stress levels didn't concern me all that much.

"Will Ezra be okay?" I whispered.

"He just needs time to cool off." Aaron sighed regretfully. "That situation was pushing all the wrong buttons for him. I should've sent him outside, but I was afraid we'd need him against the Ghost."

"Zak."

"Huh?"

"He hates being called the Ghost." When Aaron smirked, I narrowed my eyes. "Don't call him that just to be mean. Cut the guy a little slack."

"Why? Why does he deserve slack?"

"Because he dropped everything to help me when he's already up to his neck in problems of his own."

The troublemaker gleam faded from Aaron's gaze, replaced by a thoughtful crease between his brows.

Kai and Zak walked out of the dining room, the druid carrying the grimoire under one arm. He sat on the sofa beside me, all casual like this was his home, and flipped the book open to a page filled with circular diagrams, symbols, and miniscule handwritten text.

"This is the ritual they used," he said without preamble, then turned several pages. "And this is a variation for transferring a fae link, which explains why Red Rum wants you. The ritual for transferring the link is significantly simpler than enslaving a fae, and I think I can alter it to dissolve the link instead. However, it will still require a fae-created relic to work."

"So"—I sat up to get a better look at the grimoire—"we need to summon the Rat."

"The what?" Aaron asked.

"The Rat. He's the fae Zak asked that Mancini guy about. Llyrle—the fae lord told us about him, said he sells relics to humans and that other fae hate him." I wrinkled my nose and asked Zak, "Can you buy the relic we need from him?"

"I'm sure I have something in my collection that will interest him. I know all the blood summoning arrays, and I can use one to call him from a distance." Closing the book, Zak looked from Aaron to Kai. "Calling an unknown darkfae is risky. I'd have the advantage on my own land, where the local fae support me, but if I summon the Rat elsewhere, I'll need you three to back me up."

"If we help, where would you want to do it?" Kai asked.

"Stanley Park. It's the fae lord's domain. We can get the relic from the Rat, then immediately begin the ritual to separate Tori from the link."

"Let's do that," Kai decided. "Will you need sorcerers for the ritual? Red Rum used four, plus their witch."

"I *am* a sorcerer. I don't need help."

"You're an alchemist *and* a druid," I told him grumpily. "You don't get to be a sorcerer too."

"Why not?"

"Because you're hogging all the mythic points for yourself. Look at me! I've got no magic at all." I'd meant to sound flippant, but judging by the way Aaron and Kai glanced away, it had come out painfully bitter instead.

Zak made an annoyed rasp in his throat. Not a sympathetic guy, that one.

"You have your Queen of Spades," he said. "And the spells you stole from me."

"Stole? You all but gave them to me." I folded my arms. "Besides, having a few artifacts doesn't make me a mythic."

"Doesn't it? Magic is a tool. Whether you inherit it, learn it, bargain for it, steal it—it's all the same."

I scrunched my face. "Mythics have magic."

He shook his head, exasperated as though I'd missed his point, and pushed off the sofa. "I need to—"

"Wait." I yanked him back down. "I want to show you something first."

"What?"

"Uh." Glancing around, I spotted my purse on the coffee table, where it'd been sitting since Kai and I left for the gallery. I slid it closer and dipped my hand in. My fingers found a smooth, warm sphere. Yep, it was back.

I lifted the fae orb out and offered it to him. He passed the grimoire to Kai, then took the orb in both hands and gently caressed its ridged shape. His expression softened, eyes losing focus, and he lifted it to his face, crooning softly. The closest I'd ever seen him looking this open and tender-hearted was when he'd been working with his horses.

The orb twitched, then uncoiled in one smooth motion. Suddenly, Zak's arms were full of fae, and the silvery blue creature rubbed its cheek ecstatically against his face, its vibrant pink antennae bobbing. Its excessively long tail was piled in his lap, and its small wings flared open and closed.

Zak stroked its smooth neck, then looked at me with glazed eyes. "She's awake."

"I noticed," I said dryly, boggled by the sight of the creature squirming all over him like he'd bathed in catnip. I'd heard fae were drawn to druids—like vultures to a corpse, as Kaveri had so poetically phrased it—but this was my first time seeing it. "She's been following me."

"Hmm." He focused on the creature again. "The fae lord's power woke her, but she remembers your voice and scent from before that. She's quite fond of you."

"You can speak to her?"

"Of course." He tilted his head. "She doesn't have a good grasp of human language, though, and can't understand you very well."

"What is she? What's her name?"

"She's a sylph—an air sprite. Her name … hmm, not very pronounceable. It means stars … starry night … starlight? Something like that." He rose to his feet, and the fae slid around his shoulders. He listened for a moment. "She wants to stay with you."

"Me?"

"She likes you."

Uncoiling from around him, the fae weightlessly drifted down to pool in my lap, her huge pink eyes staring up at me.

"Uh." I hesitantly touched her smooth neck. "I was okay babysitting a dormant orb thing, but I don't know how to take care of a sylph."

"You don't need to take care of her. She just wants a friend." He stretched, cracking his neck. "Now can I go? I have a lot of work to do."

"Zak, why did you give her to me?"

He shrugged. "I suspected she needed somewhere safe and quiet to recover for a few months—somewhere away from me. You were a convenient solution."

"Convenient," I repeated in a mutter. Curled in my lap, the sylph blinked at me.

"What's with that tone?" His eyebrows arched. "Are you disappointed it wasn't a fated union?"

I snorted dismissively.

Zak turned to Kai. "Tomorrow night in Stanley Park, nine o'clock sharp."

"We'll be there." Kai headed for the entryway. "I'll help get my bike out of your truck."

They disappeared through the door and it clunked shut. I looked down at the odd creature in my lap, a weird blend of gecko, insect, and something wholly unrecognizable. She sniffed curiously at my shirt, then tucked her head under her chest. Her entire body curled up and shrank into a tight ball again.

Zak giving me the fae had been an act of convenience, nothing more. That the sylph had awakened while I was caring for her was a coincidence, nothing more.

Everything had been a coincidence.

All this time I'd been searching for an explanation—a reason behind my involvement in this world—but it had been dumb luck from the start. Dumb luck I'd found that printout with the guild job listings. Dumb luck I'd been stubborn enough to walk through the repelling ward on the Crow and Hammer door. And dumb luck that they'd needed a bartender so badly they'd hired a human.

Human was all I'd ever been. There wasn't a drop of magical blood in my body. I had no mysterious heritage, no secret destiny, no hidden power. I was just a human who'd bulldozed her way into this world through sheer force of will.

I raised my eyes from the fae orb to Aaron, who stood at the window, watching Kai and Zak outside. I'd gotten this far with no magic of my own. I wasn't a mythic, but maybe I didn't have to be. All I needed to do was to hang on to this life with every stubborn bone in my body.

19

THE MOST ANNOYING SOUND in the world: plastic taped over a broken car window while the car is in motion. Flapping and snapping and rippling and just *arg*. I clamped my hands over my ears, jaw clenched.

So maybe I was irritable tonight. Just a little.

In the backseat of Aaron's car, Kai and Ezra were silent, probably because they couldn't think over the sound of the plastic. Was it supposed to be this noisy? Maybe Aaron had done a crappy tape job.

Signaling, Aaron pulled the car off the Stanley Park Causeway and onto the narrow road that led to the parking lot. When the car rolled out of the trees, we saw the lot wasn't as abandoned as last time. Unfamiliar cars were scattered around, and a man and woman in running gear were guzzling water from plastic bottles.

Aaron drove to the far end of the lot and pulled in beside a huge blue truck. Its driver was leaning against the tailgate, glowering. Looked like I wasn't the only irritable one.

We climbed out, and as Aaron opened his trunk, I strode toward the truck.

"You're late," Zak barked.

"Five minutes. Quit whining." I put my hands on my hips. "Are you ready with … everything?"

"Of course. Are you?"

"The guys need to gear up."

Across the parking lot, Mr. and Mrs. SuperFit had settled in their car. The engine rumbled, then the vehicle backed out. Once its taillights had disappeared, Aaron pulled his sword and baldric out of the trunk.

He, Kai, and Ezra had gone one step further than merely bringing weapons. They wore leather pants, similar to armored motorcycle gear, and heavy boots. Aaron's sleeveless shirt was made from a shiny, fire-resistant fabric, while Kai wore a long-sleeved black shirt in the same style as his pants. Ezra's t-shirt conformed to his torso, the material padded with something I assumed was armor. His long fingerless gloves that ran up to his biceps were definitely armored, the silver plates on the knuckles and elbows gleaming.

Zak, too, had dressed for the occasion in similar clothes, and he hadn't bothered with his shadow-hood coat. Too bulky, probably.

Me, well, I wore sturdy jeans, hiking boots, and my leather bomber jacket. The closest outfit I had to "badass combat mythic." All three of my sorcery artifacts were tucked in my pockets, and the only other thing I carried was my cell phone.

As the guys strapped on their weapons, the air shimmered and the sylph appeared. She nuzzled the back of Zak's neck, then glided behind me and closed her small front paws around the collar of my coat. As I'd discovered earlier today while getting ready, she liked to be towed along like a kid in a wagon.

"She says you chose a name for her," Zak remarked as he opened his tailgate. A duffle bag waited, plus a stack of his own gear.

"We named her Hoshi. It means 'star' in Japanese." I patted the sylph's nose. "Does she like it?"

"She does." He buckled on his belt of alchemic vials, then picked up a set of three long knives. As he strapped them around his thigh, he frowned thoughtfully. "If she's staying with you, you two need to be able to communicate."

"You said she doesn't talk."

"She doesn't. She communicates with images and a few sounds, but not words." He turned to his truck bed. "Take off your coat."

I was halfway through sliding my coat off when I realized I hadn't questioned his abrupt command. Damn, I must be growing desensitized to his bossy bluntness. The glow of my rune-covered arm reflected off his shiny truck as I flipped my coat over the edge of the box.

He dug into a pocket of his duffle bag, then turned to me, a thin black pen in hand. Wait, no, not a pen.

"Is that eyeliner?"

"Non-smudging, waterproof eyeliner." He lifted the hem of his shirt to show me the bottom of a spikey, rune-filled triangle on his side. "Best product for drawing on skin."

"You don't say."

Taking my left elbow, he uncapped the eyeliner with his teeth. Hoshi hovered beside him, watching with curious fuchsia eyes.

As he drew on my arm, I whispered, "*Maybe he's born with it …*"

"Ha-ha."

Aaron wandered over, adjusting the baldric across his chest. The leather-wrapped hilt of Sharpie, his biggest sword, jutted above his shoulder. "What are you doing?"

Zak drew a swift circle on my upper arm, filled the center with a jagged rune, then added radiating lines and more runes. As he capped the liner, Hoshi stretched out her petite muzzle and touched the centermost symbol.

Heat flashed through my arm. "Whoa! What was that?"

"Now you can communicate with her. Might take some practice, though." He stuffed the liner back in his bag. "Are we ready?"

Aaron's trunk was closed, and Ezra and Kai had donned their weapons. The latter wore two swords at his hip—a long katana in a black sheath, and a shorter one. Kai usually relied on small throwing knives; I hadn't seen him bring out his swords in months.

I squinted at my drawn-upon arm, then pulled my coat back on. "Guys, are we ready?"

"No," Aaron replied. "We're waiting for the O'Conner sisters. I called them yesterday with an update, and they insisted on being present."

"Is that a problem?" I asked Zak.

He shrugged. "As long as no one calls me the Ghost in front of them, they'll have no idea who I am."

Minutes ticked by. At a quarter after nine, a familiar blue sedan pulled into the lot and parked a few spaces away. Olivia climbed out, her hair in a messy ponytail, bags under her eyes, and a greenish bruise on her cheek—courtesy of yours truly. She straightened her khaki pants, barely glancing at Zak.

"Sorry I'm late," she mumbled.

I frowned. "Where's Odette?"

"She's not feeling well. She stayed home."

"Are you okay?"

"I might be coming down with something too." She squeezed her temples like her head hurt. "Can we hurry?"

Yeesh. If she was going to be cranky, she should've stayed at home.

Zak heaved his duffle bag out and slung it over his shoulder, then reached into the truck for a small pet carrier. As he slid it out, something inside squawked.

"Uh … what is that?" I asked in alarm.

He shut the tailgate. "A chicken."

"Why did you bring a chicken?"

He started across the parking lot. I scrambled after him, the three mages following and Olivia bringing up the rear. Hoshi had vanished, but I figured she was nearby.

"Zak? Chicken. Explain."

"Did you forget already? Our plan requires a blood summoning array."

"Blood …" My gorge rose as we walked onto a dark trail through the trees. "Tell me you aren't planning what I think you are."

"It's black magic, Tori. No getting around it."

"But—"

"But the chicken will make a delicious roast."

I gulped down my twisting stomach. Right. Zak lived on a farm, and he was nothing if not pragmatic. That chicken had been destined for someone's dinner table anyway, and he wouldn't waste it.

We made our way down the sloping path toward the coast. Zak scouted around, then chose a forested spot away from the trails but close enough to hear ocean waves. The near-full moon provided our only light as he kicked the worst of the leaf litter out of the clearing, then unzipped his duffle bag.

Keeping out of the way, I watched him open a large wine bottle and stick a spout in it. When he upended it, instead of liquor, a viscous silver liquid poured out. He used it to draw a perfect circle three feet across, then marked out lines and runes. No grimoire needed.

"Who is this mythic?" Olivia whispered to Kai. "Is he a witch or—oh my sweet lady earth!"

"What?" I demanded.

"His familiar is possessing him!"

Zak glanced at her, his green eyes supernaturally bright. "And?"

"That's—that's *disgraceful!* And dangerous! Only black witches and druids would ever allow a fae that much influence over—"

"You have no idea what you're talking about." He bent over the circle again, adding lines and runes with swift precision. "Witches know less about fae than vampires."

Olivia let out another wild gasp. "You're a druid?"

"I'm obviously not a witch."

"Fae possession is taboo," she declared righteously. "Whoring yourself for power, opening your body and mind to a fae like a prostitute for a—"

The feather tattoos on his arms shimmered. "You're making my familiar angry. You don't want to do that."

Olivia snapped her mouth shut. She minced sideways until she stood beside me, then whispered feverishly in my ear, "This is why a druid's primary familiar is called a *consort*. It's obscenely intimate to allow a fae inside your body. With prolonged exposure—"

"If she doesn't shut up," Zak said coolly, "I'll silence her."

"Olivia," Kai snapped, "keep your opinions to yourself."

She pressed her lips together, glaring mutinously. Zak continued his preparations, adding various dried plants, fresh leaves, bits of precious metals, pouches with mysterious substances in them, and crystals. Finally, he brought out a scorched metal bowl, filled it with oil, and lit it on fire. Smoke curled up from the dish.

He turned to us. "I'm ready to begin the summoning. I'll stand in front of the circle. Kai, Aaron, Ezra, you three line up four paces behind me. Don't speak, no matter what I say; this will require some calculated bravado. I won't know how powerful the darkfae is until he shows up, so I'll signal to you."

He held up his index finger. "One means I don't need your help. Just look menacing." He spread his hand, fingers and thumb outstretched. "Five means we're dead if he decides he doesn't want us alive, so I'll give him whatever he wants and hope he doesn't massacre us."

"And what about two through four?" Kai asked.

Zak shrugged. "Four means we can probably win in a fight, but avoid taking a direct hit at all costs. If the fae attacks, he'll go for me first. You three should get behind him. I'll keep his attention, and you strike from the flanks and rear."

"How likely is a fight?" I asked nervously.

"Depends on his temperament. Since this fae regularly deals with humans, probably low. He'll want to see what he can get from us." Zak pointed at me. "You and the fae lord need to stay out of this. If the darkfae is too powerful for us to handle, then Llyr would cause you serious damage fighting it. You and the witch should back up—way up—and stay there."

He gave me a meaningful look and I nodded in understanding. I grabbed Olivia's arm and hauled her through the trees until we were well away from the clearing. She complained the whole way, but I ignored her. Zak wanted me to keep her from screwing things up. That I could do.

Aaron and Ezra, positioned on either side of Kai, moved out a few steps and drew their weapons. Aaron rested the point of his broadsword on the ground, while Ezra split his polearm and reattached the ends, forming a double-bladed staff. Leaving his throwing knives sheathed, Kai drew his katana, the polished steel gleaming.

Zak's voice drifted through the trees in a soft chant that verged on a song. I crouched behind a shrub and pulled Olivia down with me.

"Dealing with darkfae," Olivia hissed angrily. "No better than Red Rum."

"Which is worse?" I hissed back. "Dealing with this darkfae or letting me die? Witch ethics aside, I'd rather live."

Zak crouched to open the pet carrier. As he pulled the chicken out, I glimpsed ruffled brown feathers—and the gleam of a knife in his other hand. His body blocked my view, but whatever he did, he was quick about it. The fire in the center of the circle puffed black smoke, and the ritual lines lit with glowing magenta power.

He resumed his chanting song. The circle's eerie glow grew brighter, and Olivia fidgeted with impatience and discomfort. I pinched her arm to make her hold still.

Falling silent, Zak stood, unmoving. Aaron, Kai, and Ezra held still too, following the druid's lead. We waited, the night gradually deepening. My legs ached from crouching awkwardly, but I didn't move.

Olivia sucked in a sharp, trembling breath.

The air above the glowing circle shimmered. A shadow darkened the glow of the fire, then the shape stretched upward and solidified. My stomach clenched.

The fae called the Rat towered over Zak, twice his height. The creature stood in a hunch, his immensely long arms braced against the ground, his powerful shoulders bulging like a hyena's. A bald, rat-like tail lashed behind him, and his brownish-gray skin shone dimly in the sputtering firelight.

His large head was vaguely human, with a heavy brow and deep-set eyes, but jutting tusks stuck up from his lower jaw. A tangled black mane sprouted from the top of his skull.

"Bhardudlin," Zak said, his tone neutral. He put his hand behind his back and signaled a number to the mages. Even from fifty feet away, I could see his hand spread wide in warning. Five.

The darkfae's head dropped a few inches as he examined Zak with ebony eyes.

"Druid." The deep, bone-rumbling bass of his voice rolled through the quiet night. "The Crystal Druid, no less. I give my respects to the lovely Night Eagle."

Zak inclined his head. "Would you care to bargain, Bhardudlin?"

"Hmm." His giant head lunged down, far faster than such a huge creature should be able to move. He flung his head into the air, caught the dead chicken in his mouth, and swallowed it in one gulp. "I did not travel so far for a measly bird."

A few scraggily feathers drifted to the ground.

"As we have not had the pleasure of meeting," Bhardudlin continued, the baritone words slurring past his tusks, "I shall illuminate my preferences for you. I do not enjoy games of word, or plays of strength or strategy." His black stare slashed across the three mages. "You summoned me with a goal, so speak it. Then we will bargain."

"I seek an enslavement relic. I believe you have traded these to humans before."

"I have. Not a tool I expected *you* to desire, Crystal Druid."

"My use for it is irrelevant."

A cackling laugh. "A straightforward creature you are. I like that." He growled thoughtfully. "I demand the highest price for these relics. I accept the three warriors."

"They are not bargaining chips. I will give you no lives."

"What else can you offer? I have no use for trinkets."

"I own a variety of rare artifacts and relics. Tell me where your interests lie and I can offer you something of value."

"Hmm." The fae bobbed his head in consideration. "I seek only tools of power, druid."

"Would the Carapace of Valdurna interest you?"

A strange dark light ignited in the fae's eyes. "You do not have it."

"I do."

Lips parting, Bhardudlin ran a thick, slimy tongue across one tusk. "A good offering to start. What else would you give?"

"A grimoire of Hindarfur."

"What does it contain?"

Zak shrugged. "I don't know. I can't read it."

"Then it may be worthless."

"Or it may be priceless."

Another ugly laugh. "Bold, druid, so bold. Tell me of your other treasures. How much of the Wolfsbane Druid's collection did you steal when you killed him?"

"All of it."

"Ha! I would expect no less."

Olivia grabbed my arm, her fingers digging in. "Tori!" she hissed. "Look at the trees!"

"Huh?" I squinted around the clearing as Zak listed more of his fae treasures to Bhardudlin's greedy delight. Everything looked normal …

Olivia pointed. The trees surrounding the clearing were difficult to make out in the darkness, but I caught a flutter of movement. Falling leaves? But there was no wind. I squinted harder.

Just beyond the clearing where the four guys and the darkfae stood, the trees were dying. Their leaves were shriveling and falling, their thinnest branches melting like they'd been rotting for months.

"Is the darkfae doing that?" I gasped.

"He's building up his magic." Olivia tightened her grip on my arm, her face ghostly white. "He's preparing an attack—a powerful unleashing."

Zak had said a fae this powerful could kill us all no problem. But they were negotiating, weren't they? Why was the fae preparing an attack?

My hands clenched into fists. I wasn't letting the guys die on my account. No. Way. In. Hell. I had no power to fight, but I was tied to a fae with enough magic to defend us—even if I became the collateral damage.

Better me than all of us.

"Stay here," I told Olivia.

I crept into the undergrowth, but instead of obeying, Olivia followed. Growling under my breath, I kept moving.

The spreading wave of death reached us: the ferns turned brown and their fan-like leaves curled; the bushes shrank and their foliage shriveled; tree bark turned black; and dead leaves rained softly on my head. Bhardudlin was sucking the life out of the surrounding forest to fuel his magic, keeping it hidden from Zak and the mages.

"Impressive, impressive," Bhardudlin rumbled. "I confess I am torn as to what I want most from you, druid."

"I think we can come to an agreeable exchange."

"Perhaps." His tusks gleamed in the shrinking firelight. "Perhaps not."

Zak tensed. "Is there a problem, Bhardudlin?"

"Only that I desire everything you offer—and more. I do not want a handful of your toys, Crystal Druid. I want *you.*"

His dull pink tongue slid between his lips, then faster than a blink, he grabbed Zak in his massive hands. Bhardudlin lifted Zak into the air, thick fingers spanning his chest.

The fae dragged his fat tongue up the side of Zak's face. "A pet druid of my own."

Black wings flared off Zak's shoulders and shadowy blades surged out of him, lashing Bhardudlin's face.

The darkfae dropped Zak. He fell six feet and landed on his knees, phantom wings still spread. He shot to his feet and retreated rapidly, forcing the three mages to back up with him.

"You would betray the barter truce?" Zak demanded.

Bhardudlin heaved a guttural laugh. "I follow none of the rules of my pathetic kin. You should have realized that before calling me. Nothing you offer is as tempting as claiming you." He clacked his tusks. "Come out and play with me, beautiful Lallakai. I will battle you for your beloved consort."

Her wings flared but she didn't emerge from Zak's body.

"A shame, a shame." Bhardudlin opened his huge hands, fingers curled like he held an invisible beach ball between his palms. "Then I will force you out—unless you and your druid die first. If you do, I will know he was not strong enough to make an entertaining pet."

Dark power sparked in the space between the fae's hands. The crackling ebony light expanded, growing larger and larger—the magic he had killed an acre of forest to fuel.

I launched to my feet and sprinted toward the mages. Olivia ran after me.

Bhardudlin pulled his hands apart and power surged to fill the gap. The air turned heavy and poisonous, and the ground trembled. With an ecstatic roar, the fae unleashed his attack.

A maelstrom of black magic hurtled toward the druid. Zak thrust his hands out and shadows erupted from his palms, forming a rippling dome. Bhardudlin's attack struck the nebulous barrier. All the heaving, crackling power piled against the obstacle.

Zak had warned against fighting such a powerful fae. He'd also warned us not to take a direct hit. Now he was doing both because he had no choice.

I couldn't let him die.

Bhardudlin's ebony magic tore at Zak's barrier and bolts of black lightning cut through the edges, shearing fissures in the earth on either side of the druid. Aaron, Kai, and Ezra braced against the howling wind that blasted out from the clashing powers. A branch tore off a tree and whipped past my face, scratching my cheek.

Olivia shrieked in pain and hit the ground with a thud, but I couldn't stop. Bent against the gale, I ran toward the guys.

Lallakai's shadow magic rippled. Faltered. Started to fail.

I opened my mouth to scream Llyrlethiad's name.

A bolt of power ripped through the barrier and lashed at Aaron and Kai. It slammed into their raised swords, flinging them backward—into me. We crashed down in a tangle, the breath crushed from my lungs. I had no air to call for the fae lord.

Lallakai's desperate shadow barrier shuddered. The edges had torn away. Bhardudlin's power screamed against it, pushing harder, ripping deeper.

Then Ezra darted to Zak's side.

He pressed his palms against Lallakai's barrier—and crimson light flared beneath his fingers. The scarlet magic burst out of his hands and surged up his arms, veining his flesh and shining through his clothes. The power, a vivid red that was black at its deepest core, snaked across the inside of Lallakai's failing barrier.

The temperature plunged. The darkness thickened into an inky soup.

Blood-red power erupted in a circle around Ezra's feet. Lines spiked out of it, runes igniting in the leaf litter. A fully formed sorcery circle coalesced beneath him, red magic pouring out of it. The circle pulsed.

Then howling crimson power erupted from his hands and ripped through both Lallakai's barrier and Bhardudlin's ebony attack.

20

I COULDN'T BREATHE.

Aaron was on top of me. As the crimson magic had collided with black fae power and exploded, he'd rolled over me. His weight was crushing my lungs, and I hammered desperately at his shoulder.

He pushed off me and lurched onto his hands and knees.

Bhardudlin groaned furiously. The explosion had thrown the huge darkfae across the clearing. Great wounds raked his brownish-gray flesh, dripping dark blood over the forest floor, and the unleashing of power had torn smoking, foot-deep crevices into the earth.

Zak and Ezra, who'd been front and center for the explosive collision, were both down and unmoving.

Bhardudlin heaved to his feet and stretched to his towering twelve-foot height. His black eyes fixed on the downed druid and he hungrily licked his tusks. Ignoring the blood trickling from his wounds, he lumbered forward.

Aaron grabbed his sword from the scorched leaf litter. "Tori, take care of Ezra and Zak."

Kai rose too, katana at the ready. The two mages advanced on the injured darkfae.

I scrambled up and raced to the druid and aeromage. Ezra's face was slack, but red magic glowed across his fingertips. What the hell *was* that?

Aaron roared in challenge and fiery orange light flared. Bhardudlin snarled.

I grabbed Ezra's shoulders, but he was six feet of solid muscle and impossible to lift. Planting my feet, I heaved on him anyway.

Silvery light glimmered. Hoshi appeared above Ezra, her long body floating effortlessly. She grasped the strap of his baldric with her little paws—and half his weight vanished. I lifted his shoulders off the ground, his head hanging limply. With Hoshi's help, I dragged him into the trees, then ran back for Zak. Olivia was crumpled half behind a tree trunk, far enough away that she should be safe. I'd worry about her later.

As I took hold of Zak's shoulders, he sucked in a sharp breath. His eyes flew open, then glazed with pain. Though Lallakai's tattoos still marked his skin, his irises had no crystalline brightness. She must have used up her power.

Instead of dragging him away, I helped him sit up. "Zak, I have to call—"

"No. Bhardudlin is injured. We can finish him."

As Hoshi flitted anxiously around us, Zak staggered to his feet and snapped a vial off his belt. He pulled the cork and downed the orange-gold contents in one gulp. Within three breaths, his rough exhalations steadied. Had the potion healed him or merely dulled his pain?

He extended his hand and a red rune ignited on his forearm. A crimson saber materialized in his grip. Shadows rippled on either side of him, then four vargs took form, their fangs bared and ruby eyes glaring.

Leaving me standing there, helpless and terrified, he ran for Bhardudlin with the vargs speeding ahead of him. The darkfae whirled away from Aaron to meet the druid and his wolves. Zak swung his saber and Bhardudlin caught it with one hand. Unconcerned by the spray of blood from his palm, he grinned through his tusks.

Aaron drew his sword back and whipped it in an arc. A band of searing blue fire struck the fae's back, tearing an infuriated howl from him. Kai flung a handful of throwing knives into Bhardudlin's shoulder, then pointed his katana. Lightning leaped from his blade to the knives.

The darkfae dropped to one knee under the barrage, then flung both giant arms out. His sweeping fists missed Zak and Kai but sent Aaron and two vargs flying. Aaron hit the ground and rolled into a tree.

Panic choked me, but Zak had said not to call Llyrlethiad. He'd said they could handle it.

With Hoshi holding on to my collar, I sprinted back into the trees and crouched beside Ezra. His eyes fluttered open. He squinted blearily at me, his jaw tight. Like Zak, he was in obvious pain, but he tried to sit up.

I slung an arm around his shoulders and helped him. He breathed harshly, then raised his head, his attention pulled toward the sounds of battle.

"Where's my weapon?" he panted.

I shook my head. "You can't fight like this."

"Can." He grabbed the nearest tree and levered himself to his feet. "I'm just bruised. The fae's magic hit like a tank."

Deciding not to point out that Ezra's mysterious crimson magic had hit even harder, I stuck my head around the tree. Zak had unleashed another rune on his arm, and green bands of magic spiraled around Bhardudlin, restricting his movements—but the darkfae kept fighting. His wounds had barely slowed him. He was unstoppable.

A few yards from the edge of the battle, Ezra's double-bladed staff lay in the leaf litter, the steel reflecting Aaron's firelight.

Ezra leaned against the tree, panting for air. Whatever he'd said, he was in bad shape. He needed a minute to recover. Clamping down on my fear, I set my feet. In and out. I could do this.

"Wait here," I told him.

Before he could argue, I sprinted toward the battle.

Hoshi hung onto my shoulders like a streaming blue banner as I ran. The vargs harried Bhardudlin's ankles but seemed incapable of inflicting real damage, and Zak darted back and forth in front of the fae, preventing him from defending against the two mages. Aaron and Kai rained fire and lightning down on the fae's back.

Bhardudlin's flesh was torn and blackened. His blood drenched the forest floor. But he was still standing, still fighting, and seemed more furious than frightened.

Skidding through the leaves, I stooped to grab Ezra's weapon.

Bellowing, Bhardudlin flung his huge arms wide. A wave of black power surged out of his thick fingers, expanding in every direction. Zak ducked. Aaron and Kai dove to the ground.

But I didn't have the reflexes of a trained combat mythic. I didn't even have my Queen of Spades card in my hand.

As the crackling black power shot outward, Hoshi's long tail snapped around me and squeezed. In a rush of cold magic, my vision turned to colorful ripples. For an instant, Aaron and Kai disappeared, but I could see shadowy shapes: Bhardudlin, a massive gray monster; the black vargs; and Zak, whose body was overshadowed by Lallakai's wings.

The darkfae's attack swept right through me.

I saw its shadow pass through my shimmering chest like I wasn't even there. Then my vision snapped back to normal, and Hoshi faded out of sight. Shock kept me rooted in place—then Bhardudlin's hand shot out with super speed. He grabbed Zak around the chest.

Clutching Ezra's weapon, I spun. As Ezra sprinted out of the trees, I drew the heavy staff back and hurled it at him like a javelin.

It flew straight and true—then dropped out of the air and stuck into the ground like a crooked flagpole, halfway to him. Goddamn it! I needed to work out more.

He veered toward it, snatched it from the ground, and charged for Bhardudlin. As the darkfae lifted Zak into the air, Ezra closed in from behind. Aaron and Kai hurled attacks at the darkfae's face, blinding him.

Launching himself with a gust of wind, Ezra leaped onto the fae's hunched back. He raised his staff, the air distorting around it, and slammed the blade down. The foot-long steel sank into grayish-brown flesh, then the wound exploded like a starburst as blades of air ripped outward.

Bhardudlin screamed and collapsed.

Zak rolled free from the darkfae's grip. Glowing red saber in hand, he jammed the point under Bhardudlin's chin. Standing on the fae's back, Ezra pushed his staff into the bleeding wound. Aaron and Kai stuck the tips of their swords into Bhardudlin's sides.

"Well," Zak panted, "would you care to continue our negotiations?"

The darkfae snarled softly. "What would you have of me, druid?"

"The enslavement relic in exchange for your life."

Bhardudlin hissed. "So be it."

Dragging one arm across the ground, he clenched his huge hand. Ebony ripples danced over his fingers, then he opened his fist. A small, delicate orb of silver threads sat on his palm.

"Tori," Zak said. "Pass that to me."

I minced closer, overwhelmed by the fae's monstrous size even as he lay on the ground. I plucked the sphere from his bloody gray palm and handed it to Zak.

Keeping his saber at the fae's throat, he examined it. "It's real."

"I have met my end of our bargain," Bhardudlin growled, desperation in his baritone slur.

Zak handed the sphere back to me. "Yes, you have."

He lifted his sword from the darkfae's neck—then slammed it back down. Red light flared across the blade as it tore through flesh and bone. Bhardudlin writhed, a furious wet groan wheezing from his mouth before he went still.

"Holy shit," I whispered.

Zak opened his hand and the scarlet saber dissolved. "He knew I would kill him, though he was hoping I might be stupid enough not to." He bared his teeth. "He chose the wrong druid to make his *pet*."

Ezra slid off the fae's body, stumbled several paces away, then sank to the ground. I took an alarmed step toward him, only to falter as Aaron and Kai both dropped, landing heavily on their butts as though they couldn't stand any longer.

Zak walked to Ezra, pulled him up, and half dragged him to the far end of the clearing. As he trudged back to get Kai, I pulled myself together and hurried to Aaron. I helped him over to Ezra, where he immediately sat, breathing heavily.

Olivia had recovered from her unfortunate encounter with a flying tree branch. She sat at the edge of the clearing, one hand pressed to her head as she stared at the slain darkfae.

Leaving her, I found Aaron's and Kai's swords among the leaf litter. Zak had deposited Kai with the other two, and the electramage was slumped against a log, eyes closed. After leaning their swords against a tree trunk, I anxiously scanned them—wheezing, sweating, eyes closed, faces pale.

"Guys?" I quavered.

"Give them a few minutes," Zak said, rubbing his hair. When he pulled his hand away, slimy strings of Bhardudlin's saliva stuck to his fingers. For a second, I thought he might barf on the spot—I almost did—but he merely wiped his hand on his pants, then added, "They're done."

"Done what?"

Something like respect gathered in his eyes. "When a mage pushes to his limit, the price is steep. This is the cost of Elementaria."

I turned to the guys, taking in their exhaustion. In a few minutes, they'd gone from full strength to trembling fatigue like they'd just finished a twelve-hour Ironman triathlon.

"The only class that places a higher demand on the mythic is Demonica," Zak murmured, "and that's a very different price."

"What about you?" I asked, clutching the spindly silver relic Zak had yet to take back. "You seem okay."

In answer, he held out his tattooed forearms. The colorful runes were dark, and three had disappeared, leaving empty circles on his skin. "The cost of this magic was paid by the fae who made it. Lallakai is exhausted. So are the vargs. Hoshi used what little magic she had to protect you."

I pressed a hand to my chest. "She did something ... the darkfae's attack went right through me."

"She shifted you into the fae demesne."

"She *what?*"

"Fae have their own world ... realm ... reality. Whatever." Zak limped to his duffle bag and pulled out a beer-bottle-sized vial of purple potion. "Some fae can pull a human in with them, which makes the human incorporeal in this realm—and invisible to non-Spiritalis mythics."

I remembered, back at the art gallery, when Lallakai had swept her wings around him and he'd vanished.

"Huh." I pointed at the bottle. "Is that a vitality potion?"

"Yes. It'll get the mages back on their feet. We need to move down to the beach so I can set up the—"

An ear-shattering blast burst through the forest—a gunshot.

For an instant that lasted far longer, I couldn't understand it. Gunfire? Here? Now? In the park?

Three more shots rang out and Zak pitched forward. He hit the ground, blood misting the air above his back, and the potion bottle rolled out of his limp hand. The ringing echo blared in my ears, shock freezing me in place.

Zak made an awful wet rasp as he struggled to breathe.

The mages recovered before I did. Aaron and Kai lurched forward, scrambling to stand.

"Stop right there."

The cold command slid out of the darkness. A man appeared, his black pistol pointed at the mages—a real gun, not a paintball one. Three other men strode out of the trees after him. Even more came out of the darkness, surrounding us. Several held guns, while others wielded bladed weapons or sorcery artifacts.

I didn't move. Neither did the mages, who hadn't even managed to stand.

The first man, his gun trained on Aaron, walked to Zak and nudged him with a boot. The druid didn't stir. Using his foot, the man shoved Zak onto his back. He rolled limply, a trickle of blood running from the corner of his mouth.

"He's younger than I expected," the man remarked, studying the druid. "Interesting. His bounty is all the more impressive for his age. A shame he's worth more dead."

He turned to me and held out his hand, palm up. "The relic, young lady."

I didn't move. These men could only be from Red Rum—but how had they found us? How had they known we were here? The way they had snuck up on us like this, their arrival timed perfectly with Bhardudlin's defeat, seemed too well planned to be a lucky break on their part.

We were surrounded, and Aaron, Kai, and Ezra were exhausted from battling Bhardudlin. Zak was down, unable to help.

He was *down*. Not dead. I refused to believe he was dead. He was *the Ghost*, the most feared rogue in the city. He wouldn't die from something as lame as getting shot in the back.

"The relic," the man repeated.

Hand trembling, I placed the silver sphere in his waiting palm.

"Excellent. Now listen carefully. If you speak, we will shoot a mage. If you attempt to summon the sea lord to your defense, we will shoot all three mages. If you act suspicious in any way, we'll kill them. Do you understand?"

I nodded faintly. My heart raced so fast I could feel it throbbing in my neck.

An agonized wail made me jump. Olivia had clambered to her feet, tears streaking her face.

"I did what you wanted!" she cried, stumbling toward the rogues. "Tell me where Odette is!"

A mythic strode over and grabbed her arm, holding her back.

The leader of the rogues waved a hand, the motion sharp with annoyance. "She's of no more use to us. Get her out of here."

My chest tightened as the man dragged Olivia into the trees. When had she betrayed us? Earlier today? Yesterday? Before Aaron had shared our plans with her?

Jaw tight, I focused on the Red Rum leader. He was stocky, scarcely taller than me, but thick with muscle. He held a gun, and sorcery artifacts hung in rows from his belt. I wanted to scream insults in his face, but I didn't dare make a sound.

Aaron, Kai, and Ezra sat stiffly, guns and weapons trained on them. What could they do? Nothing. There was nothing. Even Hoshi had used her tiny bit of magic, so she couldn't make me disappear. We were out of magic and out of allies.

"Which one?" the Red Rum leader asked, gesturing at the mages.

A rogue pointed at Kai. "He protected her last night."

"Bring him, then." The leader bounced the orb in his palm. "Now, young lady, we will head down to the beach. It is time to transfer command of the fae lord to us."

As a man dragged Kai up and put a gun to his head, the Red Rum leader smiled.

"And if you resist in any way, this mage will die first."

21

STARING AT THE MUD between my hiking boots, I couldn't bear
to look up.

I didn't want to see the elaborate ritual circle carved into the
surrounding foreshore. Or the witch standing in the inner
circle nearby, waiting to receive the fae bond. Or Kai on his
knees with a gun to the back of his head, execution style.

I didn't want to see the huge luxury yacht anchored far out
in the bay, lit up like a party boat, its deck lined with people-
sized shadows—elite members of Red Rum observing the
spectacle and waiting to meet their new sea lord guardian.

The deep chant of four sorcerers filled my ears, and that I
couldn't block out. The lines of the ritual circle glowed purple.
There was nothing I could do to stop it.

Nothing. Nothing. Nothing.

The witch standing six feet away laughed, and my eyes rose
against my will. He was around thirty, with blah-brown hair

tied in a low ponytail and a scruffy attempt at a beard that made his chin look extra weedy. A pair of oversized, dark-framed glasses sat on his nose.

It was the same guy from the first beach ritual, the one I'd tackled and knocked out with a spell—spells Red Rum had confiscated along with my coat and phone. My hands were tied behind my back, my mouth duct-taped shut.

The witch grinned nastily. "I hope you had fun with my familiar these last few days. The first thing I'll command him to do is swallow you whole. It'll be an interesting way to die, don't you think?"

I said nothing—not that I could speak with my mouth taped shut. Neither did I dare utter a word with that gun pressed to Kai's head. Two more gunmen stood nearby, plus two witches and three spare sorcerers, including the leader. The remaining four rogues were back in the clearing, holding Aaron and Ezra as reserve hostages.

"After he eats you," the witch continued in a whisper I could barely hear over the chanting sorcerers, "I'll have him disembowel the Yamada mongrel—you know, because that's how Japanese samurai commit suicide, right?"

Wow. Not only a would-be murderer, but a racist too.

"I already got permission to finish off the others as well, but I haven't decided how yet. So many options."

I again considered mentally calling Llyrlethiad, but the moment the fae lord showed up, the rogues would kill Kai.

As the chanting grew louder and bolder, the witch looked across the circle. "We're almost there. Now the fun part begins."

The chanting sorcerers reached a crescendo, the final word ringing out, then they went silent.

"Lord of the Seas!" The witch lifted his hand, the spun-silver sphere resting on his palm. "Wyldfae known as Llyrlethiad, I summon you!"

Silver light glimmered across the sphere—and agony blazed through my body.

The air around us rippled, then the giant leviathan appeared inside the circle, its thick coils looped around me and the witch. Torment burned my flesh and bones, and I choked back a scream.

The fae's reptilian head swung around, fangs bared at the witch, but he made no move to attack.

"*Human girl.*"

His snarling voice slammed into my skull and I flinched violently—but the witch didn't react. The sorcerers had resumed their chant, and their chorus didn't falter either. They hadn't heard it?

"*I speak only to you.*"

Llyrlethiad, I gasped silently inside my head. *Can you stop them?*

"*I cannot inflict harm upon the relic's holder.*"

Despair crushed my lungs, cutting off my air. Llyrlethiad couldn't help, and anything I tried would get Kai, Aaron, and Ezra killed.

"*The others are safe,*" Llyrlethiad rumbled. "*The druid freed them. He is near.*"

My heart skipped a beat. Several beats. Zak was *alive?*

I peeked toward the shore. Beyond the circle, the eight rogues not participating in the ritual waited with flawless patience. Kai was still in the "about to be executed" position, and I couldn't see any sign of Zak, but I supposed that was a good thing. How he could hide on the flat, muddy foreshore was beyond me.

"*Listen, human.*" Llyrlethiad's serpentine coils stirred restlessly. "*Once the ritual concludes, this cursed bond will flow from you to the witch. It will take time—minutes, at least. If you kill the witch before the transfer is completed, the bond will fail. I—and you—will be free.*"

My eyes widened. After the ritual ended but before the witch gained complete control of the sea lord, I would have a few minutes to save Llyrlethiad *and* myself? Maybe that would be enough to—

Wait. Did you say I have to kill *the witch?*

"*There is no other way to destroy the binding magic,*" Llyrlethiad answered.

My eyes went from wide to bulging. *I can't kill him!*

"*I told you: I cannot harm the relic's holder.*" A wash of bitterness lined his voice. "*You must do this.*"

Me? Kill the witch? My gaze darted to the smirking mythic, oblivious to my conversation with the fae lord. Murdering another person aside, how was I supposed to accomplish that? Zak might be close by, but he'd been shot—I was pretty sure he'd been shot, at least. I didn't know how useful he'd be, and before anything else, he needed to save Kai.

That meant I'd have to take on the witch by myself, and there were four sorcerers within spellcasting distance. They'd flatten me in an instant. I was just a human with no magic, no artifacts, no relics, no familiar—

My thoughts skidded to a halt. No familiar? Or …

Llyrlethiad? My heart crawled into my throat and throbbed frantically. *Can you lend me your power?*

His anger sparked inside my head. "*What is it you ask?*"

The sorcerers' chant rose in volume again. We were running out of time. *Can you give me magical power the way Lallakai does with Zak?*

Llyrlethiad snarled silently.

Can you or can't you? I barked at him.

The chanting rose until the sorcerers were bellowing the words. The rogue witch, holding the relic aloft, squinted suspiciously at me over the serpent coil between us. The light glowing from the relic was brightening.

With a final cry, the sorcerers stopped.

"Llyrlethiad!" the witch cried. "You submitted to this magic and now I take your submission upon *me*. Your will, your body, and your power are mine. Obey me, Lord of the Seas!"

Flaring with painful heat, the markings on my body flashed. The sphere lit up with equal incandescence, then collapsed into dust in the witch's hand, its magic consumed.

The massive leviathan reared into the air. Shimmering violently, his body began to shrink, his long tail lashing against the mud. Pearly eyes turned to me, gleaming with deadly power.

The shrinking sea serpent lunged at me.

His head struck my chest—except we didn't collide. The serpent flowed into the same space I occupied, pouring into my body, cramming himself inside my skin. Possessing me.

Between one instant and the next, I went from being a single person to being two—regular me, and the fae lord sharing my skin. I could feel him inside me, rubbing against my soul, and Olivia's comments about the obscene intimacy of fae possession now made sense.

But it wasn't just his presence inside me. With the fae's spirit came his power. All of it.

It built under my skin, burning holes in my innards and making the world dance in my vision. I was coming apart at the seams, the power pushing against my fragile flesh— crackling electricity and torrential rain and gusting wind and roaring tides, all trapped inside my wimpy mortal body.

Almost as fast as Llyrlethiad had possessed me, lightning flashed—a bolt leaping from Kai to the metal guns pointed at him. The rogues reeled back from the shock—not a powerful bolt like the electramage normally unleashed, but strong enough to startle them.

A dozen yards behind the rogues, a shape leaped up from the mudflats—Zak, his exposed skin smeared with mud to camouflage his approach. He flung a potion vial into the rogues' midst and heavy smoke roiled out of it in an obscuring cloud.

The last thing I saw was Zak pulling a wickedly serrated dagger from the sheath on his thigh.

I focused through the spinning disorientation of Llyrlethiad's possession. I had to get to the witch before the fae bond passed to him. Without thinking, I pulled on my bound arms—and the rope snapped. Inhuman strength pulsed through my muscles.

Ripping the duct tape off my face, I whirled toward the witch. He backpedaled, hands raised defensively. A faint shadow of the markings that covered the right side of my body lit his arm. His wide eyes were fixed on me in terror, and in the lenses of his glasses, my reflection shone.

My hazel eyes were glowing like twin lamps, radiant with Llyrlethiad's power. My skin shimmered like scales and Llyrlethiad's long, finned tail trailed behind me, semi-transparent but solid enough to score the mud as it lashed.

The witch scrambled away. I had to stop him. My gaze flicked to the waterline, waves gently lapping against the mud. I could feel the ocean's power inside me and all around me.

I raised my hand, my fingers tipped with phantom claws, and dizzying magic surged down my arm.

The ocean rose like an incoming tidal wave. Roaring breakers charged toward us, and the witch spun around, panic stamped across his face.

"*Impello!*"

The desperate cry came from behind me, and force struck my back. I fell to my knees, then launched up as four sorcerers charged at me, hands filled with artifacts.

"Don't kill her!" the witch screamed. "Not until the bond is mine!"

A barrage of magic slammed me into the mud again. As I crumpled, Llyrlethiad pushed at my mind with stern encouragements—get up, fight back, use the power he was giving me.

I sprang to my feet and flung my hands up commandingly— and the ocean rose in answer. A six-foot wave smashed into the sorcerers, hurling them off their feet and covering them in frothing water.

The nauseating sensation of my body being stretched out from within worsened, and I could feel Llyrlethiad's urgency. I whirled, scanning the rushing water as it crashed over my thighs. The last wave had knocked the witch down too. Where was he? Where had he gone?

Bodies flailed in the seawater, dark and unidentifiable. I turned, searching, desperate. The fae marks on my arm weren't as bright as they'd been a minute ago.

A flash of blue. There! The witch, his markings glowing like a beacon, was slogging through the shallow ocean toward the shore. I lunged after him, fighting the water. Too slow!

I waved my hand. The water parted in front of me.

Roaring furiously, a man launched into my path—the Red Rum leader. He thrust a carved metal disc at me and screamed the incantation. My hand leaped to my back pocket, but they'd taken my Queen of Spades.

"*Ori repercutio!*"

A familiar voice shouted the words, and the sorcerer's spell rebounded. As the man went down with a splash, I jerked around. Kai stood beside me, holding my card. The genius electramage had seen them take it from me—so he'd gotten it back.

I didn't have time to congratulate him as Llyrlethiad urged me on. Commanding the water to part again, I launched into a sprint. The fae's strength filled me, and the ground flew beneath my feet faster than I'd ever run in my life.

Ahead, the witch had reached the seawall. As he climbed onto it, he shouted something.

A dark shape appeared out of the rippling air. A steel-gray horse with poisonous green eyes reared up, screaming in fury at the human who commanded it. The witch jumped onto its back and the fae horse sprang at the sheer bluff Ezra had fallen down five nights ago. It charged up the near-vertical obstacle like it was a gentle incline.

I sprang over the seawall, closing in on the bluff and thinking frantically. How would *I* get up that bluff?

Llyrlethiad cast an image into my mind—swift instructions. Gulping, I ran up to the wall of rocky clay and leaped. Water coalesced out of the humid air. A geyser of wind and water formed under me and propelled me upward. I landed on the mossy ground at the top.

The thick foliage had slowed the horse fae. It wasn't far ahead, and I cast out my hand. A band of water smashed through the trees, tearing saplings out by the roots, but the horse sprang out of the bush and onto the trail. It veered left. They were heading toward the lookout point—the restaurant and parking lot. Would the witch try to flee by car?

I charged after him. The fae marks on my arm had faded even more.

As the horse galloped up the trail, Llyrlethiad poured more dizzying magic into my limbs. Running even faster, I slashed my hand again.

The band of water struck the fae horse's hindquarters. It lost its footing and fell, tumbling across the trail. The witch flew clear and landed hard, but he scrambled up and fled on human legs.

I tore past the downed horse, but my speed was flagging. Llyrlethiad's magic was weakening—and the marks on the witch's body glowed brighter. He dove into the bushes before I could summon more water.

Cutting through the trees after him, I came out at the edge of the parking lot, aglow with multicolored lights that flashed and spun, but I scarcely noticed. The witch bolted past the parked cars and closed restaurants. As I gave chase, my desperation twined so closely with Llyrlethiad's that I didn't know whose was whose.

The fae's magic was ebbing. His dizzying power was fading.

I ran harder, lungs screaming, legs burning. The witch was heedlessly sprinting toward the lookout point—a dead end.

There was nowhere else to flee. I would reach him. I would stop him. I stretched my hands out, calling on Llyrlethiad's magic.

With a whisper of despair, his presence disappeared.

The final shadow of the fae marks on my outstretched arm faded to nothing. Gone. The bond was gone.

At the lookout point's edge, the witch skidded to a stop and spun around, his back pressed to the rail as he gasped for breath. Magic glowed across his right side, shining through his clothes. He threw his head back and laughed in maniacal delight.

I was still running. The ground sloped down, urging me on.

"Llyrlethiad is mine!" he crowed. "Llyrlethiad, I command you to—"

Before the witch could complete the order that would end my life, I ran into him at full tilt.

My shoulder slammed into his sternum and he flipped backward over the railing. I caught the metal barrier before I fell over too, my chest heaving.

With a breathless grunt, the witch hit the steep, rocky ledge on the other side. He scrambled desperately for purchase on the crumbling rock and spindly weeds, sliding in slow motion over the edge.

Hanging half over the railing, I watched him slip out of sight.

His scream tore through the quiet park. The sound went on and on—then cut off as his body met the beach three hundred feet below. I stared at the spot where he had disappeared, eyes unblinking and mind blank.

The ocean shimmered. Waves broke across a finned, scaled back as the sea serpent surfaced. The leviathan lifted his head from the water and gazed across the distance between us with ivory eyes. Then he dove beneath the surface, vanishing without a trace.

My hand was stretched toward the cliff edge, but I didn't remember reaching out. My fingers trembled so badly I couldn't move them.

A boot scuffed against the pavement behind me. "Put your hands in the air!"

Confusion twisted through my numb thoughts. I'd expected Zak. Maybe Aaron or Ezra. But not …

"Put your hands in the air!" the older male voice bellowed again.

I lifted my quivering arms and slowly turned around.

Standing in a line on the next tier of the lookout were four police officers, their guns drawn and pointed at me. Flashing red and blue lights from the parking lot reflected off the restaurant's windows, and at the top of the sidewalk, two frightened late-night joggers clutched each other's arms.

Joggers. They must have heard something—the sounds of a mythic battle, perhaps. Or the gunfire when the Red Rum rogues had shot Zak. Whatever it was, they'd called the police.

And those four officers had just watched me chase a man to the lookout point and shove him off the cliff to his death.

22

MOST PEOPLE who know me—meaning people who know my temper—would be surprised to learn I've never been arrested. Well, my clean record was garbage now.

Sitting in the back of the police cruiser, I stared out the window. My whole body shook from exhaustion, but adrenaline kept me awake—adrenaline and throat-crushing dread.

Outside the car, a dozen officers and investigators bustled around the parking lot. An ambulance, its lights flashing, was parked in the corner, but the paramedics had yet to return from collecting the witch's body from the bottom of the cliff.

A dozen yards away, Aaron, Kai, and Ezra stood amongst a cluster of cops, handcuffed like me. Kai was speaking, the sharp movements of his head and shoulders betraying his anger. Olivia sat on the curb, also handcuffed and bawling her eyes out. A confused paramedic knelt beside her.

Two cops had a sniffer dog in the back of Zak's truck. I wondered what they'd find. The druid was too smart to leave evidence in his vehicle, and the license plate would be a dead end. He wasn't here with the mages—no, he was far too wily to get arrested. Like the Red Rum survivors, he'd disappeared.

All the doors of Aaron's car were open as several officers sorted through the contents of the glove box. One cop held my purse, already searched. I'd seen no sign of the guys' weapons, so they must have stashed them in the woods somewhere.

I leaned my heavy head against the glass, dizzy from the flashing lights reflecting off everything nearby. My chest hurt, but I didn't know if it was lingering pain from Llyrlethiad's possession or the weight of my conscience.

An hour ago, I had killed a man.

He'd been an evil man. He'd planned to murder me, Kai, Aaron, and Ezra. He'd been seconds away from commanding Llyrlethiad to kill me. By pushing him, I'd saved myself, my friends, and the fae lord. It had been the right thing to do … but logic was failing to calm my churning gut.

I had ended someone's life, an action that could never be undone. An evil man or not, the witch's death was a burden I'd have to bear for the rest of my life.

My lower lip trembled. Right about now would be a great time to get a hug from the guys. To hear their soothing assurances—that I'd done what I had to, that I'd saved everyone, that it had been the only way.

But I couldn't talk to them. I pressed my face to the glass.

Kai was still speaking angrily. Aaron took an aggressive step toward an officer and the man pushed him back. The disagreement reached a pitch, then an officer pulled out something small. He walked behind Aaron, fiddled for a moment, then stepped back, holding a pair of handcuffs.

Aaron rubbed his wrists, outrage radiating off him. The officer removed Kai's and Ezra's handcuffs, then pointed sternly at Aaron's little red sports car in obvious command. Instead of obeying, the three mages turned to the vehicle where I waited, their distress as obvious as a flashing sign.

Two officers walked away from the mages, heading toward me. They opened the cruiser's front doors, letting a wave of chaotic noise into the vehicle. They climbed in, settled into their seats, and the driver started the engine.

The cruiser pulled a slow U-turn and drove toward the exit. I pushed my nose into the glass, mentally reaching for Aaron, Kai, and Ezra as the car carried me past them. They stood helplessly in the middle of the parking lot. They were mythics. Police didn't arrest mythics.

But they could arrest a human, and there was nothing the guys could do to stop it.

THE ONLY QUESTION NOW was whether the charges would include first- or second-degree murder.

I slumped in the uncomfortable metal chair, staring blankly at my damp, haggard reflection in the mirrored window across from me. The interrogation room looked just like those in movies, except the table was smaller. They'd even chained my handcuffs to the bars on the tabletop.

Justin sat on the second chair, massaging my shoulder with one hand. I'd almost burst into tears when he walked in. And by "almost," I mean I'd wept like a baby for a solid five minutes.

Crumpling a tissue in my hand, I sniffed back the last of my meltdown and drew in a shaky breath. Squeezing my shoulder, Justin glowered at the mirrored window, then leaned close to my ear.

"Tori," he whispered. "What happened?"

I dabbed my tear-streaked cheeks with the tissue, handcuffs clinking. "It's all a mess."

He flattened his lips into a severe line. "Did you really push a man off—no, don't answer that. Wait for your lawyer."

Did I have a lawyer? I hadn't called one. Wasn't I supposed to get a phone call? Maybe this wasn't like the movies after all.

"This is bad, Tori," Justin went on. "Four officers and two civilians swear they saw you chase a man to the lookout point and shove him over the railing. That's a lot of witnesses with the exact same story."

My hands clenched into painful fists. I said nothing.

He rubbed his forehead, and when he looked up again, anguished concern wasn't the only emotion in his eyes. "The others found at the scene—there were three men, including an 'Aaron Sinclair.' That's your boyfriend, isn't it?"

Again, I said nothing. He didn't need my confirmation.

Justin leaned even closer, voice dropping to the barest whisper. "He had a mythic ID."

My gaze snapped up to his. He studied my expression, his mouth twisting.

"So you know." He brooded for a long moment. "As soon as I heard your boyfriend is a mythic, I realized that attack in Chinatown was no coincidence. You knew what those people were."

I bit my lip. "I didn't know what to tell you. I didn't know how much *you* knew."

"I only know what my training has covered." His eyes narrowed. "Seeing as you're *dating* one of them, I expect you know more than I do. What were you thinking, Tori? Getting involved with *them*?"

He said "them" like he was talking about the mafia. I opened my mouth to protest, but he went on in a low growl.

"I thought you were smarter than this. Of all the things to get involved in—"

"Stop," I hissed. "Just stop it, Justin. You have no idea what you're talking about."

He glared at me. "I would … if you'd ever mentioned it. Why didn't you tell me?"

As the hurt in his eyes overshadowed the anger, my shoulders hunched. I'd told so many lies recently that it had started to feel normal, but I hadn't needed to lie to Justin. I could have shared my recent crazy experiences with him. He already knew magic and mythics existed. I'd had no good reason to deceive him.

"I … I didn't think you'd understand."

He looked away, his jaw tight. As the silence stretched, I questioned every decision I'd made in the last few weeks.

"You should have told me," he muttered. "Maybe I could have prevented this … but now it's too late."

I sagged forward, too exhausted and emotionally spent to respond. This time, he didn't speak. One hour dragged into two, then three. Justin shifted in his seat, as uncomfortable as I was. He could've left, but he didn't. Even angry and betrayed, he stuck by my side.

Fighting through my shame, I took his hand in both of mine. He squeezed my fingers, holding tight, and grateful tears pricked my eyes. I blinked them back. All week, I'd been freaking out over MagiPol's investigation as though getting kicked out of the mythic community was the worst thing that could happen to me. Instead, I'd ruined my life. What would prison be like? Not fun, I knew that much.

After what felt like fifty years, the door opened and an older cop stepped inside. "Officer Dawson."

Justin released my hands and crossed to the older cop. They put their heads together, whispering.

"What?" Justin jerked back. "But they have no jurisdiction over—"

The older cop hissed something, then took Justin's arm. My brother shot me a panicked look as the man drew him out of the room. The door snapped shut.

I stared at the mirrored window, too weary to panic. Llyrlethiad's magic had done a number on me. I'd never felt this tired and worn out in my life. My head was too heavy to hold up. Breathing took conscious effort.

As I was contemplating taking a nap on the table, the door opened again. A female officer walked in, a set of keys in her hand, while a male officer lingered in the doorway.

The woman detached my handcuffs from the table. "Come with us, Miss Dawson."

I dragged myself out of the chair, every muscle throbbing. "Where're we going?"

"This way."

I followed the pair into a sterile hallway. We didn't go far— only a few doors down. The lady officer indicated I should go first, so I stepped into the room.

It was another interrogation room, smaller and without the one-way glass. And unlike the last one, two people were already seated behind the table, waiting for me. I blinked at the vaguely familiar man, trying to place him. The officers didn't follow me in, and instead closed the door behind me.

"Take a seat, Miss Dawson," the man said.

His voice was even more familiar than his face. I minced forward and sank into one of the two chairs facing the duo, cuffed hands resting awkwardly on my lap. His brown hair was buzzed short and hers was slicked back in a boring ponytail. They both wore black suits, like Hollywood FBI agents.

The man pulled a pair of dark-rimmed glasses from his pocket, unfolded them, and placed them precisely on his nose. He flipped open the brown folder in front of him.

"Victoria Dawson, goes by the name Tori. Twenty-one years old. Five-foot-seven, red hair, hazel eyes. Born in Peterborough, Ontario, to Michael and Carol Dawson." He flipped the top page over. "You've fallen into unfortunate company, Miss Dawson."

"Who are you?" I asked hoarsely.

He slid a finger down the page. "Tell me, Miss Dawson. When did you first learn about the Crow and Hammer guild?"

At the word "guild," my tired brain put it together. All the air vanished from my lungs. Not FBI agents.

MPD agents.

These were the same two agents who'd gatecrashed the guild's monthly meeting, tried to arrest Ezra, questioned half the guild, searched the premises, and stalked the guys in an attempt to unravel the mystery of who had helped them apprehend the River couple four weeks ago.

While I sat in stunned silence, the man—Agent Harris—adjusted his glasses. "It is in your best interest to speak, Miss Dawson."

"Remaining silent will gain you nothing," the woman added with all the emotion of a fax machine.

My mouth hung open. I closed it, silently panicking. "I want a lawyer."

Agent Harris *tsked* softly. "You seem to be under the impression that we function like the human justice system. We most certainly do not. Lawyers have no role in our system, and the MPD is both prosecutor and judge. It is *your* responsibility to prove your innocence."

He flipped to a new page in his folder, also full of typed notes. "Let me help you out, Miss Dawson. We already know you've been associating with the Crow and Hammer for at least three months. You've been present on the premises and involved with several of its members on a daily basis. You've inserted yourself into mythic investigations. You've obtained and used illegal artifacts—on your fellow humans, no less."

"We're also in the process of proving your association with the wanted rogue known as The Ghost," the woman said, tacking it on like an afterthought.

"Tonight, you killed a man in front of four police officers. The fact he was a rogue mythic will mean nothing to the human courts." Agent Harris leaned back in his seat. "However, if you cooperate, we'll certainly put in a good word for you. Perhaps they'll even believe you acted in self-defense."

He wanted me to betray the Crow and Hammer for the slim chance I could avoid a murder charge. He wanted me to throw them all to the MagiPol wolves.

I bared my teeth. "Go to hell."

Agent Harris snorted. "You fit in well with the Crow and Hammer mythics, I see. In that case—"

The door handle clacked and a breeze hit my back as the door was swung open with enthusiasm. I didn't look, too busy glaring at the agents to see which cop was butting in on our—

The chair beside me pulled away from the table. "My apologies for being late."

I knew that voice. Unable to believe my ears, I jerked toward the man settling into the seat beside me.

23

DARIUS, GUILD MASTER of the Crow and Hammer, snuck me a wink as he dropped a thick folder on the tabletop. I gawked witlessly. Despite it being the middle of the damn night, his salt-and-pepper hair was neatly combed, his short beard was groomed, and his casual dress shirt and slacks were crisply ironed.

"Brennan, how are you?" Darius flashed a polite smile. "Your hours this week have been intense, haven't they? I hope you qualify for overtime pay."

Agent Harris glared through his glasses. "You are not invited to this meeting, Darius. We'll summon you for questioning when we're ready."

"On the contrary, I have every right to be present while you're interrogating one of my guildeds."

"She isn't a member of your guild—or any guild," Agent Harris snapped.

"*Pending* guild member," Darius clarified with easy cheer. "Which means, as you know, I can choose to exercise my full rights as her GM."

"She—is—a—*human*," Agent Harris ground out. "She can't be a guild member, pending or otherwise. Humans can *work* for a guild—*with* MPD approval—but they cannot be inducted as members."

"Very true, very true. However"—Darius put his elbows on the table, fingers steepled—"Tori is a mythic."

Agent Harris's mouth fell open. So did mine.

I recovered fast, pretending that hadn't been a bombshell equivalent to a cattle prod being jammed up my ass.

Outraged, Agent Harris looked between us, then slapped a hand against his open folder, his professional façade evaporating. "I won't tolerate your bullshit, Darius, not this time. We *know* she's human. We already checked her background, lineage, and family history. She's as human as it's possible to be."

"It would seem that way," Darius replied, unfazed, "but she was merely undiscovered. It's rare, but—"

"An undiscovered *what*?" Agent Harris interrupted.

"A witch, of course."

I clenched my jaw to keep my mouth closed. Ha-ha, funny, right? I waited for the punch line.

"She is a witch," Darius repeated into the terse silence. "For a mythic who's lived her entire life in cities, it's not surprising she never saw a fae before arriving at the Crow and Hammer. Indeed, when she stumbled into my guild, she believed she was human. But"—he tapped his nose slyly—"I had my suspicions. I hired her as a bartender—"

"You didn't file the paperwork for that!"

"I admit I delayed her paperwork. I didn't want to trouble your busy administrative branch with unnecessary forms when I was expecting to submit different ones in short order." He smiled. "And lo, Tori soon displayed her aptitude for Spiritalis."

Uh, no. I definitely hadn't.

Agent Harris barked a harsh laugh. "Too ambitious, Darius. If you wanted to pretend she's a mythic, you should have picked a better class. Psychica is far easier to fake. Hell, you could have signed her into a demon contract if it was that important to induct her into your guild."

Darius opened his folder, lifted out a form, and continued to lie so smoothly that I was left in awe of his skill. "This, as you can see, is the preliminary paperwork for her registration as a mythic. Signed and dated four weeks ago, though I'm afraid my overworked AGM hasn't had a chance to submit it."

I peeked at the form as he slid it to Agent Harris. There, at the bottom, was my signature in a big ugly scribble like I always did. I would kiss whoever had forged it so perfectly.

"And this"—Darius handed over another thick packet—"is the documentation for her induction into the guild. You'll find my handwritten notes from our interview, dated three weeks ago."

Clamping down on the urge to hug Darius, I tried to look like none of this surprised me.

Agent Harris flipped through the forms, then shoved them aside. "Impressive forgeries, Darius. Do you really expect me to believe any of this?"

"If you have doubts, we can proceed to an arbitration panel, as per MPD policy. Though," Darius added with a smile that held all the warmth of an arctic storm, "I don't see how you or anyone else could prove these documents are fake."

Agent Harris bared his teeth. "The documents don't matter. What matters is this woman is *not* a witch. You can't prove she's a Spiritalis mythic. Without proof, she's headed straight to a prison cell. We will not allow you to play us for fools."

Darius swiveled in his chair to face me. His expression was solemn but his eyes sparked with fierce enjoyment. He *loved* messing with the MPD. "Tori, could you please summon your familiar for Brennan?"

My familiar? But I *didn't have a familiar.*

I'd scarcely begun to panic when the corner of the room inexplicably darkened. A hulking shape emerged from the shadows—stubby snout gaping to show a mouthful of teeth, red eyes blazing like they were about to shoot lasers.

The six-foot-tall Godzilla roared loud enough to rattle the door.

Agent Harris leaped out of his chair, sending it crashing to the floor. His partner remained seated, blinking bemusedly.

I stared at the mini Godzilla. "Twiggy?"

The monster's form blurred and shrank. Green skin and branchy limbs solidified, then the small faery leaped onto my lap, his huge eyes bright and his expression a mixture of pride and apprehension.

A flicker of warmth ran through my upper left arm. Air rippling, a long bluish serpent emerged from nothing. Hoshi hovered above my head, her tail sweeping down to curl around my shoulders.

"Behold," Darius announced dryly, "Tori's familiars."

Agent Harris looked from the faery to the sylph, then angrily righted his chair and sat. "How do we know those are *her* fae?"

"Tori is my human!" Twiggy squeaked, thin chest puffing with anger. "We live in our house and she plays movies for me and I chase the fat man out when he comes in to snoop."

"The fat man?" Darius murmured curiously.

"My landlord," I whispered back.

"Where's your familiar mark?" Agent Harris demanded, smugness crossing his face.

"Do you need to get your glasses checked, Brennan?" Darius tapped my arm. "It's right here."

I looked at my left arm. The rune circle Zak had drawn stood out sharply against my pale skin.

"That's black pen," Agent Harris barked. "Go on. Wipe it off."

Darius licked his thumb and rubbed it vigorously against my arm. The liner barely smudged. I would've told him it was waterproof, but I was terrified of what would happen once someone washed it off and this whole façade crumbled.

Silently, the female agent lifted her purse off the floor, pulled out a packet of makeup remover wipes, and handed me one. I squinted at her face. Why was she carrying these? I couldn't see a trace of makeup on her.

Twiggy wrinkled his nose at the smell and hopped off my lap. Nerves pounding in my throat, I pressed the damp towelette against my arm, my wrists held awkwardly to accommodate the handcuffs. I counted to ten, then wiped downward.

The black washed away—and in its place were aquamarine lines in the exact shape of the fancy spell Zak had drawn. As I lifted my arm to peer at it more closely, the blue markings gleamed with pink tones. Hoshi gently squeezed me with her tail, a silent reassurance.

As I wiped off the rest of the eyeliner, Darius beamed. "A clever way to disguise her familiar mark, don't you think?"

Agent Harris seethed for a long minute, a vein pulsing in his temple. Jerking his glasses off his face, he shoved them in his breast pocket. "We'll be confirming her familiar bond as soon as we can get a witch out."

"Of course."

"Don't think we're done, Darius," the agent snarled, shoving all the forms into his folder and snapping it shut. "You hired a human at your guild without clearance, identified an undiscovered mythic without registering her, and involved that unregistered mythic in supernatural activity. We haven't forgotten the River case either. *And* there will be an investigation into the events at Stanley Park tonight."

Darius nodded placidly.

Agent Harris stood. "Expect a full list of the charges and fines against your guild by Monday."

"I'll eagerly await them," Darius replied. "In turn, I expect you to eagerly inform all appropriate parties that Victoria Dawson and the rogue's death are now under the MPD's jurisdiction. The police will need to cease their investigation and expunge all records of her arrest."

Agent Harris grunted and strode to the door, the female agent on his heels.

"Oh, and Brennan?" Darius propped an arm on the back of his chair. "I think it would be in everyone's best interests for you to expedite the processing of Tori's registration and guild induction paperwork. You already have the forms."

The agent snarled something incomprehensible, stormed through the door, and slammed it shut, almost clobbering his partner. She had to open the door again to leave, but unlike Harris, she closed it like a mature, emotionally stable adult.

Silence fell over the small room. Her tail draped over me, Hoshi undulated placidly. I stared at Darius, stunned and speechless.

"How are you feeling, Tori?" he asked kindly.

"I—I—I'm not sure. Relieved? I think?" I twitched my wrists, jingling the metal cuffs. Twiggy watched me anxiously. "Also confused. How did you … all that stuff …?"

Darius rubbed his beard ruefully. "It's been a hectic few hours, I admit. Once we realized there was no way to clear you of the impending murder charges, the only solution was to shift you out of the human justice system and into our own. The paperwork wasn't an issue, but what to register you as …"

"A witch?" I muttered, shaking my head.

"It wasn't the first thing to occur to me." An odd smile tugged at his lips. "As we were debating whether you'd learned enough taromancy to fool an MPD agent, I received a call from an unknown number.

"The mysterious caller gave no name. Not one for small talk either. But he made a few highly salient points. He said a human who contracts with a demon is considered a mythic, so a human—like you—who has a familiar bond with a fae should also be considered a mythic. I agreed that sounded reasonable, and he told me to convince the MPD of the same. Then he hung up."

Every part of that, especially the rude hang up, sounded like someone I knew. I looked down at my arm, Hoshi's magic glowing faintly over my skin. A familiar mark. That sneaky druid.

"I confess I was worried when it came time to call your familiar," Darius added thoughtfully. "I wasn't sure you had one."

I turned to Twiggy, who didn't normally venture far from the house. "How did you know to come here?"

"The Crystal Druid called us to him!" Twiggy chirped happily. "He told us to find you and wait for the right moment. Was it the right moment?"

"It was definitely the right moment," I replied, cautiously observing Darius's reaction to Twiggy's mention of "the Crystal Druid."

Darius gave me another wink. Of course. He was too smart not to suspect who his mysterious caller had been—or who had helped us summon a darkfae in Stanley Park, assuming the guys had filled their GM in on that part.

Anxiety trickled through me. "Darius, what about the charges against the guild? What about—"

"Don't worry about that, my dear. Dealing with the MPD is *my* job. It's one of the many privileges that come with being your guild master."

A slow roll of emotion left me dizzy. "My guild master …"

His mood sobered. "I must apologize, Tori. I couldn't ask you in advance if you wanted this, but it was the only way to keep you out of prison. You're registered as a mythic, meaning all our laws, both good and bad, now govern your life."

Laws, shmaws. That wasn't what I cared about. "Am I a member of the Crow and Hammer now?"

"Yes, you are."

A grin spread across my face, so wide it hurt, and tears pricked my eyes. Tossing decorum out the window, I threw my handcuffed wrists over Darius's head and hugged him, doing my best not to strangle him in the process.

"Thank you," I choked out.

He returned the hug with an extra squeeze. "I'm delighted to welcome you to the guild. Our very own mythical human."

"Mythical human," I repeated as I sat back in my chair, equally amused and amazed. "Can we make that an official class?"

Chuckling, Darius gathered up his folder. "Shall we? I think dear Agent Harris has had enough time to clear you for release."

Ten minutes and one handcuff removal later, I walked out of the station and into the gloriously fresh air, the horizon stained by the orange tinge of dawn. Vaguely missing the feel of Hoshi's little paws, I rolled my shoulders. I'd already sent her and Twiggy home, where they couldn't shock any policemen.

Standing at the bottom of the steps and casting long shadows across the sidewalk, three figures waited.

A spurt of energy revived my flagging strength, and I sprinted down the steps two at a time, arms outstretched. In the next moment, I was engulfed in a three-way hug and I hardly knew who I had my arms around.

"Guys!" I gasped. Then I burst into tears. Again.

"Tori!" Aaron half laughed.

I gulped back my hysteria after one sob, and Kai produced a handkerchief to dry my cheeks. I squeezed Aaron's and Ezra's necks, refusing to release them.

"How'd it go?" Aaron directed the question over my shoulder, and I looked around as Darius joined us.

He smiled like a proud father. "I arrived just as she was telling dear Agent Harris to go to hell. The rest went about as planned."

Aaron clamped me against his chest, his strong arms squeezing the air out of me. "Then you're a mythic now."

"Darius says I'm a mythical human. My very own class. Pretty cool, huh?"

He laughed exuberantly. "I love it. You're a misfit just like the rest of us Crow and Hammer myth—"

"Tori!"

I peeled out of Aaron's arms as Justin ran down the stairs, his hair rumpled and stress lines around his eyes. As his wary gaze snapped across the four men, I stepped away from them.

"Justin! Did you hear? I'm a free woman—"

"Tori," he interrupted tersely, grabbing my arm and pulling me farther from the others. "They said you're under *their* jurisdiction."

"Yes, that's right."

His hazel eyes were frantic. "But you're not one of *them*."

"It's a long story." And I had no idea where to begin. Was I *allowed* to explain? Didn't matter, because I was telling my brother the truth whether MagiPol liked it or not. "I'll explain everything later, okay? I need to go. I'm beat."

"Tori," he tried again. "You don't—do you have any idea what you—"

"Actually, I do." I took a deep breath. "Justin, I'm sorry I kept secrets from you, and I promise I'll tell you all about it. But now isn't the time. They're waiting for me."

Justin's expression darkened. "I'll take you home. You don't belong with them."

Anger sparked through me and I struggled to keep my tone even. "That's my choice."

His jaw tightened. "You killed someone, Tori. Don't pretend that had nothing to do with these people. Even if you don't go to jail, *you killed someone.* Is this the road you want to go down?"

My stomach twisted painfully. I pulled my arm out of his hand. "I'll call you this evening."

"Tori—"

Each step hurt me, but I walked away. Making Justin understand wouldn't be easy and I didn't have the time or energy to talk him through it now. I'd smooth things over with him later.

When I reached the guys, I slung my arms around the two nearest me—Aaron and Kai—and together we walked away from the station.

24

AFTER THIRTY HOURS of sleep in the last forty-eight, you'd *think* I'd be well rested.

I stifled a yawn as the instructor described the class syllabus and major assignments. After missing the first three days of the fall semester, I'd refused to skip my Friday class. I was kind of regretting it, though. Nothing could put me to sleep faster than the droning of an old man who spoke at the same pitch as a distant vacuum cleaner.

Glancing at the clock—fifteen more minutes—I stretched my legs out and slipped my phone under the long table. It blinked with a new message.

I rolled my eyes. It had to be Aaron, reminding me that he planned to walk me to work. He, along with a healer and two alchemists, had tried to convince me to skip school *and* work today so I could start fresh on Tuesday instead. But I'd already missed two weeks of work since that first MPD raid, and I wasn't missing another day. My bank account was alarmingly low.

Opening my messaging app, I read the brief text.

I'm in the atrium. Get out here.

Halfway through the thought that the pyromage sounded awfully grumpy today, I checked the sender. The message wasn't from Aaron.

A startled yelp escaped me. As the instructor squinted in my direction, I rammed my laptop into my purse and shoved back from the table.

"Sorry," I called as I rushed to the door. "Family emergency. Have to go!"

I bolted into the hallway. The atrium, he'd said. I zoomed to the nearest stairwell and descended to the second level, then jogged down a long corridor of classrooms. The hall opened into a two-story space with huge windows that arched over the roof like skylights.

At the staircase railing, I looked down. A couple dozen students wandered through the lobby-like space below, coming in and out of the library that bordered it. A few more were seated on the U-shaped banks of seats along the wall and—

There. A man in a gray sweater, the hood drawn up, leaned against a wide pillar.

I sprinted down the stairs and across the tiled floor. He glanced up from his phone, sunlight striking his handsome face.

"Zak!" I slid to a halt, scanned him from head to toe, then grabbed him in a hug.

He grunted as I squeezed him. "You're strangling me."

"You're alive!"

"Not if you keep strangling me."

I released him and stepped back—then smacked his shoulder with enough force to sting my hand. "Why didn't you text me sooner? I was afraid you'd died."

"Of course I didn't die." He rolled his otherworldly green eyes. "Who do you take me for?"

"I seem to remember you getting *shot*—multiple times!—so excuse me if I was concerned about your survival."

Since he'd called Darius on the night of my arrest, I'd known he made it out of the park alive, but with nothing but radio silence since, I'd been having nightmares about him dying from his untreated wounds.

"I didn't get shot." His mouth twisted. "Well, yes, I did, but being attacked from behind is a possibility I usually account for. I wasn't entirely prepared for bullets, but the damage wasn't life-threatening."

A zing of realization ran through me. Back in the parking lot, before we'd summoned Bhardudlin, Zak had pulled his shirt up to show me the spellwork drawn on his side. Protection sorcery?

"If you *weren't* severely injured," I demanded, "why didn't you contact me?"

"I was busy."

"Too busy to reply to a single message?" I planted my hands on my hips. "You're an ass."

"So you've told me. I'm here now, aren't I?"

Indeed he was, and that was the most surprising thing about this impromptu meeting. "Why *are* you here?"

He scrutinized my face. "Hasn't that guild been giving you vitality potions? You're still pale."

"I'm always pale. And yes, they have." I wrinkled my nose. "Theirs taste terrible compared to yours."

His lips twitched up like I'd surprised him with a compliment.

"I brought you a few more doses." He swung a backpack off his shoulder—deliberately or not, he resembled a student more than I would've expected—and pulled out a paper bag that clinked with bottles. "Here."

I groaned as I took it. "This looks like you're delivering booze to a minor."

"You're not a minor."

"That's beside the point. How did you find me, anyway?"

"There was a time when I had reason to investigate everything about you. Also, Twiggy told me you were at 'the boring place.' I figured it out from there." He slung his bag over his shoulder. "Did your GM sort things out with the police?"

A grin overtook me and I dug into my purse. Whipping out a blue and white ID card, I proudly displayed it. "Ta-da!"

He peered at the card and a slow smile curved his mouth, warming his eyes. "You have an MID number now. Good."

"In part thanks to you." I stuffed the card back in my purse. "I can't believe you made Hoshi my familiar without telling me."

"Did they register you as a witch?"

I bobbed my head in a nod. "I wish I was a real one, but fake is better than nothing."

"You are a real witch."

My good humor evaporated. "Don't screw with my head, Zak."

He scowled. "Your relationships with fae aren't fake, so why would you be a fake witch? Weren't you listening when I said you can be human *and* mythic?"

"When did you say that?"

He huffed in exasperation. "Magic is a tool, not a birthright. If we were limited to what we inherit, then witches and druids wouldn't have familiars—we aren't born with those, are we? There'd be no such thing as contractors. Mages wouldn't use switches. Sorcerers would only use artifacts they made themselves."

As his meaning sank in, the floor shifted under my feet.

"A mythic is anyone who *uses* magic. You"—he rapped his knuckles against my skull—"are just as much a mythic as I am. The only difference is you started at zero."

I swallowed hard. "But the MPD says—"

He leaned down, meeting my eyes. "You chose this, Tori. Choice is more powerful than fate."

I goggled at him. He was right. I had *chosen* to take up magic and learn to use it. Was I so different from a witch or a sorcerer just because I couldn't sense energies or create spells myself?

Zak straightened and rolled his shoulders. "I need to go."

"Already?" I jiggled the paper bag of bottles. "You came all this way to give me a few potions?"

"I also came to say goodbye."

Alarm shot through me, and I remembered what he'd said back at Aaron's house. "You're going into hiding?"

He nodded.

"What about Nadine? Did you find a safe place for her?"

"I put her on a plane an hour ago. She has a surprising number of relatives in England eager to take her in. She'll be safe there."

Wow, England. That would be fun for Nadine. But ... "What about you? Where will you go?"

"Off the grid—into the mountains first, and after that …" Shrugging, he held up his phone. "I won't be taking this or any other method of communication."

My throat constricted. "For how long?"

"Long enough for my enemies to forget about me." He pushed off the pillar. "Now you know, so don't expect me to respond to your weekly insults."

"You never responded anyway," I said hoarsely. "Zak …"

"It's been interesting, Tori." He stepped away from me. "Stay out of trouble—if you can."

"Zak—"

Shadows rippled off his shoulders—Lallakai's wings sweeping around him.

"*Zak!*"

My shout rang through the atrium, but it was too late. He'd already disappeared from my perception.

Ignoring the stares from the nearby students—none of whom had been paying enough attention to realize a man had vanished into thin air—I clenched my hands. How could he just *leave* like this? I dropped onto the nearest chair. At least he'd said goodbye before going off on a secretive druid sabbatical.

A slight smile turned up my lips. He'd said goodbye like a proper friend—not that he'd ever admit we were friends.

I sat for a minute longer, then checked the clock on my phone. "Shit!"

Shoving the bag of potions into my purse, I speed-walked to the main entrance and out the doors. Clouds dotted the sky and the sun peeked out, golden beams streaking toward the ground. At the top of the steps, I paused.

Aaron stood beside a blocky cement planter, gazing idly at the passing students. His copper hair gleamed, his rugged jaw clean-shaven, and his blue shirt clung to his torso in just the right way. Every woman who walked by snuck an admiring look; his biceps had a magnetic force all their own.

I hopped down the steps. He spotted me, a grin flashing over his face. The bruise-like circles that had lurked under his eyes since the battle in Stanley Park had almost faded.

"Hey!" I said brightly, catching him in a one-armed hug. "Sorry I'm late."

His grin melted into sorrow. "I'd drive you to work instead of walking, but my baby is still in the shop."

The problem with older cars: mechanics didn't have spare rear windows lying around.

As we headed down the sidewalk, he told me about the fit Agent Harris had thrown after Darius had weaseled me out of trouble. By all accounts, it had been spectacular. The Crow and Hammer, however, wasn't the only guild on the MPD's shit list. The Stanley Coven was also in trouble for failing to report the Red Rum activity in their territory.

Speaking of the coven, I hadn't seen Olivia or Odette since the whole fiasco, but the day after, I *had* received a monster-sized gift basket overflowing with organic baked goods. Both sisters, as well as a dozen other witches, had signed the accompanying card. So far, Twiggy had eaten about half its contents. When he woke up from his food coma, he'd probably eat the rest. I should've hidden the chocolate muffins to save for myself.

Aaron asked about Justin, but I quickly changed the subject. I'd talked to my brother twice since my arrest, and neither conversation had gone well. He didn't want to hear anything good about mythics; he wanted me to move in with him again so he could go full Big Brother on me.

As Aaron and I talked, one topic failed to come up. I didn't expect it to, but the fact neither he nor Kai had mentioned it hung over me like a little cloud, its shadow catching my attention every now and then.

Neither of them had mentioned Ezra's terrifying crimson magic that had laid out a monstrous darkfae.

Whatever Ezra had done, it was part of his secrets—his power, his temper, his scars. I understood I wasn't supposed to ask. I wasn't supposed to bring it up. So, I buried the questions down deep, vowing not to think about it. I would willfully forget until the day came for me to learn the truth.

My steps picked up a happy bounce as we neared the guild, and Aaron chuckled. "This excited to work?"

"Hell yes. I don't do well with idleness."

"Idleness? Is that how you describe getting bound to a fae lord, battling a rogue guild, and giving MagiPol their worst migraine of the month?"

"Not that. The whole bed-rest-recovery thing. Also, I did a lot of sitting around before the exciting stuff."

"Well, you won't be doing much sitting around after this." His grin stretched his lips as we stopped at an intersection, waiting for the light to change. "You'll be busy learning how to be a mythic."

Remembering Zak's words of wisdom, my chest swelled with happiness. "I'm okay with that."

"We'll start with defense training," Aaron mused, starting across the street. "And I'll talk to Ramsey about artifacts we can set you up with."

"Uh." I stood rock-still for a moment, then jogged to catch up. "Wait, wait. Defense training? I thought you meant, like, learning the rules and stuff."

"That too, but you need training. You can't rely on a couple of artifacts and Hoshi for protection. She's not a powerful fae." He tapped his chin. "You should resume martial arts as well. You used to take taekwondo, right?"

"Why do I need protection?" I yelped, grabbing his arm to slow his pace like that might slow his ideas about my "training."

"Mythics tend to ignore humans, but you're in the system now. You aren't invisible anymore."

"What, are other mythics going to attack me?"

"No, but you should be able to hold your own." He smiled eagerly. "That means we finally get to train you!"

My eyes narrowed. "Finally? What do you mean, *finally*?"

"Well ... Kai and I may have already discussed routines to start you on."

"When was that?"

"Uh ... a couple months ago."

I might've berated him, but the guild's three-story building had come into view down the street. Eagerness swept through me and I felt as bubbly as a kid on her first day of kindergarten. I tried to extend my stride, but Aaron pulled me back.

"Tori, there's something I've been meaning to talk to you about."

My inner child tripped and fell on her face. I attempted to look curious instead of panicked by his reluctant tone. "What?"

He stopped, and I nervously faced him. His gaze traveled across my features, lingering on my eyes. "We've been sort of dating the last couple of months and, well ..."

My heart skidded across my ribs. No, no, no. He was going to ask me to be his girlfriend. Or to be serious about our relationship. Or ask what my problem was. I wasn't ready for any of those questions.

"I know how you feel"—he flicked his hand back and forth between our chests—"about us. It's okay, I get it."

"You … you know?"

"This isn't going anywhere, is it?" He studied my face. "I've been thinking it's time to call it quits. What do you think?"

"Me?" I struggled to pull my thoughts together. "I—I mean, I don't … I didn't …"

Amusement touched his eyes. "Wow, you're terrible at this."

I really was, and I needed to do better. He deserved a proper explanation. "Aaron, it isn't anything you did. You've been nothing but amazing and—"

He stepped close and cupped my chin with one warm hand. Tilting my face up, he placed a soft kiss on my lips. "Don't freak, Tori. It's fine. Having great chemistry doesn't make us a perfect couple, and if it isn't working, then it isn't working. Let's not destroy our friendship trying to force it."

"Our friendship," I repeated softly.

His intense blue eyes met mine. "We're good, right, Tori?"

"Yeah." A relieved smile pulled at my lips. "We're good."

His mischievous grin flashed. "Glad that's over with. I was worried I'd take too long and you'd dump me first. I'd never live *that* down."

"I wouldn't have—wait." I squinted indignantly. "Are you suggesting *you* dumped *me*?"

"Um, by the way, Kai totally betrayed your confidence and told me everything you said."

"*What?*" I growled, knowing he'd derailed me on purpose but unable to ignore it. "He didn't! And why are you telling me? Now you've betrayed *his* confidence."

"It seemed fitting." Aaron linked our arms. "We need to get in there before you're late."

"I'm not late. It isn't even three thirty."

"Actually"—Aaron stopped in front of the Crow and Hammer's door, painted with a fierce crow perched on a war mallet—"you *are* late. I told them I'd have you here by twenty after."

"Told who?" I asked blankly.

Grinning, he grasped the handle. "Welcome home, Tori."

Then he swung the door open.

"*Surprise!*"

The blast of sound hit me like an ocean wave and I stumbled back. Aaron pushed me inside.

The familiar dim interior, with its dark wood finishes and beamed ceiling, was filled with mythics. Over half the guild was assembled, every person cheering at my appearance. Hands reached out and dragged me into the crowd.

Faces spun as I was passed around for congratulatory hugs. Girard, the first officer, his thick beard almost hiding his broad grin; Zora and Felix, the mismatched married duo; Ramsey, the cook and artifact expert; Kaveri and her witch boyfriend; Andrew, the team leader; Lyndon, the counter-magic sorcerer; Sabrina and Rose, the two diviners; Liam, the telekinetic, his round sunglasses crooked on his nose.

Even more faces blurred together until a pair of hands caught my waist and pulled me from the chaos. Strong arms—and a heavenly scent—engulfed me. I looked up into Ezra's grin. Kai stood beside him, his smile equally as broad.

"What—what—" I babbled coherently.

"New member party," Ezra informed me. "It's a tradition."

"It is?"

"No," Kai corrected. "We've never had one before."

My brow furrowed. "Then why now?"

"Because it's you."

Oh jeez. Was someone cutting onions in here? I blinked rapidly.

Aaron fought his way through the boisterous crowd and half collapsed against the bar. "Gah. The gang is rowdy today. Hey Cooper!"

Cooper, our lazy cook and part-time bartender, popped through the saloon doors. "Huh? What?"

"Are you serving drinks or what? Why do you think we called you in for this?"

"Of course I'm serving drinks." He waved vaguely at the gathered mythics. "Where d'ya think they all got their glasses?"

"Well, get us some—"

"Cooper!" Gwen hollered from the other end of the bar. "Sylvia is buying me a Manhattan. Hurry up and make the gob-spitting thing before she changes her mind!"

Stumbling in his haste, Cooper rushed away. Aaron heaved a sigh.

Ezra pulled a stool out for me, and I'd scarcely sunk onto the seat when a streak of blue hair announced Sin's approach. She popped out from between Taye and Delta to swoop down on me for a hug.

"You're back!" She squeezed the air out of me. "How are you feeling? Are the potions working?"

They were working, but at the cost of my taste buds. Thank goodness I had Zak's sugary ones tucked away in my purse.

"Yep. I feel almost back to normal." I flexed my measly biceps. "Aaron is already planning my new workout routine so I can handle the next fae lord better."

She snickered. "You have a familiar now, right? Where is it? And where'd you get it? No one seems to know."

The three mages ignored her squinty-eyed look.

"My familiar is shy," I replied quickly. "I'll introduce her another time."

"Tori!" Clara rushed over, her brown hair spilling out of its bun. "Welcome back! We missed you so much!"

"Thanks Clara," I wheezed as she hugged me. I wasn't sure how many more hugs I could handle. Someone called for Sin and she moved away from the bar.

The assistant guild master beamed like it was my high school graduation. "Before I forget, I have something for you. After you, ah, left the park on Tuesday night, our team tracked down several Red Rum rogues who couldn't get away fast enough. They all had outstanding bounties, so I divvied up the payout."

"But I didn't …"

"You earned your share!" She stuffed a plain white envelope into my hand. "Also, Darius decided your time off was paid personal leave, so your paycheck hasn't changed—oh, except I deducted your guild membership fee. I figured that would be easier for you."

"Y-yeah."

She smiled distractedly. "Darius is waiting for me upstairs. We're still figuring out paperwork for … stuff. I'll see you later." Three steps away, she called back, "And Cooper is taking your shift tonight, so enjoy the party!"

Holding the envelope like it was a live bomb, I looked at the guys. "Um, speaking of Red Rum, how scared should we be?"

"Not very." Aaron shrugged. "It's gonna take them a while to recover."

"What do you mean?"

"Didn't you tell her?" Kai smiled evilly. "The Red Rum yacht set sail after the ritual fell apart, but later that night, the ship capsized. The Coast Guard is still searching for survivors."

My eyes went huge.

"It's a big, deeply rooted rogue guild," Aaron added. "The bastards will bounce back, but here's hoping they'll be more worried about the sea god they royally pissed off than our little guild."

Wow. Go Llyrlethiad! I hoped he was angry enough to sink every Red Rum boat he found for the next, oh, ten years ought to do it.

Still absorbing the news, I opened the envelope Clara had given me and peered at the stack of crisp bills. Ah. Look at that. Hundred-dollar bills. Lots of them.

"You can get your apartment fixed," Aaron said.

"Or you can get a tattoo," Ezra suggested, tapping the fae mark on my upper arm. "How about a full sleeve? A skull would look great."

"A skull?"

"With a rose in its teeth. And a crown of thorns." He nodded to himself. "You should get something fresh and original like that."

I snorted so hard I almost choked, and his grin came to life.

"Tori," he began.

A burst of cheering drowned him out.

"Whoa!" Aaron pointed across the room. "What is Bryce chugging?"

The guild's telepath was pouring an entire bottle of something down his throat while half a dozen people chanted his name. Aaron hurried over to catch the action, and Kai followed with a smirk.

I turned back to Ezra. "What were you saying?"

As the noise level increased, he stepped close to my stool and put his mouth to my ear.

"I promised everything would go back to normal. I was wrong. It didn't." He leaned back to meet my questioning gaze, his mismatched eyes warm. "But I think this is better."

Another roar from the drinking group drowned out my attempt to respond. Laughing, I caught his hand, conveying my thanks with a touch instead.

Aaron and Kai reappeared, shaking their heads.

"Crazy bastard," Aaron remarked. "Anyway, we were planning to do a round of celebratory shots, but it might be a while before Cooper makes it back over here."

I glanced down the bar. The man in question was flailing through a set of cocktails. Sylvia had her arms folded, her mouth twisted in a familiar disapproving scowl as he botched her precious Manhattan.

Throwing my shoulders back, I leaped off my stool. "I'll do it!"

"No way," Aaron protested. "You're—"

"It's my party. I can do whatever I want." Sticking my tongue out at him, I grabbed the bar top and vaulted over it like I'd seen him do a dozen times—except whatever muscles or coordination he used, I didn't possess. I belly-flopped on the wooden top, slid awkwardly across it, and half fell off the other side.

Popping upright, I tugged my shirt down and pretended I'd totally meant to do that. Aaron coughed violently, and I applied my powers of delusion to also pretend he wasn't laughing.

"Okay, Tori." Kai's dark eyes sparkled with mirth as he scanned the room. "Thirty glasses ought to do it."

I twitched. "Uh, thirty? Not ... four?"

Aaron cupped his hands around his mouth and shouted, "Oy, noisy dipshits! It's time for shots!"

The rambunctious conversations paused for about two seconds, then everyone surged toward the bar. Cooper grabbed the bottle of special-occasion whiskey and raced over. Eyes wide, I whipped out shot glasses, and together we poured one for every mythic in the bar.

Girard, Felix, and Tabitha squeezed through the mass to take the last three shots. Everyone quieted expectantly, all eyes on the three guild officers. Grinning mischievously, Girard nudged Tabitha with his elbow. Her regal mouth thinned, then she faced the crowd and raised her glass.

"It isn't often we welcome a new member into our ranks," she said into the rapt silence. "She has a lot to learn, but she's already demonstrated our most prized qualities: courage, determination, and loyalty."

Tabitha turned to me, a subtle but sincere smile on her lips. "To Victoria—"

"Tori," Felix corrected in a loud whisper.

"To Tori, the Crow and Hammer's newest member!"

"*To Tori!*" thirty voices shouted.

As they lifted their glasses, my heart swelled to bursting. Sorcerers and alchemists. Mages and witches. Psychics and healers. Mythics with power I didn't have and couldn't match, but that didn't matter—not to them, and not to me.

Magic was a tool, and I was learning to wield it. I was a mythic by choice instead of birthright, and this was my guild. This was my life—the one I'd chosen for myself.

Aaron, Kai, and Ezra held their shots, waiting for me. My three best friends. My guardians, companions, allies, family. They had so many secrets, and trouble followed them everywhere they went, but that was okay. I didn't mind a little trouble. Or a lot of trouble.

Everything was changing and though I could scarcely grasp the consequences, I'd known for months what I was getting myself into—and I had no intention of backing out now. I was the Crow and Hammer's mythically human bartender, and this was exactly where I belonged.

I raised my shot, and the guys raised theirs. Together, we tossed the whiskey back and slammed our glasses triumphantly on the bar top. Then I threw my hands in the air and cheered, my voice joining all the rest.

Want to learn more about the three mages?

FOUR SHIFTERS AND A STRANGER
A GUILD CODEX SHORT STORY

When a bounty hunting job goes wrong, a mysterious aeromage saves Aaron's life … and Aaron is determined to return the favor.

Delve into the mages' pasts in this exclusive Guild Codex short story.

Download your copy at
www.guildcodex.ca/fourshifters

TORI'S ADVENTURES CONTINUE IN

DEMON MAGIC AND A MARTINI

THE GUILD CODEX: SPELLBOUND / FOUR

When I first landed this job, I didn't know a thing about magic. These days, I'm practically an expert, but there's a class no one ever talks about: Demonica.

Turns out they have a good reason for that.

My guild is strictly hellion-free, but some people will risk life and soul to control the biggest bullies on the mythic playground. And now a demon has been loosed in the city. Aaron, Kai, and Ezra are determined to slay it, but even badass combat mages are critically out-magicked. And that's not all. The monster they're tracking—it's not hiding. It's not fleeing. It's not leaving a trail of corpses everywhere it goes.

The demon is hunting too. And in a city full of mythics, it's searching for deadlier prey.

If we can't unravel the demon's sinister motivations, more innocent people will die, but finding the answers means digging into dark secrets ... and learning truths I never wanted to know.

www.guildcodex.ca

ABOUT THE AUTHOR

Annette Marie is the author of YA urban fantasy series *Steel & Stone*, its prequel trilogy *Spell Weaver*, and romantic fantasy trilogy *Red Winter*.

Her first love is fantasy, but fast-paced adventures, bold heroines, and tantalizing forbidden romances are her guilty pleasures. She proudly admits she has a thing for dragons, and her editor has politely inquired as to whether she intends to include them in every book.

Annette lives in the frozen winter wasteland of Alberta, Canada (okay, it's not quite that bad) and shares her life with her husband and their furry minion of darkness—sorry, cat—Caesar. When not writing, she can be found elbow-deep in one art project or another while blissfully ignoring all adult responsibilities.

www.annettemarie.ca

SPECIAL THANKS

My thanks to Erich Merkel for sharing your exceptional expertise in Latin. Any errors are mine.

THE
GUILD CODEX
SPELLBOUND

Through a mix of pure chance and bullheaded determination, Tori has become a permanent part of the magical world—for better or for worse. But she's only scratched the surface of what it means to be a mythic ... and she still has some dangerous lessons to learn.

Welcome to the Crow and Hammer.

DISCOVER MORE BOOKS AT
www.guildcodex.ca

STEEL & STONE

When everyone wants you dead, good help is hard to find.

The first rule for an apprentice Consul is *don't trust daemons*. But when Piper is framed for the theft of the deadly Sahar Stone, she ends up with two troublesome daemons as her only allies: Lyre, a hotter-than-hell incubus who isn't as harmless as he seems, and Ash, a draconian mercenary with a seriously bad reputation. Trusting them might be her biggest mistake yet.

SPELL WEAVER

*The only thing more dangerous than the denizens of the
Underworld ... is stealing from them.*

As a daemon living in exile among humans, Clio has picked up some
unique skills. But pilfering magic from the Underworld's deadliest
spell weavers? Not so much. Unfortunately, that's exactly what she has
to do to earn a ticket home.

A destiny written by the gods. A fate forged by lies.

If Emi is sure of anything, it's that *kami*—the gods—are good, and *yokai*—the earth spirits—are evil. But when she saves the life of a fox shapeshifter, the truths of her world start to crumble. And the treachery of the gods runs deep.

This stunning trilogy features 30 full-page illustrations.

Printed in Poland
by Amazon Fulfillment
Poland Sp. z o.o., Wrocław